CROSSING BULLY CREEK

Also by Margaret Erhart

Old Love
Augusta Cotton
Unusual Company

CROSSING BULLY CREEK

MARGARET ERHART

MILKWEED EDITIONS

The characters and events in this book are fictitious. Any similarity to real persons, living or dead, is coincidental and not intended by the author.

Published in 2006 by Milkweed Editions
Printed in the United States of America
Cover design by Brad Norr
Interior design by Linda Koutsky
The text of this book is set in Perpetua.
06 07 08 09 10 5 4 3 2 1
First Paperback Edition

ISBN-13: 978-1-57131-053-8
ISBN-10: 1-57131-053-3

Milkweed Editions, a nonprofit publisher, gratefully acknowledges sustaining support from Emilie and Henry Buchwald; Bush Foundation; Patrick and Aimee Butler Family Foundation; Cargill Value Investment; Timothy and Tara Clark Family Charitable Fund; Dougherty Family Foundation; Ecolab Foundation; General Mills Foundation; John and Joanne Gordon; Greystone Foundation; Institute for Scholarship in the Liberal Arts, College of Arts and Sciences, University of Notre Dame; Constance B. Kunin; Marshall BankFirst; Marshall Field's Gives; May Department Stores Company Foundation; McKnight Foundation; a grant from the Minnesota State Arts Board, through an appropriation by the Minnesota State Legislature, a grant from the National Endowment for the Arts, and private funders; an award from the National Endowment for the Arts, which believes that a great nation deserves great art; Navarre Corporation; Debbie Reynolds; St. Paul Travelers Foundation; Ellen and Sheldon Sturgis; Target Foundation; Gertrude Sexton Thompson Charitable Trust (George R. A. Johnson, Trustee); James R. Thorpe Foundation; Toro Foundation; Serene and Christopher Warren; W. M. Foundation; and Xcel Energy Foundation.

THE LIBRARY OF CONGRESS HAS CATALOGED THE HARDCOVER EDITION AS FOLLOWS:

Erhart, Margaret.
Crossing Bully Creek / Margaret Erhart.—1st ed.
p. cm.
ISBN 1-57131-042-8 (hardcover : alk. paper)
I. Title.
PS3555.R426C76 2005
813'.54—DC22
2004021884

This book is printed on acid-free paper.

For the people of Elsoma Plantation

And in memory of James and Annie Kate Hill,
and Miss Sallie Brown

CROSSING BULLY CREEK

1969

1929–1968

1969

1965–1968

1969

1929

1969

PRINCIPAL CHARACTERS

LONGBROW PLANTATION: one of Georgia's great plantations, on the southern border of Thomas County

RUTHA BROWN: employed on the Longbrow estate; Lewis's wife

HENRY DETROIT: patriarch of the Detroit family; owner of Longbrow Plantation

LEWIS BROWN: a hired hand at Longbrow

ROWENA DETROIT: Henry's second wife; granddaughter of General William Tecumseh Sherman

BYRDINE DEAN: proprietor of Etta's, a café

COLE JONES: manager of Longbrow; married to Karen Jones and father of Debby and Cherry

QUINN VALENTINE: wife of Billy Valentine, Rowena's son from her first marriage

FRANKIE DETROIT: granddaughter of Henry and Rowena

ROOSEVELT DAVIS: the young son of Osee and Pearly Mae Davis; works for Henry Detroit

CHARLENE DAVIS: Roosevelt's younger sister

DALLAS DAVIS: Roosevelt and Charlene's older brother; Vietnam veteran

RAY LUKEN JR.: a hired hand at Longbrow; married to Rosemary Luken and father of Brenda

BRENDA LUKEN: Ray and Rosemary's young daughter

CROSSING
BULLY CREEK

RUTHA BROWN

1969

On the sickbed there was no difference between man and woman, white and colored, rich and poor. The rich man set in his Yankee ways held out his hand to death like it was a done deal between gentlemen, held up his hand like it was a taxi to hail on an urban street, while the colored man taught by his father and his father and his father raised up a hand to ward off blows and kicks and the murderous heat of the sun, the shadow of his hand falling like a cool cloth across his eyes, a moment of respite. But the hand, thought Miss Rutha. That hand. That old man, young man, white man, Negro, poor man, rich man, overseer, slave, fat man, thin man, singing or silent man, Christian or devil's man—that hand. Its bones all looked the same and that's what it would come to soon as death stopped by. On the sickbed the hand of Mr. Henry Adams Detroit turned the color of old cooked turnip and this, not the labor of his breath, told her he was going sure.

It was Miss Geneva ordered Mrs. Detroit away from that bed. Came and got her herself, took her arm and walked her to the kitchen and set her down and put a bowl of clear soup and buttered bread in front of her. Made her sit and fill herself with something other than the breaking of her heart. No one said one word. Pearly Mae in the corner with her polishing cloth, touching up the silver. She, Miss Rutha, hissing the iron back and forth over a pair of Mr. Detroit's pajamas. Miss Geneva bringing an orange cake out of the oven, fanning a cloud of heat that made her eyes smart. Mrs. Detroit sitting small as a child at the table, her face long and sad and slow. Finally she said, "I can't leave him there. He's just lying there alone."

"Rutha'll go in," said Miss Geneva, and Rutha went, carrying his fresh pajamas folded flat with the collar starched just enough to keep it from looking limp. His eyes were closed. He seemed still enough to be peaceful but she knew better. Six years his body had moved from supple flesh to stone and this now was the end of it. She felt a casing around him, brittle and transparent like the stone had thinned to a layer of mica that held him in place. It would not hold him long, it was thinning and thinning. The light was already seeping through the cracks of his prison so she had to blink and cover her eyes and steady herself until the sight of him dulled down and she got used to it.

Like an old rattler slipping out of its skin, skinning itself free of that old good-for-nothing body. A body made of itch and pain and inside it, caught inside it like some miracle, that milky light. Sharp at first like venom, then soft as milk. She approached the bed and watched his breath pour in and out of his chest through the slack mouth. She put his pajamas away in the drawer then pulled them out again and set them at the foot of the bed. She brought two clean towels and a washcloth from the linen closet outside the bedroom door and put them at the foot of the bed. Talcum powder and a basin of warm water from the bathroom. His razor and shaving cream. Life-giving lotion for his paper skin. A rubber sheet beneath him and the heavy linen oversheet pressing him down for a few more rounds of life. She stood close to him and stooped and said, "This ain't the final washing. We got some time to go so this ain't that." She knew how to lay out a body, had learned from her aunt when the scarlet fever had taken her own mother. Two coins for the eyes to keep the lids down. Eyes are the last to accept death. They seem to close then slide open and you feel the look and it agitates you and you turn to scold. She had witnessed one old dead woman cry.

"I got to turn you," she said.

"I'd rather you shoot me."

He was light as a husk. Her arm under his shoulder, her other arm cradling his head so he came rolling into her embrace, his voice caught in the bosom of an angel.

"Shoot you?"

"Yes."

"No one gonna shoot you."

"I'd like to be shot." He frowned. "For mercy."

He was naked under the sheet, his undecorated body a candle of unused light. Rutha had not looked at any white man but this one. He himself didn't look up but beyond her into a corner of the room where two pale gray walls met.

His teeth chattered as she washed him. His skin peeled off like the label off a can. The body was going, washing away. She covered him with lotion and powder in the crevices and laid him back on the pillow so he might rest before she shaved and dressed him.

She thought to shave Lewis once when they were first married. Took him by surprise after a night of love. Sat him down on the bed and brought the basin and without a word took up his straight razor. He bowed his head and said, "I'll never lay a hand on you again. Though I done it in love." He saw his own throat cut like Isaac, like the lamb. He saw the basin there brimmed with his own blood. She kneeled before him ashamed and made him take back his words. But later she thought of her childlessness as a curse for the vow he'd made and broken on the altar of sacrifice.

Mr. Detroit said, "I don't have my clothes on."

"We gonna take care a that."

"I'm buck naked."

"Get you shaved first."

"Who are you? You're not my first wife."

"Nosir."

"She was a thin girl. She loved the pantry. And a horse. She had a horse. No children, though. It was too cold for children. Too electric."

"Yessir."

"She tried though."

"Yessir. I know she did."

"She had one child and then she had two. They galloped in the pasture, it was a mad sight to see. Wave after wave. The heat like fallen soldiers, the way they do."

"Yessir."

"You aren't my wife?"

"Nosir. I come to wash you up and get you shaved and dress you in some clean pajamas. Set you up comfortable in the bed."

"Well, I haven't a thing on."

"We gonna tend to that. Right now we gonna tend to it."

She slipped him into his pajamas and he seemed to ease some. She laid a dry towel under his head and his eyes caught fire and his voice cracked like he had ripped open his throat and found a fountain of ice. "Breathe for me, will you, when it's time? Say yes. No, I know it's not even foolish out, but the clock needed its meat and bread. Yes," he insisted, shaking his head. "Yes, yes, no more."

She laid her hands solidly on his cheekbones, his entire head less than a melon's weight. "No one gonna hurt you now," she said, and it was what he longed for. He quit fighting right then and became a man whom death does not struggle to take. It was then, right then, he began his slow, muffled walk toward it. A long walk—there were days yet—but he had been handed the road and behind him life would soon shrink down to one flat plane, then one long line, then a black dot and let him go.

She did get those whiskers off him. How a dying man can grow hair! He seemed to dream through the shave until she came to the place, all bone, beneath his right ear. "I came upon them in the trees," he said. "No live oaks there, they used a pine. They hung good and straight from the same branch, their bare feet licking the ground and a terrible mess of blood on their hands like they had served themselves that brute injustice. Their parts stripped from them. Their body hair burned off them either before or after—I prayed after. Left there like meat, boiled men, no name or home, their eyes gone. When I close my eyes I see them. I don't see the others. I don't ever look for them. The liquor they used to set them on fire mixed with the young hope I had. I was no one. They touched shoulders when the breeze stirred them to. I sat all night and after a while the crows came and I had to shoo them away with a stick. My two had gone and I took these two instead and mourned them until by morning I was mourning the men they were and the ones getting up now without them. Cool place in the bed. You lie down on a sheet of snow and scan the heavens for her and she gives nothing away and the boy doesn't either." Mr. Detroit gripped her wrist which was holding the razor. "You must believe it. Not even a bird sings. I can show you that place."

But Rutha thought she knew and when she was done and he was quiet, even asleep, all clean and smooth and swept out inside, she put away the bathroom things and set aside the damp towels to carry to the laundry later and took up a chair by the door. The night he spoke of was hard as jagged glass inside her and she knew it like today though it was forty years ago. The two men hanged and burned and brought to her aunt's house in the last hour of the night, brought by an anonymous citizen rumored to be a white man. There they washed and scraped the smell off them, dressed them in a neighbor's borrowed clothes. Her aunt packed the eye sockets with wax and when they were done it looked like death was a gentleman. Though the whole South knew then and still that death was a beggar at the feast. And the North knew it too, or ought to. And the beggar looked worse than the man in the casket but better than the colored man on the street. Yet the more they hanged you, cut you, spat upon you, cursed and threw fire at you, the more you rose up and walked. The more you loosened your rope and stepped onto the earth and claimed it, with your hands at your sides, neither up nor out, not asking, not begging, but telling the truth of your right to live through another day and a night and on into your own new history made by you and not by the shadow of your death. Made by the raw light of you spilling out into the woods and fields and roads, and onto the bed of your family and future.

HENRY DETROIT

1929

The baby died in the spring, right before burning, and Henry came down to shake the shadow off him by working alongside his men. Working his body hard until it gave him the peace a machine can give, all its parts moving without thought, making something from nothing, although, as Lewis said, the burning seemed to make nothing of something, and then something grew up stronger in the wake of it. Lewis was a married man now, his wife a north Florida girl half his age, three times his size. She might have been all of sixteen. But it meant he went home to someone, while Henry went home to a cold clean slate of a bed.

The first day, with the wind out of the south, they burned the Florida line. That fire got up into the live oaks instead of chewing up the ground. Too much wind and the ground too soft and wet. It was a hard day of work, and Henry worked harder than he ever had in his life. They took wet croker sacks and beat the flames out of the trees but the fire wouldn't run, it just slunk in the shade of the trees like it was looking for someplace cool to rest. Lewis said it would run tomorrow, he promised it. The next day they returned and it ran alright, ran north in manageable acres, a perfect day of fire. They followed it up past fields of Abel Davis's shining green oats and into the lowland around Lake Walter. The third day was Cullis Jones's. Lewis's sister, a soot-black woman at least the size of his new wife, brought out a dinner pail and a pot of gray coffee at noontime. She plopped them down on the ground and went off, her big bare feet sturdy as hooves.

They ate with their backs up against the old cabin where Cullis Jones had raised his twenty-six children, twenty-six children out of three wives, all of whom died in childbirth. Lewis brought out a flat tin of tobacco and rolled himself a cigarette. He sat there smoking with one leg up, bent at the knee. Then he said, not looking at anyone, "Three days you ain't et a thing. I can get her to bring out something you like. Whatever you want to eat, she can learn to cook it."

The other two men had each finished off two plates of venison stew and cornbread, and they were drinking their coffee. They looked at the air around their tin cups, then drank some more. Henry said, "It's food fit for a king, Lewis. You tell your sister there's nothing the matter with this food."

Lewis looked at his cigarette. "Then it's the king ain't fit."

Henry said nothing. He could see the sister through the trees, just the back of her passing through an old grove of black walnuts.

Lewis said, "We coulda gone on, not set and et here next to that place."

"It doesn't matter."

"You been moving toward that place these last three days. Might as well set here with it."

He told the other two men to go and check the fire, make sure it wasn't lying too low, make sure it got in the thickest brush and burned hot there and ran good through the tall grasses. They might need to build more firebreak or set more fire. Keep it big but not too big, and moving. After they went off, he said, "How long I knowed you, Mr. Detroit?"

"A long time, Lewis. We met sometime in the last century."

"Yessir, we did."

"I think I'm older than you."

"You could be."

"I think I'm five or ten years older."

"Could be, five or ten years."

"I remember you came up to the house one time, you and Aunt Annie. It was my birthday. Remember that?"

"I remember."

"You were a little boy. You told me you didn't have a birthday, and I said, 'Go on and take mine, I've had quite a few.'"

"You said it weren't no good, a birthday so close to Christmas. But I kept that day."

"You still call it your birthday?"

"Yessir, I do."

"I didn't know that, Lewis. That makes me happy."

Lewis poured a cup of the gray-blue coffee and handed it to him and he took it and held it to his face and let the heat of it soften his hold on things. "You don't mind getting older?"

"Nosir."

"That's what birthdays do, they make you older."

"Mine don't do nothing like that."

"They mark the next year of your life."

"It don't come in years, Mr. Detroit, it come in minutes. It come in less than minutes. It come in pieces so small you don't hardly know it's come before it's gone. That's why you ain't et nothing for all these days, you still trying to go back and catch them pieces you didn't even know was there till they wasn't no more. Miz Detroit and that little baby, your little boy, they come and gone, and as much as you had them is all you gonna have them. You got to quit trying to have them more and go on and have someone else. You a young man. You ain't a old man yet. You get to be a old man, I'll tell you, 'cause I'll be right behind you."

He brought out the tobacco tin again. He took the last quarter-inch of his cigarette and pinched out the fire and unrolled the last shred of tobacco into the tin. He said, "You never did smoke?"

"No," said Henry.

"Miz Chubb, she still smoke?"

"Yes."

"She showed me how to smoke."

"Mary did?"

"She still smoke them Pall Malls?"

Henry laughed.

"That may a been the only smoke I ever had I didn't roll it myself. Your daddy, he liked a pipe, I remember that. A pipe or a nice cigar. He bought them cigars right there in town at the factory. That's how I always think a your daddy, with a big old cigar coming outta his mouth, or that pipe a his. And your mama. I seen your mama smoke a cigar. She said it was to keep the flies off. She was setting in the dove field and I was picking up for some of her company, and I smelled that cigar and I thought, Mr. Detroit got to be around here somewheres, then I remember he been dead a year or two. Old Isaac, he always pick up for your mama, he pick up for her till he went blind. Well, he start to laugh and I seen he's trying hard not to but he can't help it. Miz Detroit she's setting there with that cigar, and every time a dove come in she give the cigar to Isaac and pick up her gun and shoot the bird dead, then she take up the cigar again and he go out and pick it up."

Henry laughed. "I don't believe it."

"It's the truth."

"It's a good story."

"It's the truth."

"She can still hit anything, can't she, Lewis?"

"Yessir. Long as it fly."

"And my wife. She was a damn good shot, wasn't she, Lewis?"

"Yessir. She was."

"She was a damn good shot, Caroline."

"She was good. She was real good."

"She could outshoot Mother."

"Yessir, she could. The only one could."

"I'm a lousy shot."

"You ain't that bad."

"I hate to think of that day, Lewis."

"Don't think of it. That day is come and gone. They ain't one thing gonna happen different than it already happen."

"Timmy's death made her death more complete. I know I should be thinking of him, but I can't do anything but think of Caroline. Her pain, her physical suffering. I've never seen anyone suffer the way she did. Physically. I don't even want to think about her mind."

"Don't think about it."

"That includes the war, Lewis. Never did I see that. Or I saw it and wouldn't let myself remember it. I must have seen it, men torn apart by guns. Never their own gun though. And men. Not a woman. Not my wife. Not here. This was her place, Lewis. She loved it here. I mean here, around this old cabin and back in the live oaks at the foot of the hills. Only hills on the plantation, she loved them. Gray-green. She loved the color here. The ground more yellow than red and the view open and the birds—the place so full of birds. She loved it. Walking with the dog, that useless dog of hers. She was always trying to turn him into a real bird dog. You couldn't turn that dog into anything. Not really. Not a real anything. That goddamn dog. Ran all the way back to us. That must have been ten, twelve miles. Cut through the plantation then ran the road. That was a sorry sight, old Chad coming in. I'll never forget the sight of him, running the driveway alone. He was wild, Lewis. He didn't need words to tell us. He told us, that dog. Goddamn it, Lewis. What do you do?"

He was rocking back and forth like a baby, sitting cross-legged on the ground with his arms hugging his chest. "What do you do, Lewis? What do you do? What am I going to do?"

Lewis reached over and put his hand on the ground between them. "You alright," he said. "You doing what you going to do. Right now you doing it. You working hard, you talking a little bit, you out here in this place. Like you say, she had a real strong feeling for this place. Sometimes that's where we gonna die and we don't know it, but we feel it strong all our life, and when we die we died in a place we want to be, a place we know like we know a person."

Henry shook his head. "I don't have such a place."

"Not everyone do."

"Do you?"

"Yessir. My old bed. That's where I gonna die, right in my old bed." He laughed. "Here come my sister back now. You better eat."

"I'll take some of that cornbread in my pocket."

"You'll take some of this stew too. I'll fix you up a plate."

But Henry was looking out toward the walnut grove. "I think I'm ready to walk out there, Lewis. Would you come with me?"

They got up. Lewis said something to his sister in their own language, and she gave him a cool look and started packing the dinner things. "She don't like it when people ain't finish their dinner, but she gonna leave you a plate."

"What's her name?"

"Cordelia." It was the sister who spoke. "I reckon I know my name better than he do. Some calls me Big Cordelia on account a my mama was also Cordelia, and she a tiny woman, skinny like Lewis here. But she dead now."

She picked up the pail and coffeepot and gave the two men a nod and said to Henry, "Y'all eat that food I left for you. Stew's cold, cornbread's cold, coffee's cold. It's all cold, but it won't kill you. Fire's hot. Now that'll kill you." She headed off toward the road.

They went the other direction, into the trees. They were newly leafed and gave a watery canopy of shade that eased Henry's mind, made him feel like a swimmer in a green pool. He'd never thought twice about this part of the land until she'd thought about it for him, and then he'd seen it through her eyes, felt the lift of the hills and the spaciousness, the spareness of the woods. He loved the deep woods, especially after burning when all the undergrowth was gone and walking was easy and the birds came in abundance after the seeds exploded by the fire. But down here around Cullis Jones's you didn't have the pines in such numbers, you had live oaks and around the cabin itself you had some of the oldest magnolias in the state of Georgia. And you had the black walnuts, planted by Jones, planted before the Civil War, and you had young beech trees big around as elephant legs. He felt himself moving forward like a machine, and Lewis moving along next to him, a step or two behind him, and when they came to the place where the wire fence lay on the ground, lay where its old posts had rotted, he suddenly saw her and saw her feet get tangled and heard her gun go off and saw her right shoulder open up and her amazement bloom out of her, and he heard the dog barking, running circles around her, and he knew her attempt to comfort the dog, and it was the last thing she could do on this earth. "Here," he said to Lewis. "This is where she lay."

"She was alive yet?"

He nodded. "She died back there in the cabin."

Neither of them knelt down or made any Christian sign. They stood and looked at the tanglement that had taken her life, and then they walked back through the trees that reminded one of them of water and brought to mind in the other a sweet walnut pie his mother, Miss Cordelia, used to make.

LEWIS BROWN

1929–1968

Every evening he came up to the house to clean the guns. He got out his rag and his gun oil and the long bristle brush he used to clean the bore. He picked up a shotgun, cracked it apart, oiled the stock until it shone like water or ice and the barrel as well. If it was the Purdey he'd take a look inside the barrel before he cleaned it, see if Miss Caroline was having a good day or a bad one. Now Miss Mary's husband, Mr. Chubb, when he started using that gun and bringing nothing home to show for it, he always talked like it was the gun's fault. But Lewis, looking inside the barrel, same barrel as had been Miss Caroline's, could see he was a man without the mind to shoot twice at the same bird or at a second bird. A covey of quail, it scattered out and sometimes you were left aiming at the wind and nothing else and that was when you had to keep your mind steady and move your attention (which boiled down to the end of your gun) and look for something to shoot at and fire that second barrel. Mr. Chubb, his second barrel was always clean. Miss Caroline, she most of the time killed a bird dead first shot and often went on and fired again to kill another, and if she didn't she would turn to her gun (he had seen this) and stroke its barrel the same way he had seen Mr.

Henry lean from the saddle after a poor jump and stroke the neck of his horse. Looking down the bore of that Purdey he could see the difference between the nature of Mr. Chubb and the nature of Miss Caroline, and when Miss Caroline went he was for many reasons sorry to see her go and every time he cleaned her gun he was sorry all over again.

Then he cleaned the boots. Mr. Henry's mama she liked a polishing paste but his daddy liked an oil and they fought about that sometimes, all the way up until the old man died. Mr. Henry's second wife, Miss Rowena, she come along and she liked a hard-bristle brush while old Mrs. Detroit she wouldn't have nothing but a soft one. And she didn't like much color on the boot. Miss Rowena, she liked color, she liked a little red. Not a red red but a blood red. Lewis wasn't fond of that red. It wasn't the color a boot should be and on this matter he went with Mrs. Detroit. But when she died it was Miss Rowena's house 'cause Mr. Henry's sister, Miss Mary, she didn't come down much and when she did it weren't boots or polish that interest her, only thing that interest her was a party. Miss Rowena, she was a person who went for a little red and that's how it had gone. For a long time it had gone that way. And then the son, Mr. Harry, him and his wife Miss Kate they'd started to say this or that and Lewis could see it was them now, it was them saying hard or soft bristles, red or no red. They said that and they said more. Their opinions went on to build the house he and Rutha lived in. Raise it up said one, let the air get under it. Leave it lay on the ground said the other. Ground'll cool it in summer, keep it warm in the winter. No one said ask Lewis, it's his house, and no one did. But the boots they got shined and polished like they always had, and the guns they got cleaned, and soon it was Osee Davis did all that 'cause the doctor say Osee he can't work outside no more. He have stuff in his lungs that don't much like the stuff in the air. It don't like horses nor mules nor dogs nor dust but it don't mind guns and it don't mind boots and it don't mind laying the fire for Miss Rowena or driving Miss Geneva the cook from town. Before Miss Geneva it was Miss Rachel, and Lewis would get up, dress in the dark, ease the car out the back past the slave shacks behind the plantation house (it was at that time the old house on the Tallahassee Road). He'd drive slow and easy into town to Peach Street where Miss Rachel lived. It was the Negro part of town and it was awake at that hour and in many of the houses people had already eaten their breakfast and gone. They worked in town and walked or took the bus or they worked out on the plantations and waited as Miss Rachel did for someone like Lewis to come and collect them. In the winter Miss Rachel waited inside the house. Lewis tapped the horn twice and she came out and down the porch steps and got into the car. He'd open the door for her but she didn't like that, said she didn't need no chauffeur like the fancy folks. Chauffeur do the driving, he told her. Maybe you like to do your own driving. Naw, she said. I ain't never drove and I'm too old to learn. One thing I can do though is I can open my own door.

They often spoke not one word until they turned onto the road that came in back of the plantation house. Then she'd start to say a thing or two that was on her mind, and she always did have something on her mind, something new since the night before when he took her home. How's Rutha? she'd say.

'Bout the same.

Same as when?

Same as last night 'round nine o'clock, last time you saw her.

Some people never change.

They'd pass through the old quarters and sometimes Miss Rachel she'd sigh or press her fingers together or shift her pocketbook and say, I wonder why don't he put this place to rest. What good do it do, standing here in ruins? Tear down these spoiled shacks and plant something green and new.

Right now we got to fight Mr. Hitler, Lewis would say. Or he'd say, Now we got trouble with the Russians. Miss Rachel, she'd look at him and say, Lewis Brown, what in the world your Russians got to do with these old rundown memories here, rats and raccoons living in them. Someday a child gonna come looking in here and the roof gonna fall and that gonna be a lot worse than any old Russians. And ain't them Russians in Russia? And ain't Russia an awful long way from Longbrow Plantation?

Used to be.

Well, you 'splain that one to me.

I will, he'd say. When I take you home tonight I'll 'splain it.

But nine ten o'clock in the evening she'd get in the car, set her body down, pull her old legs in, and doze all the way home. In front of her house he'd stop the car, walk around and open her door and wake her. She'd jump a little and ask, How long was I out?

Just a minute or two.

That'd be 'bout right. I don't believe in sleeping during the day.

It's night now, Miss Rachel.

Well.

She'd refuse his help and pull herself up holding onto the door. Ooh, I feel stiff as a stick tonight. Thank you kindly, Lewis. No, I reckon as long as I'm alive I'm fit enough to walk up onto my own porch.

And then one night on the way home she was restless and she got to talking. Lewis Brown, she said, I think I got my own answer.

I guess you got your own question too.

It's about them Russians.

Them Russians?

They changed it all around.

Who did? What'd they change?

Used to be, said Miss Rachel, people lived separate and stayed separate and over there was them and here was us. You know how that was, Lewis, right here in our own place, right here where we was born. But now we got the integration. We got people calling for the colored children and the white children all together in the same school. The people start thinking, and once the people start thinking there won't be no unthinking. So that day is gonna come. I won't see it but it's gonna come. Just like it come with the Russians. Russia ain't over there in Russia no more. It's right here.

It ain't exactly right here.

Hush, Lewis. Yes it is. You woulda told me that yourself but I went and figured it out. It's right here. There ain't nothing a man can do that don't affect every other man, and that's what Jesus was trying to tell us. Way back when, He was trying to tell us. But we didn't listen. Now we got to listen. It remind me of the time I pass through the house looking for Miss Caroline and I hear her in one of her tempers, calling Mr. Henry all kind a evil, and later I hear him crying in his room—a grown man crying, and a white man, that surprise me, and I say to myself, Rachel, you go in there, say a kind word to him, you been in this family longer than he has—why, you spanked his little bare bottom. But he's a white man, Lewis, and I don't go in, and then I see that French girl, the little boy's nurse, she hugging Mr. Henry and kissing him and doing like this to his hair, and he hug her and kiss her back and I think well, there ain't no sense in a man being lonely but then I think there ain't no good can come of that. And there weren't.

It was a accident, said Lewis wearily, for he was tired of thinking. A accident was what it was.

He got out of the car and went around to open her door if she'd let him, but before he got there he noticed the back tire on the driver's side looked low so he got down close to it in the dark and moved his hand across the tread trying to feel the head of a nail or some other such thing. But she was waiting. He went all the way around and was surprised to see her asleep inside. Just like that she'd fallen asleep. He opened the door and told her, If the Russians give you your answer or if Jesus do, I'm happy you found it, Miss Rachel. And then he saw she was too still and he saw the old eyes fixed open and he felt her wrist though he didn't need to and he closed the door again and stood for a minute trying to feel what she would wish him to do. She said *Carry me into my house* and he did. She said *Lay me on my old bed* and he did that too. The iron bed with its sour sheets and crocheted coverlet and above it a picture of Our Savior crowned in thorns carrying His own cross through the streets of a city, and beside it a low table holding a glass of water and some cloudy green medicine in a clear bottle stoppered with a cork, and beneath his feet a braided rug she set her feet upon every morning in the dark and every evening after he brought her home again. And again he waited to hear what she wished him to do but she was far away now and no longer needed him. He walked outside and checked the tire and it was nothing but a pool of rubber attached to a rim and he changed it right there in front of her house on Peach Street.

ROWENA AND HENRY

1933

He confessed to her one night and afterward Rowena understood what she hadn't before and felt a kind of bitterness to her love which strangely satisfied her more than the sweet. She finally saw him as a flawed man. It gave him a meat and heart he hadn't had before—or hadn't offered to her. He offered it that night like a packaged ham, its juices meant for her and sealed by the smoke-sweet crust.

It was early in their marriage, the second winter, her second New Year's at Longbrow. Harry, a colicky infant, and Billy a nine-year-old, slept upstairs with Mrs. Beauchamp, the nurse. Henry and Rowena on the first floor in the conjugal bed that had been his mother and father's. His mother, when she came, enjoyed the guest room with its view of the garden.

She waited until he went to sleep then got up and walked outside and found herself on the road that led back through the old slave quarters, a dozen empty ghostly shacks uninhabited, their sour doorless entryways a fright to her—had she never imagined how people lived? And there in the towering darkness the plantation house a looming ship bearing down on her and those mawkish, hapless shanties. Suddenly she saw them for what they were, saw the whole South for what it was, and the knowledge depressed her. Henry's confession angered her. She was out in only her dressing gown and slippers and knew she should turn back but she was restless and bored and continued on, surprised—almost ashamed—that she had never walked here before. She had no idea where the road would take her.

As she walked she conversed with Henry in her mind, as young wives will do. Though she wasn't young, she was thirty-seven and had lived through one marriage, one child, and now seemed fated to repeat it. Which mostly suited her, especially the lack of a daughter. She didn't want a daughter, didn't know what she'd do with one. The elder Mrs. Detroit assured her it was perfectly natural to want sons. She herself had had one of each and preferred her son to her daughter. (Rowena was shocked by such an admission. She hoped never to favor one child over the other and knew if she did she would keep it to herself.)

It was easier, she found, to carry on a conversation with Henry when he wasn't there. She often found him difficult to talk to, a little above her in his concerns. There was a hollowness to his responses, and his means of expression went beyond her as well. He was a man unaccustomed to intimate communication, to the language of marriage as Rowena thought of it, and this disturbed her. Young wives—new wives—were tossed about at the beginning of their sea voyage, thinking always that the next day would bring the fulfillment of their happiness, conversation with the beloved being the key. But more often the ship dragged itself to port, threw down its gangplank, released its weather-worn passengers, and left happiness undiscovered off in the deep somewhere, perhaps never to be experienced. So the new wives buckled down to their task of creating a satisfactory contentment from the raw materials at hand, which meant they carried on their longed-for conversations, achieved their coveted intimacy, but alone, in their minds, and it often was—or became—enough.

It had not been enough for Rowena in her marriage to Leland Valentine, but in Henry Detroit she had sensed a potential. She saw it in the way he spoke to his sister Mary, and to the Negroes, especially those older than he who had known him as a boy. He spoke of certain animals with an animation and reverence that was not intimacy itself but its fraternal twin. (An old dog Chad never failed to excite a melancholy in him, and his horse Midas might have been the Emperor Napoleon himself.) Children seemed to bewilder him, as did wives, but Rowena believed she could work with what she was given, scratch the soil here, water it there, throw a fish in with each seed and suddenly—or someday—he, Henry, would approach her in the night and part his lips not for kisses, but for conversation. So many men didn't understand the heart's great ability to express itself on the tongue. They thought instead (and eternally) of sex.

So he had spoken to her at last, and she had left the bed and felt her anger rise and now before she returned to him she wished to find a place to bury her discomfort lest he find in it a warning never to share his heart again. *But Henry dear, my only wish is to have more, to know you more, to hear you speak sooner!*

No, I shouldn't have told you. It was foolish—selfish of me. After all these years, how could it matter?

It's all that matters. Our words, Henry. Language. You read your books for the same reason. They tell us about ourselves. We create ourselves over and over again in our language, our thoughts, our stories.

But that man, that me—he's no one I want you to know. He's not the husband I want you to have.

Ah! Then I have no husband at all.

I don't understand. I'm a better man than he.

But he lives here with us, dear. Better to give him a name.

You've lost me. A name?

Claim him!

But I want him to be forgotten.

Better to tell! Have it done with! Have it out!

Why, Rowena? Why?

Why? Oh, you're impossible! Thick! Thick in the head!

And on and on it would go, his reason pitted against her emotion. That is the way he would see it, wouldn't he, and never speak again?

The road ended abruptly at a wide ditch damp and foul-smelling. Something slid across it, rat or muskrat, and she wondered, was this where they did their business, the inhabitants of those shacks? Did their defecating and urinating? In an open pit? Why, it was no better than deepest darkest Africa! At a distance she could make out the new stables and barn, could hear the horses moving against the pasture fence, shaking their fine heads, swishing their tails. Two of them whinnied back and forth, Midas and the pretty little Arab, Miss Belle Walker, Rowena's horse. The mules huddled together by the trough, still and sleeping, and she thought of her grandfather Sherman, old Tecumseh, old Cump, how he liked a mule, preferred a mule to a horse for everything but travel, called them good soldiers and praised their steady nerves. He would have ridden a mule to war if they'd let him. She'd never given much thought to that war, the war that claimed him as its hero. The man himself she'd never known. She'd seen the last portraits, stood in the room where he died and imagined him, and did not understand how the gaunt old thin-haired figure, blue-lipped and smelling of cardboard, spittle on his collar, asleep in his padded chair, added up to the Civil War general astride his mount. She guessed the photographs lied. Henry had been the one to point out that in fact the man was a savior. Many believed it. And just as many, he was quick to add, knew him to be the greatest villain of the war. That war or any other (a postscript Rowena felt to be unnecessary).

She felt her wakeful angry energy waning. Her legs beneath the dressing gown were chilled. Her thin nightgown served only as a sheath of propriety. She turned and started walking home. Along the road the live oaks dangled Spanish moss and she walked with her hands up, dragging the gray beards down, draping them across her hair, her shoulders, even tying a length at her hips, as if to wrap herself in a sort of enchantment. She felt regal, smooth, invisible, and untouched. The slave quarters seemed insignificant now as she passed through, and as she approached the house Henry's confession lost its mass and power. She found it, frankly, predictable, and he in his telling of it sweetly naive. Should she pinch his cheek, pull him by the ear, and scold him? *No, Henry. No. Bad boy. Bad.* Did he honestly think he was the first man to fall in love with a buxom young nanny? All men fell in love with their child's nurse—unless their wives had the wits to choose a Mrs. Beauchamp, a Mount Rushmore of a woman whose prodigious capability seemed to neuter a man. And married to a policeman besides! But Rowena's predecessor had not had the wits—or the will, was her guess, though she would never suggest it to Henry—to pick a suitable caretaker for their little one, their little Timmy. Instead, an inexpensive strumpet fresh off the boat from France, lying about her age, and suddenly she's caught the master's eye because, poor master, his wife's unceasing melancholy has rendered him incapable of feeling love. Or giving love. And she, *la jeune fille,* is frightfully happy to receive *amour* of any sort, and besides, she's for all intents and purposes the mother of the child who hangs all day at her hip and sleeps with her at night and when he cries he cries for her. *Waa, waa, where is my Juliette* (or whatever her name was)? He had fallen, had Henry, as any mortal would. He had taught her to ride and those rides had brought them closer, brought them to love, though he did not say it. But of course they had, and when his wife shot herself it was neither accident nor her own long desire to die but the fault of his adultery? Foolish Henry. She, Rowena, had taken his head in her hands, pulled him down to her in the bed, cradled his poor head in her arms, and said one word to him: no.

Lying there that way, comforted by the breathing of this wife and the smell of her breast and her fingers slowly combing his hair, Henry had let himself believe for the eternity of one minute and the first time since Timmy's death that he was not the shadow of the sun in the world. That shadows crossed the earth and fell upon this man or that man but the nature of a shadow was a changing nature, like the nature of death or sleep. And he had slept and awakened to find her gone, his wife gone, and he had dressed quickly and gone upstairs but she was not with the children. Only Mrs. Beauchamp snoring sonorously on her narrow bed. Outside then, to the garden. But no one. Through a thick stand of bamboo he caught sight of a whiteness. It approached. She was wearing her dressing gown and seemed to be tangled in a net. He ran toward her, calling her name, not wanting to frighten her. "Oh, Henry," she said. She looked strangely mad, her hair draped with Spanish moss, her slippers ruined. "You're awake."

"Darling—"

"Isn't it a beautiful night?"

"I didn't know where you were."

"I've been for a walk."

"In your slippers?"

"I didn't know where I would end up. I've never walked back there and I got as far as the ditch and had to turn around. It was too smelly. It was their latrine, wasn't it?"

"Whose latrine, sweetest? Where?"

"Past the shacks." She pointed. She seemed tired and slightly out of breath, though happy, cheerful.

"We'll go look in the morning."

He took her arm and at her insistence they walked once around the garden. "Oh, smell the tea olive!" she whispered. "Isn't it lovely out! Let's make a bed outside! Let's sleep outside one of these nights. Before your mother comes," she added.

"One of these nights," he agreed.

In bed his body led him to her and she took him in and for the first time since the death of his son he wanted with a wanting as fierce as anything he had ever known to create another child. He had made Harry with indifference. He would like to make this one now from all the pieces of himself that life and death had brought together, the pieces of darkness and light, the shadowed, shadowy, and luminous molecules that comprised him, always had and would forever until the end. He wanted to be worthy of his wife, of Rowena. She had frightened him that night, walking out of the house, walking away from the safety he had tried to construct around her and the boys. The happiness and safety. Anything that money could buy, he bought for them. A cupola and seven stone deer. Peacocks, ponies, a perambulator for Harry, a bicycle for Billy, a child-size wagon pulled by a goat. Furs, silk dressing gowns, soft Italian shoes. A man to garden and rake the pebbled pathways. Women to cook and clean and care for the baby. And yet there was no money he knew that could keep his loved ones from death. They would walk out with the weapon his money had placed in their hands, a Purdey gun, so magnificent in its precision and lovely to look at (the fine metal engraved with a delicate vine terminating in her initials). Or they would go to sleep in the little blue room his love and money had created, and in the morning (terrible—he would never forget it) lie as still and blue as the walls. There was no fortune—none in the world—that could prevent misfortune. This humbled him. It made him careful. It made him a man unimpressed by rank and rhetoric, a man neither soothed nor tempted by the pleasures of the city. And God—God had never thundered in the private heaven of Henry Detroit, though he yearned for the kind of elastic mind he sensed in those who did believe. He yearned for belief, but in truth he felt closer to an understanding of Zeus and the Olympians than the God of Israel and His son. His first wife dragged him into a church to marry, but Rowena begged for a garden wedding. And like anything she set her formidable will to, it was accomplished—though it was December. A wintry garden. They'd had to brush the snow from the chairs. And Chauncey Chubb had gotten through the whole event without singing the *Un bel di vedremo* aria from *Madame Butterfly* in a falsetto, nor grown morose or maudlin (he had loved Caroline), and in the end he carried the honeymooners away in a hired trap and put them on the train to Montreal. As far from Longbrow as Henry could conjure up—chill winds, gaily-lit streets, handsome couples drinking mugs of steaming chocolate behind frosty café windows, snow everywhere, horse-drawn plows, the cry of vendors—Chestnuts! *Marrons!*—and at night, in the Hotel

Charlemagne, the map of his future unrolling across the small limber body of his wife. Her gaze upon him as they joined themselves in love. Never had he watched a woman watch him before, even in circumstances less intimate.

On the last glorious night as he lay reading and waiting, Rowena stepped from the bathroom and came to him on the bed, her silk dressing gown open, showing the pale flat flesh, long breasts, dark nipples, navel, and hair. "One more night," she said. He was conscious of the slight weight of her beside him and the lemony smell of her skin and the lack of control he felt when he was near her and she was naked. "Then we go home," she said.

"I hate to."

"Darling, let's not!"

He laughed, threw his book aside. She was his sprite, his wood nymph. He reached his arms around her waist but she pulled away and stood up. "Oh, Henry, wouldn't that be lovely? To have our Christmas down South instead of in smelly old New York? Nobody's working next week. There's no work for you to go back to. I'm perfectly serious. Let's go to Longbrow. I've heard so much about Longbrow. We'd have it to ourselves before your mother came, and Mary and Chauncey never make up their mind about anything until the last minute. And it would be fun to be there with them. Wouldn't it be fun, darling?"

Henry frowned. It seemed too soon to bring another bride to Longbrow, and yet he longed to be there, longed to take Rowena there, imagined them sitting outside in the garden after supper, touching hands in the darkness. He could sense the night air soft and redolent of tea olives. He could hear the wind in the tops of the pines. December was the worst because the memory of her . . . the memory came to him unbidden and he had no heart to send it away. Three years this year. He looked at his wife, his Rowena, and shook his head and said, "I'm afraid I can't." Her expression softened and he realized suddenly that he was in love with her. He must be. It gave him such joy to love her.

They arrived on Christmas Eve and stayed on past the New Year. They did sit in the garden at night and the air was like felt on the skin and did bring them the smell of tea olives as well as the fragrance of pine smoke, roses, a fresh-cut lawn. Mary came, dragging her husband, and the two of them were very gay and went to a different party every night for four nights and then in a state of utter exhaustion caught the train home. His mother came. She withheld judgment on the new wife, for which Henry was grateful. She hadn't liked the old one and told him so a few days after the funeral. In general, she admitted, she didn't like women. She disapproved of her daughter's prodigious social life yet found it charming that Chauncey would follow along "like Mary's little puppy." Henry was less charmed, having seen his puppy brother-in-law in his cups one too many times, playing master of ceremonies or court jester or, one unforgettable night, the night Henry met Caroline, performing a water ballet in his underwear and shoes while a sad tuba wallowed in accompaniment.

This was no longer the kind of amusement Henry could enjoy. Instead he found solace in the moon, in all its changing forms, and in the cool stars, and pleasure in the rank smell of a working dog and the oaty smell of horses, and in the sudden pink flesh revealed when the mules lifted their tails and pushed out manure, and in the soft body of a quail struck by a hail of shot, a body but moments before alive, now dead in his hand—and by his hand. And in the overhead whistling of ducks before dawn, and the kick of a gun, the snap of the trap that sent a clay pigeon flying. The blind green of oats in a field and the black green of swamp water. The voices—Lewis's, Rachel's, old Aunt Annie's, the cry of herons waking in the darkness, and in the darkness his son, too, awake and furious with hunger. And Rowena's boy Billy out on the water learning to row, lifting off the seat of the boat with the effort and the fat blades deep, rising up through the gloom with a groan from the serious child, "Dad, they've been down in Davey Jones's locker!" And the sight of his wife in almost any light, but especially the pale liquid light before the honey light of January, February. The light that matched her skin and marked the end of light, November, December, when he needed her.

ROOSEVELT DAVIS

1959

Byrdine Dean slept fitfully, her palms burning and itching. Finally she went to the kitchen, stood in front of the Frigidaire, and wrapped her hands around a cold bottle of milk. She went and lay down again and sank into the kind of sleep that feels like a trough of dark water. There she stayed, a drowned soul, until a knock woke her and she rose up, her long black hair wild about her shoulders, her eyes puffy, her skin a fish-belly white and shiny for lack of rest. At the door a colored woman with a little boy in her arms. He seemed to be about three years old. The woman was talking to him and stroking his hair. She was almost as wide as Byrdine though taller by a head. A big, tall woman, neither young nor old, with a high forehead covered with little black freckles. Her hair poked out from under a yellow wool hat that looked homemade.

Byrdine got them inside, out of the dark and cold. "It's a mean night," she said. The woman nodded for answer. Byrdine motioned to the boy. "How 'bout you set him down on the couch so he can stretch out and sleep. Give you a rest," she added. But the woman clutched the child harder. She got them sitting down at least and went to make some coffee. It was three o'clock in the morning and she couldn't see anyone, no matter what their state of mind, refusing a cup of coffee. For the boy she warmed a little milk with Ovaltine.

It was the boy who did the first talking. He was dressed in pajamas and a red jacket big enough to fit him twice. It was pinned together in the front with pink and blue diaper pins. Byrdine brought him his Ovaltine and he said, "Zipper broke."

"What's that, honey? Your zipper broke?"

"Mama can't fix it 'cause she's got a baby."

Byrdine looked at the woman who shook her head. "Where's the baby now?" she asked the boy.

"Baby's home with Mama."

"Home with Mama?"

"Yeah."

"Where's that, honey?"

The boy hesitated, then he said, "That's where we live."

"You best blow on it," said the woman. She blew in the boy's cup, showing him how to cool the chocolate.

"I never make it too hot for the young ones," said Byrdine. She gave the woman her coffee. "I got cream and sugar if you like that."

"Thank you," said the woman and handed the cup back. Byrdine made it white and sweet, the way she liked it too. She came and sat down on the couch across from the two of them in the chair.

"Behind them curtains the shades is pulled," she said. "Pulled in the kitchen too. When there's a knock in the middle of the night, I pull the shades. I do it before I come to the door." She blew on her coffee, which made the boy laugh. "Who dropped you off?" she asked.

"No one," said the woman.

"It's alright. You don't have to say."

"We done walked," said the boy.

"Walked from where, honey?"

"For a long time."

Byrdine looked at the woman. "On these roads?"

The woman looked away. "Yes ma'am. We kept off the road, but we followed it. I hate to walk in those woods if I don't have to."

"Lord," said Byrdine. She rubbed her forehead.

"Now on the way back I'll have to. It'll be light."

"On the way back you'll ride with me," said Byrdine. "How many miles did y'all come?"

"Fifteen, twenty," said the woman. "He mostly rode on my back."

Byrdine shook her head. She stood up and said to the boy, "What's your name, honey?"

"Roosevelt."

"Well, Roosevelt, we got to feed your horse. Feed you too. How 'bout a nice piece of raspberry pie? You like pie?"

He nodded, but the woman said, "Thank you, but we ain't hungry." She had something with her, an old kerchief knotted at the top, and Byrdine figured it might hold a few biscuits and a couple of hard-boiled eggs.

"Alright," she said and sat down again. "But before we do any talking we got to come to an agreement. You at least got to let me get you home."

"We'll walk home," said the woman.

"No you won't," said Byrdine, "not carrying this little boy."

"We walked here," said the woman.

"I know that!"

"Miz Dean—"

"Deedee. That's what everyone calls me."

"—I know you don't have no car."

"I got a good friend with a car."

"We don't know your friend, and your friend don't know us."

"*I'll* drive you," said Byrdine. "I'll borrow a car and drive you myself."

"Well."

"That's settled. Now this boy at least ought to lay down and rest."

She'd never seen a boy sleep the way he did. It was immediate and too sound. She sensed something not right in the way he disappeared in sleep, like his self had got up and left the room. She said to the woman, "It's the boy you've come about, ain't it?"

The woman looked down and up again. "Yes."

"Who sent you? Odetta Jackson?"

"Yes ma'am."

"She couldn't do nothing?"

"Some people afraid to try."

"She was afraid to try?"

"No ma'am. She did try a time or two, did some spells when his first tooth come out."

"His first tooth? How old is he?"

"He just turn five."

"He looks more like three."

"Yes ma'am. He always been small."

"What's your name?"

The woman looked surprised. "I'm his aunt."

She laughed. "That don't give you a name."

"It's Rutha. Rutha Brown."

"Rutha. You mind me asking something?"

"I don't know if I do or I don't."

"I'll ask it, and maybe you'll answer, maybe you won't." Rutha smiled, her first smile. Byrdine went on, "If I figure right, y'all left around nine last evening. Ain't that awful late to start out?"

"I work until then," said Rutha. "And ain't no one got a car. We had to do something. His mama's got six other childrens at home. The good Lord ain't given me a one, so I tell her I be the one to go, and here I am. The boy's bad. He don't seem too bad, just you live with him you see how bad he is. Fits and all. He been that way since he was born. His mama say before that. Say she could feel him acting strange inside, like something took hold of him inside her and he'd kick and kick like he was kicking his way out of a trap, then he'd stop sudden and she'd feel like he was dead."

"Dead?"

"Yes ma'am. That's how still he got."

"He's that still now. Look at him."

Rutha sighed. "I know it. I don't know which I like better, him still like that or wild-like the way he gets. The fits and all, they knock him to the ground and sometimes you think some animal inside of him's coming on the outside of him, like he's turning inside out and the thing has claws and a big old waggy tongue and a voice like a bark and a mouth like one of them mad dogs, all foamy like he's been drinking soapsuds. You can't hold him then, itty bitty as he is. You'd do better holding down a greased hog."

"I tried that once at a county fair," said Byrdine.

"You did?"

"I like to try everything once." She looked at the boy. "I got an idea he's made for something else besides this world."

"Yeah. I know what you mean. I have dreams. He's in most of them."

They were quiet awhile, then Byrdine said, "Did Odetta tell you what I do?"

"No ma'am. Miss Odetta just said come and find you, and she told me where."

"I read the hand. That's all. I can't give you no cure. Your own people got cures. They the ones I go to. Just like you, I get up and go to them in the middle of the night."

"You do?"

"Sure I do."

On the couch the little boy moved onto his belly. His sleep seemed lighter, more human, and Byrdine knew if she didn't do it now she'd miss her chance. She went over to him and got down on the floor, which was no job at all compared to getting back up again. His skinny arm hung over the edge of the couch, his palm toward her. She said to Rutha, "I'm going to need more light. There's a flashlight in the kitchen. Get it for me, please." Rutha brought it. The whole little hand could fit in its beam. She liked to hold a hand to read it and she took the boy's lightly and a chill passed through her at that moment, as she suspected it might. She took in what she saw there and also what she didn't have to look to see. She turned the flashlight off and asked Rutha to put it back in the kitchen.

"I guess I ain't done enough toting," said Rutha, getting up slowly out of the chair.

"Don't bother," said Byrdine. "But I do got to have a minute alone with him."

"What do you got in mind? The boy's asleep."

Byrdine looked at her and said, "I don't tell you what to dream, do I? Or what those dreams mean?" Rutha shook her head and Byrdine said, "Thank you."

She wasn't much of a one for prayer, ordinarily. She said one now though, after Rutha went to the kitchen. She leaned over the boy and whispered God's name first, then His son Jesus because He had been a boy once too. "Protect this child," she said. "Let him live to be a man." She put her hands on Roosevelt's head and said, "In the name of Mary, whose boy was lost."

She tried to get up off the floor then. Rutha heard her scrabbling around and came in and said, "That ain't no bigger than my kitchen."

"I bet it ain't half as clean, either. Help me, will you?"

"He still asleep?"

"He'll be out till morning."

"It's getting on to morning now."

"We got some time."

BYRDINE DEAN

1963

The night she took Roosevelt to the swamp it was pitch dark with no moon, and a whippoorwill called at them from behind the wall of pines along the road. He was nine then, still a small boy. He looked no older than six. He came out of his house shirtless, wearing only a pair of overalls he shared with his sister Charlene. Nothing on his feet.

"You go back in and put some shoes on," Byrdine called from the car and the boy looked at her, said not a word, but made no move. Finally she said, "Tell me you don't have none."

"Yes ma'am," said Roosevelt, "I got 'em."

"Then what's your idea, standing here barefooted? Plenty a snakes out where we're going. Plenty a hungry cottonmouths. Haven't seen a boy your size for quite some time. You ever been snakebit? It ain't no picnic."

"I ain't been bit," he said. "And I ain't gonna be bit."

"Suit yourself."

They drove a couple of miles on the Old Magnolia Road, turned east on the Lower Cairo toward Metcalf. On both sides the low shapes of houses, Negroes living poor with a chained dog or two protecting their poverty. Barren yards. A few outbuildings—

sheds, coops, and privies—hunched in the darkness. The smell of motor oil and tea olive and sweet waves of pig shit coming in on the woman and the boy. Neither of them said a word. Finally Byrdine pulled the car to the shoulder and turned it off. They sat there listening to the cooling tick of the engine. She pointed across the road, "There's Florida." They got out and caught a ragged dirt track headed north.

He was a good walker, he kept right up and walked along quiet and seemed to know his place in the night. The whippoorwill called, beat them over the head with its side of the argument. A poor way to catch a wife, thought Byrdine. Without it they might have heard an owl. They'd gone a mile or two when she kicked up an armadillo, scared it out of the grass beside the road. It ran like a cat, head down, close to the ground, tearing along with little dismayed grunts. She laughed aloud. "You'd think they'd move slow. They got all that stuff to carry around. That armor."

"Nothing out here go slow," said the boy.

"Gophers do."

"Maybe a gopher."

They started walking again, the road rising slightly until they stood on top of an earthen dam. In front of them the low water of a duck pond fed by Bully Creek, the shapes of half a dozen blinds built up on stilts on little islands of clay. Beyond that another lower dam, and then the swamp's looming cypress. "Come on," she said. "Let's go see if my boat's still there." They circled the pond, startling an egret out of the shallows. It flew up behind them with a coughing croaking cry, disappeared into the trees.

"Magic birds," said Byrdine.

"They give me the spooks."

"What's spooky about them?"

"What ain't?"

"You ever seen snow?" she asked.

"Yeah, on TV."

"You find that spooky?"

"Naw, it look pretty."

"It looks pretty alright. For the first half hour. You ever heard of Wyoming?" Roosevelt shook his head. "Well, I once was fool enough to follow a fellow up to Wyoming, and you talk about snow." Byrdine whistled. "They got enough snow there to kill the thrill. I look at one of them egrets, it reminds me of the color of that first snow, before you had a chance to go crazy looking at it all the time, never knowing if there was a ground still under there or not. Spring came and I'd about forgotten what green was. I'll never do that again. Live where there ain't no green."

"He died," said Roosevelt. It didn't seem to her a question.

"You mean the fellow?"

He nodded.

"Yes he did. He did."

They found her aluminum boat pulled up on the back side of the lower dam, the oars a few yards away, hidden in the briars. Whoever had used it had forgotten to flip it over so she set the boy to bailing. "Just get enough out so we can raise it and pour out the rest. I'm going looking for my pole."

There wasn't much rowing in a cypress swamp. A pole was what you needed. Hers was nowhere to be found, which meant an unexpected hardship unless she could lay her hands on a downed limb of the right length and strength and heft. That old pole of hers was precious to no one else. She didn't fear theft. But it boded ill, the loss of it. She couldn't help feeling it was somewhere within spitting distance but she was spitting in the wrong direction.

She came back to the boy and told him, “I’m wasting my time out there. It’s too dark to see. How you coming?”

“A lot of water in here.”

“Had a lot of rain, that’s why. Look over there.” She pointed to the southwest corner of the sky where the stars blurred. “More on its way, coming up from the Gulf. It’s a good thing I like shrimp. Gulf shrimp’s what makes up for all this wet Gulf weather.”

Roosevelt had finished his bailing and together they raised the boat on its side until the last of the water ran out. She said, “I sure don’t like it, you with your bare feet. I shouldn’t’ve brung you.”

The boy shrugged.

“Just promise me you won’t get bit.”

“I won’t get bit.”

“I’ll hold you to it.”

The boat, it seemed, took on water on dry land, even with no rain falling. Byrdine’s cockeyed solution was to float it quick, and for some reason it worked. She got Roosevelt in and shoved out into the swamp, using one of the oars as her pole. “You get going fast enough,” she told him, “the water can’t keep up with you and what’s already got in drains out the way it came.”

“This boat got a name?” he asked.

“Sure it does. It’s bad luck not to name a boat.”

“What’s its name?”

“Odetta give it its name. It was her boat.”

“Miss Odetta?”

“She’s the one first brought me here. Now she’s off her feet, I come out here and get the stuff she needs.”

“What kind a stuff?”

“Don’t be asking so many questions.”

"I ain't asked but one to start. It's the name of this boat." He looked down into the water. "Wish I could get an answer."

"It's called *Moses,*" said Byrdine. "Now go and ask me why."

"I know why," said the boy. He kept on looking into the water. What did he see there? The bones of Pharaoh's army? Could be. She'd seen stranger things—faces known and unknown to her, glowing like coal fire just below the viscous skin of the swamp; gold-bearing galleons dressed with Saint Elmo's fire, drifting ghostly through the cypress; an ancient Cherokee called Sow Purse, long associated with her visions and imagination, climbing arduously onto the bare back of an emaciated pinto and disappearing down into the mud-water as if descending a steep liquid hill. Byrdine no longer cared what was real and what was not. Nor were the apparitions, if they were that, important in themselves. They were remembered for the emotions they conjured in her, like the humming of air after a struck bell.

"What do you see down there?" she asked.

"Nothing."

"Well, what're you looking at?"

"I said, nothing."

"Looking at and seeing are two different things."

"I know it, but I ain't looking at nothing and I ain't seeing nothing. I got my eyes closed."

He brought his head up and showed her. She couldn't see in the dark and didn't need to look and thought only that she had been wrong to bring him. Nothing she could do about that now, short of turning back, and she didn't like to turn back. They were going now, they were on their way. Even the steady leak of swamp water gaining on her ankles, all that told her was to come out during the day and fix the holes and find her pole. None of it said one thing about turning back.

He was frightened tonight. It made him tuck in like an old gopher, scared back into his shell. The fright could do you good if you were old enough to sort out what could hurt you from what could not. Fright didn't always measure a source of harm, and what could harm you, God knew, didn't always frighten you. But he was a boy, and these things were a grown person's knowledge. Was he a boy?

Byrdine looked at the back of his bowed head, the hair sheared short, the ears too large, standing out from his skull, and she thought how strange she might seem to him now that he was no longer clearly a child. Her feelings for him, already unbidden, might be unwanted as well, seeming only like a rude kind of curiosity, the kind whites were always guilty of around Negroes. For the white and the black did think about each other, did wonder about each other all the time. No, she decided, this boy who could see through solid walls, who could walk right up to wild animals, who could sort the living from the dead in conversation and draw out snake poison with his own hand, all the stories told of him drew a picture of someone who sensed motive as easily as others saw physical features—fat and thin, man and woman, color. He would know then that her pursuit of him came unbidden to her as well. That she felt she must run beside him with food, a blanket, warm clothes, shoes, ready to lift him, to warm him, to squirrel him under her coat, to carry him hidden across borders, but she did not know why. His own people cared well for him in those ways. Was it a reach back into a time many years ago when she was a child and her own gift lay on her like pinched clothing, noticeable and laughable to others, leaving her unprotected? It was his illness that lay at the core of her grasping toward him. But unlike his kin who wanted him safe, she knew he could never be and wanted only to help him find a fit road, one that surely led away from them but possibly—and she prayed about this—possibly led him back to them as well. She imagined it circular, a round road. She at least wished it so.

Out of all this she managed to tell him only, "Hey. You know I ain't quite all I look to be." He turned and she could make out his frowning puzzlement in the dark. She laughed. "What I mean is I got Indian blood. One-quarter Cherokee."

"Then you're more than you look to be," he said and turned back to his silent mooning.

After a while she said, "You were a kid, you liked to talk to me."

She poled them forward, the water feeling more and more solid beneath them, the cypress trunks heavy and creaturelike on all sides. Now the Spanish moss started up in earnest, curtaining them from one another in places. In one of these places, his form hidden from her, his young voice coming from behind a mossy, old man's beard, he said, "Ain't I a kid now?" Then the boat jerked forward and that same cloak covered her eyes.

He insisted. "Ain't I?"

"You ain't exactly anything," said Byrdine. "Not man nor child."

She pushed them deeper and deeper into the swamp. He faced her, watching her work the oar. Sometimes the Spanish moss covered her hair, made her hauntlike, the swamp a great big witches' pot she was stirring. In it were venoms enough to kill everyone he knew. A slick of starlight shone on the water surrounding the boat. The trees above him alive with large dark birds. A sound like a cough, then a molten glob of shit fell on his shoulder, greasy and fishy, with little bones in it. Quick she gave him an old kerchief rag and told him, "That's as foul a thing as you'll find, anhinga shit. Them birds is so old they got fur instead of feathers. They go back before the time of flowers, like most things in this swamp. You and me, we're like babes in the woods. You won't find no greater collection of antiques than we got here. We're just poling around in an old museum and every now and then the stuff jumps off the walls and reminds us we best know our place here. We ain't lived a minute next to these old dinosaurs."

She produced a flashlight, told him to hold it up to his forehead and scan the water ahead where the swamp opened up some. "What am I looking for?" he asked.

"A set of red eyes. Look like the devil's eyes."

He didn't believe in the devil, not any devil that lived out here in a swamp. His Aunt Rutha loved to talk about the devil. She quoted Scripture enough. Seemed like she loved the devil. He was an angel, and the most interesting of them as far as Roosevelt could tell. *Angels and devil both, fed out of God's pocket,* that's what his mama said, though it drew a dark look from his daddy. Was it God did the feeding? If so He loved the devil too. Or the way Roosevelt saw it, the angels and the devil all formed up in a bunch like second lunch at school when the colored children ate. They bunched up and rolled toward God with their bellies growling and their Scripture forgotten, and they dipped into God's pocket that held the stuff to fill them, the fried chicken and mashed potatoes and Jell-O and golden cake, the cartons of milk and juice and the pans of hot dry cornbread served by the skinny lady with but one tooth, her hair in a net, the skin on the back of her hands melted and terrible, and on her face the scars of what Aunt Rutha claimed might be a thing called leprosy. He was never, ever to touch her. If he did he would live without a friend in the world like she did. And no doubt lose his teeth. In Roosevelt's understanding, the devil and his angels set upon God and took what they needed, and the strength of their need fueled the boldness of their act. They did not wait to be given. Might they not wait forever that way?

It startled him, Miss Deedee speaking out of the dark, like a snake uncoiling. "Hide your light," she whispered. "We got company."

He heard it then too, the whine of a truck coming over the dam, making its way around the pond in low gear. It traveled dark, without headlights, a sure sign of trouble. It stopped, the engine clunked a couple of times, and some men's voices rolled out of the cab, all going at once in an argument over something Roosevelt couldn't make out. They were white men. He could tell that. One started laughing but he was the only one and he quit as quick as he started.

"They'll be looking for the boat," he whispered.

"Hush. It ain't their boat."

Miss Deedee had worked them back into the cypress, behind a thick fall of moss. Without movement now the boat was leaking hard and Roosevelt felt around for the bailer. "It ain't in here," he told her.

She was up on the seat, scouting. "What ain't?"

"That tobacco can."

"It's sitting where you left it back by the dam. Now hush."

"What are we going to do? We're leaking bad, Miss Deedee."

She took her shoes off, a pair of old worn sneakers, and gave one to him and started bailing with the other. It was slow, and hard to do without making a sound. Over by the truck the men were unloading a boat. "Hear that?" she said. "It echoes. It's aluminum. If I was doing what they're doing I'd use a wood boat so it didn't boom like that and paint it black or green so it didn't show up in the dark."

"What are they after?" asked Roosevelt. He was gaining on the swamp in the boat and now he could feel half a dozen holes in the floor where the water kept coming in. They felt like bullet holes.

"What they're after is money."

"How they going to get that out here?"

"That devil-eyed creature," she said. "They're going to find it and kill it and take it over to Florida, and Florida's going to sell it up north and some fine fancy lady in New York City is going to get up in the morning and slip her feet into gator-hide shoes and take a hold of her gator-hide purse and never know she's walking out to do her shopping wearing the old man of the swamp. It don't mean nothing to her but money, like it do to them." She quit her bailing, rested a minute. "It's the money makes them mean. They ain't meant to be out here shooting them. They done shot all but a few anyway. They're going to shoot themselves right out of business, even if they don't get caught."

"They're poaching?" asked Roosevelt.

"That's the word for it."

"Whose land is this?"

"It's the southern end of Detroits', about seven miles from your house as the crow flies, but we ain't crows so we got to go the long way around on the roads."

"What'll they do to us?"

"Who?"

"Them? If they find us?"

"They ain't going to find us." But she didn't sound as sure as she wanted to be.

With the water out she had the boy sit down on the bottom of the boat. They plugged the holes with Spanish moss mixed with anhinga shit. She sat where she could look out and see the poachers' progress, for now they were on the water they were quiet, intent on their sorry business. There were three of them. The man in front held the light and the rear man poled. The one in the middle had a rifle ready—she couldn't see it, but she could imagine it. They came quickly across the water which had lost its mystery, its ancient feeling of refuge and covenant. Why had she not prepared herself for such a night? Poachers were a dime a dozen, usually trespassing for coon or possum or deer, pest animals the plantation owners would just as soon have them take. But gator hunters were a different kind. First off, they were white. This was not a colored man's game. There was too much money in it. And all that money meant risks. It gave the whole business a desperate edge she didn't like being this close to. But here they were. The men came toward them, their light aimed elsewhere for the moment. All they had to do was catch the stark aluminum side of *Moses,* they'd give up their gator hunt to save their own hides. And that fellow with the gun wouldn't ask before he got off a shot. She knew that. It made her sick to her stomach.

Suddenly the boy moved in the bottom of the boat, a violent recoil that set them rocking, set the water sucking at the sides of the boat. She looked at him in the dark. What did he think he was doing? She saw him reach up, what looked like a living vine wrapping his arm. He shook it off and a great big cottonmouth went over the side and oiled away across the swamp.

"*Roosevelt!*" she whispered.

He said nothing.

"Honey, he get you?"

"Naw."

"You best get up on the seat with me."

He didn't answer, and he didn't move.

"You're right," she told him. "Stay where you are. Keep your head down."

The men had gone on beyond them, unaware, their light leading them forward like a blade in a meat cutter's hand. It slid to the left and right, thin slices of swamp all struck by its brilliance—black water, hanging vine, cypress knee, floating baskets of humped ground—all struck and gone. The light left her blind. She could see nothing out there but what they pointed her to. Everything between her and them, including the boy, was a blank darkness. She could hear him breathing. He sounded scared. He was a smart boy.

Then like a bedsheet caught by the wind that light came back at her, threw itself against the curtain of moss. She felt suffocated by it. She put her hands up to her face. It sought and found the holes in the curtain, gleamed off the side of the boat and she said to the boy, "Get here behind me." Roosevelt moved up quick and the shot came right after. It went straight through the boat, one side to the other.

A man called out, "I believe we found us some poachers, boys." The light came harder and brighter as the man with the pole pushed furiously toward them. Byrdine could hear him grunting and panting. Another man said, "Shoot 'em again, Ray. Ain't we out here for sport?" But the third man said, "Shit, I ain't signed on for murder." He was the man poling. He talked like he was running hard uphill. "Shoot 'em," the second man said again.

Byrdine called out, “We’re a woman and child. We ain’t seen your faces, we don’t know who you are. Go on back and get in your truck and go home and we’ll do the same. Never seen you, you sorry sonsabitches. Never heard of you. Never were here at all.”

She was shaking hard. The boy was crying into her back, little wet hiccups of sound.

Old Ray laughed. “She got a tongue on her.”

The man poling stopped his poling and said, “She made us a deal. Let’s take it.”

The third man said, “You shitbrain, Floyd. You think she ain’t got the sheriff in there, hiding behind that toad-sucking mouth of hers?”

“I think she ain’t,” said Floyd.

“You think she ain’t?” The man guffawed. “Tell me what’s a girl and a baby doing out here in the middle of the night? It don’t add up.”

Ray said, “Tate, give me that light.”

“What for?”

“Let’s see it.”

“It’s my light.”

“I want to come in close,” said Ray. “See who all’s in there.”

“You crazy?” said Floyd. Byrdine knew then that she knew that voice. It was the same voice he’d had at seventeen, when he was afraid like he was afraid now.

Tate said, “What’re you worried about, shitbrain? It’s just a bitch and a baby.” He laughed. “She’s lit up all she can be, Ray. We cain’t see nothing till she comes out a there.”

“We’re going in,” said Ray.

“No way,” said Floyd.

Tate said, “I don’t know, Ray.”

"I'll tell you something," said Ray, "both you young shitbrains. If she had a man or a gun in there, we'd a been dead some time ago. I ain't going to leave her set here while we go running off like whipped dogs. I know she don't know us, she ain't seen our faces, but I intend to know her. She's smart. Maybe she's pretty too." He laughed. "Though I ain't counting on it. Take us over there, Floyd."

"Put your pole down, Floyd," said Byrdine. "Not one inch closer. And don't let them talk to you the way they do. Ain't I taught you nothing? Stick up for yourself, believe in yourself. Remember that, Floyd? Remember every time one of Mama's boyfriends took you out and beat you till the blood come out your ears? Every one of them did it 'cause she told them to and they were scared of her. You'd come home and I'd patch you up but it didn't make you no good. I see you're still working for a beating. Maybe you get some money out of it this way. Or maybe you land yourself in jail again, do a little more time. I tell you what, Floyd. You don't owe me nothing, you never did, but if you want to help me some you can call off your friends, pole that boat out of here, and go home. I ain't going to ask but twice. This here's the second time."

She parted the moss, showed her whole self to Tate's light, and said, "This is all I am. I'm old and ugly and this man here's my brother, haven't seen him in twenty years. Don't know nothing about what you're up to and don't care. Me and my boy here's out looking at the starlight. That's all."

To her surprise, the light went down and Tate said, "We got no one to mess with here."

But Ray said, "Floyd, don't you want to say hello to your nephew?"

"It don't matter," said Floyd.

"Bet you didn't know you had a nephew."

"Didn't think much about it one way or the other."

"Your sister married?" asked Ray.

Tate said, "Lay off, Ray. Leave the boy out of it."

Ray said, "This between me and Floyd. 'Less you tell me she's your sister too."

"She ain't my sister."

"Then what's your hurry? Ain't we having fun? Ain't you curious, Tate? See what a big old ugly fellow like Floyd come up with for a nephew? I fear it ain't a pretty sight."

"Leave it," said Tate. "Let's go home."

"If I were that boy, I'd want to meet my long-lost Uncle Floyd."

"It don't matter," said Floyd.

"That all you can say? Well, I got an idea. We'll get your sister here to do a little talking. She's a good talker. Bet there's a whole lot she could talk about, like where that boy come from and why he ain't poked his head out yet like Ray Junior woulda done when he was a boy, or Tate's boy, or any boy who ain't ashamed of who he is and what he look like. Wouldn't surprise me, no, it wouldn't surprise me at all if that boy had a drop of nigger blood in him. Maybe more than that. What do you think about that, Floyd? Your sister with a nigger child?"

"It ain't no nigger."

"Now you're talking."

"It ain't."

"That's right, it ain't. So let's go in there get a look at him."

"She wouldn't go with no nigger."

"And from what I seen, no nigger'd go with her."

“Quit, Ray,” said Tate.

“Quit? You telling me when to quit? Now that ain’t smart. I guess I’ll quit when I said enough.”

“If I can get home before Aileen, I won’t have to explain things, is all.”

“That wife a yours got a terrible hold on you, Tate. She pulls the graveyard shift every weekend and you’re so dumb you believe her.”

“Shut up, Ray.”

“Ain’t that true, Floyd?”

Floyd said nothing. Then he said, “It don’t matter what’s true. It’s Tate’s life. It ain’t our business.”

Byrdine watched him slowly, in slow motion, lean on his pole and push them away. He didn’t look at her and she didn’t want him to. She leaned down and touched the boy whose instinct for survival had brought him to the floor of the boat again. “Come up, Roosevelt. They’re gone.”

COLE JONES

1964

One morning, one of the last mornings of uncomplicated life, Cole was later to think, Billy Valentine, having fired an arsenal of shells without hitting a single bird, rowed around the duck pond collecting everyone, a grace to his figure and the light lifting up behind him like he was coming forward out of his privacy, his unknowability, to the center of a watery stage. The man could row, Cole realized. He looked at home at the oars, balancing the heavy wooden boat as if it were one of those weightless things that real rowers rowed. He looked like a man out of an English movie, rowing a lady on some river somewhere, though in this case the lady was a husky chocolate Lab by the name of Man.

"Ahoy!" called Billy, scraping the mound of the island on which the duck blind was built. "Any snakes this morning?"

"Not a one." Cole shook his head. "You find any?"

"One."

"Under the blind?"

"Curled up on the bench."

"No fooling?"

"I heard it sliding away in the dark, caught it in my flashlight. A great big water moccasin." He grinned.

"Well," said Cole, "that was some way to start the new year."

Billy came forward in the boat and Cole handed him his gun and shell case. Five long-necked ducks swung low over the blind and Billy, still standing, reached for his own gun.

"Merganser," said Cole. No one in his right mind would shoot a merganser. They were fish eaters, and the meat had a strong fishy flavor.

"I don't care what they are," said Billy. But it was too late to get a shot off. He sat down and took the oars and Cole pushed them off and got in, facing Billy's back. "Man brought in two of yours," said Billy. He nodded at a pair of male mallards on the bottom of the boat. "Another one went down over by the dam, but I didn't see where the fourth one went."

"I've got my eye on it," said Cole. "You're just about lined up with it. Pull on your left oar. Another ten yards. Yeah, that's it. That's it. I got it." He lifted the duck out of the water into the boat. Man whined and tried to leap over Billy, and Cole laughed and handed him the bird. He mouthed it until Billy told him "Give!" and he gave it into Billy's hand and Billy dropped it next to the mallards in the bottom of the boat.

"A teal," said Billy. "That's pretty."

"No, it's another mallard. A female."

Billy said nothing. He rowed without moving his shoulders. He rowed with his whole back, the plane of his back, and with his legs. He rowed without thought, Cole was certain, the way he, Cole Jones, shot without thought. A high, long shot, he just cleared his mind and let his body take over, not a single feeling about it, he just let the gun go up and do what it did. He'd tried to explain that to his wife once and she'd accused him of being irresponsible.

"Irresponsible? Why?"

"You could lose control of the gun that way, just letting it go like that."

"It's no different than playing a game of catch, Karen. You don't aim the ball, now do you? You don't stop and look at the other fellow's glove and line it up and pitch the ball, you just pitch the ball. The ball's part of your body, an extension of your arm, and after a while it's as accurate as if I was to reach out right now and touch you on the nose."

He reached for her and she said, "Don't, Cole. And I don't know one thing about baseball so I can't follow that argument and it's beside the point."

He looked at Billy again. This time he saw that the oars were part of Billy's body, as the gun was part of his. He'd remember that about Billy from now on. Billy said, "I'll drop you and the dog, then I'll go back and get Harry and Frankie. You can go and find the one that went down by the dam."

"Alright."

"If the alligator didn't get it first."

"There's some big ones in here this year," said Cole.

"That's what I hear."

"I don't believe everything I hear, but I do believe Osee Davis."

Billy nodded. "I wish we could get Mother out here one of these mornings."

"She sure liked it, didn't she, a duck shoot? She liked a turkey shoot too. The size of those birds. The speed of them. A dozen going over your head at once. Just about give you a heart attack."

"That 410 of hers," Billy laughed.

"She'd surprise you," Cole said. "Every now and then she'd hit something. You never shot turkey, Billy?"

"I liked my sleep too much."

"I was lucky. I always liked this time of the morning. It doesn't mean much to most people, but I like getting up in the dark. And you know what? If you'd have told me then in ten years there wouldn't be a turkey left on this place, I'd have bet good money against it."

"They'll come back," said Billy.

"That's what they said about the blackbirds. Now, no one cares about a blackbird, but the truth is they didn't come back. And there used to be a lot more quail, you used to see a lot more quail. There was a time, you remember it, Billy, when we had a lot of wood duck. Nothing tastes like a wood duck, does it? It's been a long time since I've seen a wood duck."

"They'll come back."

"I don't know how they can. With people being the way they are, there won't be much to come back to."

"People are the way they are because we make them that way, Cole. I learned that in advertising."

"It's the demand that drives the market."

"But we create the demand. People only really want what you offer them. You build a lot of homes and take away the trees, well," Billy shrugged, "you can guarantee there won't be much to come back to."

Cole smiled. "I know what you're saying, but the way I see it, we live here, I live here, why shouldn't everyone have a chance to live here? There's a miracle called plywood, and the way it's going, I'd be a fool to sit around and watch some stranger come in, buy up all the land, and develop it. Shoot, why not me?"

"And I'm not trying to stop you. You've got the head for that kind of thing. That's why my brother's got you running this place.

Harry's a little dictator, he's not a manager." Billy looked over his shoulder, scouting for the best place to land. "I'll tell you what, though. This is what I think. I think people will change. In twenty years they'll see what they've lost and they'll try to get it back again. At least on the plantations. Life's a whole different bag of tricks on the plantations. They'll become parks, that's my guess. Game parks. Twenty, thirty years."

They bumped the shore and Cole got out and the dog jumped over the side into the shallow water. "Thanks," said Cole.

"*De nada,*" said Billy.

"What's that?"

"Spanish. You're welcome."

"*De nada*. I'll have to remember that. *De nada*."

"Look," said Billy, "I want to ask you something." He turned around and leaned forward in the boat. "Feel free to say no."

"Alright."

"It's about a shooting lesson. I want to order up a shooting lesson. Does that sound like something you'd be interested in? I want to pay you for it, too."

Cole shook his head. "You can have me but not hire me, Billy. I won't let you pay me."

"No deal then."

"To do something I like? It would be like paying you to—"

"I don't work for free," said Billy. "I never work for free. You think about it." He took the oars again, took a few strokes out on the water and turned the boat around. He called back, "It's not for me, Cole. It's for Quinn." Then he rowed hard, set his whole body into it, and Cole thought he knew that exhilaration. He felt some of it himself, watching full daylight hit the tops of the pines. In a minute it would ease down across the pond and illuminate the signal-white faces of the hunters. The morning was over, though for some it had just begun. Quinn, he thought. He hardly knew Billy's wife. Quinn. It was a strange name. He called the dog and headed for the dam with a sense of anticipation now, and when they had both searched and the dog finally returned to him with the wood duck, a male in all its courtly colors, Cole thought he had never seen such a beautiful sight—the young dog, the bird in every way perfect, sunlight descending the dam. He stood still, barely breathing. The only thing moving was the light. The dog came to him, waiting to be told to give it up, and Cole took the bird. It was cool and stiff in his hand, a small, chubby duck with a head of brilliant green, the open eye the color of blood. He put it in his game pocket and suddenly he thought of Karen and how she would not see what he saw, she would see something dead, she would see something she was expected to cook. She would say nothing, but she would be blind to what made him happy.

He stood behind her, his arms around her shoulders, his hands covering hers on the gun. "Like this," he said, holding the barrel steady as she swung left to right across the dove field. "Don't let the gun drop. It'll want to drop, it's heavy, but don't let it."

He stepped away from her and watched her shoulders let go. She was a lefty. He'd never tried to teach a lefty before. "What about the bead?" she asked him.

"The bead?"

"The . . . you know. The thing at the end of the barrel."

"Don't pay any attention to anything but the target."

"Well, get me a target."

He grinned. "Let's go over and hit a pinecone out of a tree."

"Pinecone? That's no target. I want a moving target."

She missed the first clay pigeon and hit the second, but it was just a lucky hit, he could see that. She missed the third and the fourth, and then the next one she nicked, not a solid shot. She turned around and said, "What am I doing wrong? I should be hitting these and I'm not."

"You're only five shots into your first shooting lesson."

"Two out of five, Cole. I'm better than that." He laughed and she said, "No, I mean it."

He could see she did and he came up behind her and stood with his arms around her shoulders again, his chest lightly touching her back. He placed himself against her as impersonally as he could, like a stamp on a letter. He had trained himself to make that contact businesslike, but some couldn't tolerate it and he sensed it might be where he would lose her. He knew there was talent there, could see it right away and it was exciting, so he was as careful as he could be.

He told her to raise the gun and she did and he could feel her angle was wrong. "You're leaning back," he said.

"Show me." He angled forward and she had to move with him. "Yes. I can feel that."

"Feet closer together."

"Closer?"

"You need to be ready to spring."

She laughed. "I'm not catching these birds, I'm shooting them."

"The whole body shoots."

She lowered the gun. "What about the mind?"

"Forget your mind," he said. He was speaking into her hair, which smelled of the shampoo she used. He knew he shouldn't be thinking about her shampoo. He let go of her and asked her to raise the gun again and this time she was balanced correctly and he was satisfied.

She hit the next three clay pigeons but missed four in a row after that. "What *is* it, Cole?" she cried.

"You're aiming. Don't aim."

"What do you mean, I'm aiming?"

"Just watch the target."

"I don't under*stand*."

"Don't line anything up. Just watch the target."

She tightened her jaw and missed the next two shots and he wasn't sure what he saw but he saw something, a catch in the motion as the gun went up, almost imperceptible, like a twig in a river. He went to her and she raised the gun for him, then he saw it and was sure. "It's your ring," he said.

She looked at him blankly.

"Your wedding ring. It's catching the trigger guard on the way up."

She yanked it off and put it in her pocket and for the rest of the afternoon she shot consistently and accurately. He was pleased and wanted to push her and at the end, without warning, he sent out two clay pigeons at once. He watched her. He found that he enjoyed watching her move and react. Her face tightened with concentration. He knew she would have to learn to relax. That might be the hardest lesson for her. He wasn't sure he could teach it, though he would like to. He thought he would like to teach her everything he knew. He watched her see the two targets, a slight jump of her right hand, but she recovered and hit the longest shot first—a good instinct—then the closer one, taking her time. This was important, that she didn't hurry. He'd forgotten to tell her not to hurry but she seemed to know it already. She turned to him and smiled and said, "You sneak."

"Nothing sneaky about it. Two birds get up at once."

"You knew I could do it, didn't you?"

"I knew you'd want to try."

She was happy and talkative, walking out in the dove field with him to pick up the few targets she'd missed. They could see the kennels through the trees, and then the hill to the house. He felt miles away from that house, across an ocean, on an island with her. It was neither a good feeling nor a bad one. He remembered something Karen had once said to him in the cooling-down time after one of their fights. She had told him how she hated not to feel proud of herself, and how seldom she felt proud of herself. She was asking him to feel proud of her if he could. He wondered if Quinn had feelings like that. He wondered why Billy wasn't teaching her himself. Billy was as poor a shot as his wife was a fine one, but he could teach her. Cole knew anyone could teach her. And he wondered why she hadn't taken up a gun until now. They walked back across the field, toward his car, and he asked her this and she said, "It's a complicated answer. It's two answers. The one I give out freely is that I needed to wait until Leo didn't need me anymore, didn't cling to me. He's four and a half now. He's more sure of himself. I feel like I can begin to have a life of my own." Cole nodded, and she went on. "The other answer is more confusing. It has to do with Billy. Billy likes to be good at what he does, and if he can't be good at what he does he'd rather I didn't see it. He certainly doesn't want me to be better at it. But I think I've convinced him it doesn't matter how many birds he kills. He's in advertising. That's its own form of hunting."

Cole guessed differently, that Billy would take more convincing, that competition died slowly in a man, if it truly died at all. At the car he offered to take Quinn up to the house but she said no, she would walk home. He told her she was an A-plus student and she nodded and said, "Thank you. We'll see, won't we?"

He watched her go. Her form already seemed familiar to him. Her form brought back the smell of her hair and the sharp angle of her shoulder blades against his chest and the perspiration of her hands as he covered them, things he had no business thinking about, and yet all the way home he thought about them.

QUINN VALENTINE

1968

A blind is a structure as old as thinking man. Deadwood lashed to a sapling frame. Reeds poked upright into the dark mud of a shallow lake. Pampas grass bundled like sheaves of wheat arranged in a circle. A platform of boughs in the Y of a tree. A net of vines like a stiff hammock suspended over a water hole. A tumble of well-placed boulders, glacial debris, an earthwork thrown up. The sheltering carcass of a large animal. The body of an enemy, the body of a friend. Body as structure, thought Quinn. Body as the house we inhabit. Or the cage that inhabits us. Hadn't she seen it in the last months of her own father's illness? His skeleton seemed to rise from his flesh as if the bones themselves were spirit and the Holy Dove envisioned at the end was but another perpetuated falsehood. The dove roosted in her father's heart and its cage lifted out away from his body and the bird stayed and would never fly from him, only sing as its shackles flew.

At a great distance it seemed, Lewis mumbled *Mark Miss Quinn* and she raised her gun with effort and as was expected of her dropped a high fast one stone dead out of a churning sky. Lewis laughed—he whooped really. She liked that, an old man whooping. He walked on out and flicked his cigarette away as he went and picked up the bird and held it like a clean wad of socks and brought it back and put it in the game bag. It was a business arrangement, she reminded herself. They gave you a gun and you brought down dinner. But she'd rather buy dinner in a store. It's a sport, she told herself, and besides, you bring this black old man pleasure.

She was not used to inhabiting her blind alone. To herself she said, Ask him in, ask the old man in. But she knew she could not, that his duty to please would conflict with his duty to watch the sky, and more than that he would be ruined for presuming to step into the circle of a white woman. If she asked him to, he would have to and be ruined. It shocked her suddenly to think that in her lifetime she had become someone who could destroy someone else with a request.

Instead, though she had not smoked since before the conception of her second child, she asked Lewis for a cigarette.

"Ma'am?"

"A cigarette," she said. "Whatever you're rolling there, roll me one."

He wouldn't light it for her, she knew. He would pass it with a book of matches over the top of the blind. He did so, all the while looking at the sky as if awaiting judgment from the scudding clouds. It was harsh tobacco and she said so. She drew on the cigarette again then held it away exhaling, observing the length of the first two fingers of her left hand and the cigarette tight and thin white as if she'd taken her own finger bone and lit it. In her right hand the barrel of the gun that stood upright on the seat of the blind.

"I used to chain-smoke," she said. "I was addicted. Two packs a day. Isn't that awful?"

"Yes ma'am," said Lewis. "But you enjoyed it. Long as you enjoyed it."

"My lungs didn't enjoy it."

"Well," said Lewis.

"I stopped before Leo was born. I haven't smoked in ten years. I don't miss it. Did you ever try to quit, Lewis?"

"No ma'am I never did."

"Maybe you can't get addicted to your kind of tobacco."

Lewis laughed.

"People tell me now how hard it is to quit. I didn't find it hard at all."

"Mark Miss Quinn. Over by Mr. Billy's blind coming this way."

She didn't want to, but out of respect for him and his working eyes she placed the cigarette on the edge of the seat and lifted her gun to the place she'd carved out for it inside her left shoulder. Her husband shot and missed and scared the bird quickly out of the field and away from her duty to kill it. She picked up the cigarette again.

"I found it easy in fact," she said. "There was nothing to it. One day I was a smoker, the next day I wasn't. Did you ever hear of that, Lewis?"

"No ma'am. I don't know no one who tried to quit."

"Billy said if I quit he'd give me a new kitchen."

"Well," said Lewis.

She could not say the truth to this man whose manners built a wall between them, who had historical reason to protect himself from her and did so with the most acceptable weapon at hand: propriety. She wanted to say it to humanize her and amuse him. If they hadn't been who they were, if he had been a white man, if he had been Cole Jones or even Ray Luken, she would have. She would certainly say it to Cole. Where was he anyway? He had promised her this day. This morning, following her brother-in-law Harry out to the rose garden where Detroit family business was conducted, he had nodded at her and activated the lax corner of his mouth and shown her that she might expect to see him in the dove field where late arrivals were duly punished by having to share a blind. And now the afternoon had turned, a few dove flew erratically out of range along the tops of the loblolly pines at field's edge. Lewis kneeled on one knee. She looked at him over the top of the blind. He looked like a retired long distance runner, slumped and smoking. Billy said if I quit he'd give me a new baby, she thought. Abstinence. That's where babies come from. She pulled the last coarse plume of flavor from her cigarette, letting the hot ash all but touch the skin of her fingers.

It was unusual to place your two best guns in the same blind. Cole couldn't remember how it started though it pleased him to think it was Quinn's doing. He knew he had not in any way suggested it. In that company he was not a man who suggested, he was a man who bowed his head and listened. He took orders. But he made sure on the business end of things that the rightful orders were there to be taken. In Harry Detroit's head he planted a seed, a whole field of seeds, and he did it stealthily under cover of darkness so the master at daylight looked out upon a crop of money—a cash crop, Cole smiled to himself—and though it was but an idea planted by him in the master's eye, it looked exactly like a product of the master's own mind. Harry Detroit was a complicated fellow and not to be toyed with, but to the temptations of easy cash by another man's labor he succumbed like any fool.

Cole had met Harry's father Henry in the fifties when Longbrow Plantation ran east and west of the Old Magnolia Road, from the outskirts of Thomasville right on down to the state of Florida, and he as a seed salesman covered a territory vast and various as God, called south Georgia. Detroit had impressed him, the Yankee coal baron himself, but more memorable to young Cole was the eleven-thousand-acre enterprise called Longbrow. Of course there were larger plantations, all Yankee owned and operated, run on the profitable sweat of northern Negroes and poor white immigrants—fodder for the factories of Cleveland and New York. But Longbrow had a feeling to it that was lacking in a great estate like Melrose or Suwannee. Longbrow's land seemed a confluence of the best south Georgia had to offer, as if tributaries of all good traits met and swelled there and became one river bearing with it the great privilege of clean pine forest and grassland and sharecropped oats and winter wheat and drained swampland planted with corn and dammed and refilled to make duck ponds. Cole himself had once sold the benne that brought the dove to the fields. Now those fields and every other inch of that fine plantation was his to manage. He thought of this every time he stood in a blind and raised his gun.

In the early sixties, Detroit the elder and his sister Mary had drawn a line down the middle of that magnificent accomplishment of man and nature and parted ways. Brother and sister each built their own house on their own land, and the original plantation house on the Tallahassee Road had been sold. Cole knew someone who knew someone and they'd got it sold and he'd bought the fifty acres of longleaf pine around it and bulldozed the slave shacks and timbered it for good money and built the first housing development in Thomas County, then the first whites-only school to go with it. It was a turning point, one he would never forget. It gave him the shape of his fate the way an architectural plan gathers futures out of space and line. He saw that even in the simplest situation it is almost always possible to profit twice. He called this the law of complementary resources and it became the law he lived by.

Lewis Brown could with one shot drop three blackbirds out of the sky looking at the ground with his gun held upright back when those birds flocked in numbers immeasurable. Back when flocks of darkness descended and did not lift and the sky took on the aspect of black gravel and to kill meant to drop a stone from a street of heaven. Now as an old man he hires on as pickup for Miss Quinn and her company, squatting in the dirt outside her blind and keeping watch over the corners of the field where bullet-shaped dove swing in to feed. Their habit of hunger palpable, pink breasts throwing back the end of daylight as they whine closer and closer and close enough to kill. *Mark* says Lewis, low guttural groan of that single word warning both hunter and hunted that a window of transforming possibility has opened. Death to death to death.

It's his business to know what goes on behind his back. The whole sky is his business. If there's one dove written on it he better read it. He sits down now out of his squat, smoking and looking at his business. It's a gray business today, low-ceilinged like his own house and hard to read. A glare comes off it like someone lit a white fire behind the clouds. One dove comes in from the southeast. He's lucky to catch it and he says *Mark Miss Quinn* in enough time but it stays a long shot and she raises her gun and sights but lowers it again. Mr. Jones facing northwest laughs low and says,

Alright Lewis, find me one now. Miss Quinn says, That last one didn't count. It wasn't in range. Mr. Jones laughs again. Miss Quinn says, It wasn't, was it, Lewis? Could you have hit that bird? Well ma'am, no ma'am, I don't believe I could. Well then no one could, says Mr. Jones, and Lewis knows it is not the truth and he knows that Mr. Jones knows. It is a kind of flattery not meant as a gift to Lewis but as a demonstration of Mr. Jones's ability to flatter. A dove comes in fast from the northeast and Lewis says *Mark Miss Quinn* and both guns lift and swing toward it and Mr. Jones backs down. She fires and misses and at an impossible distance he fires and the bird drops whirling like a propeller. Mr. Billy two blinds up hoots and says, I've got it Cole. Good shot. Wow. He runs out prancing like a boy as the winged bird rights itself and starts walking with the focused patience of the doomed.

Roosevelt Davis with a blind at his back reads the page in front of him, reads it like his uncle reads the sky. "Fellow called Langston Hughes," he says. "You know him?"

"Sure," says the girl. "Let's hear it."

"You want me to read it?"

"Unless you want to trade places and stand here with this gun."

"You got a dove coming in, Miss Frankie." He points over the trees. "See him?"

"I see him." She knocks on the wooden bench of the blind with the butt of her gun and the bird flies straight up, startled, and veers away.

Roosevelt sighs. The dove flies out of the field toward the barn and pasture. Horses and mules with their necks down drinking. "How come you don't want to shoot nothing, Miss Frankie?"

"You've got to quit calling me 'Miss Frankie,' Roosevelt. It makes me feel like Scarlett O'Hara."

He doesn't know any Scarlett O'Hara. "It's just what we do."

"I know it, but let's start not doing it, you and me. What do you think will happen?"

He hears his uncle at the other end of the field crying *Mark Miss Quinn* and two shots like a tree falling twice. The same sound kills the dove kills a man, thinks Roosevelt. Same sound, same gun, same human hand. White hand on the trigger, black hand pointing to the sky. Black hand pointing a prayer that says *Spare me, and take my brother the dove.*

He reads her the poem called "Troubled Woman." A dove comes in, it comes into the field threading its way through the guns, then startles upward, frightened by the guns but still flying low enough. He tells her, "Dove, Miss Frankie. Frankie."

She raises her gun and says, "What do we do if I kill it?"

Roosevelt laughs and says, "Just shoot at it."

She shoots and the bird keeps on going and she could shoot again but he knows she won't.

"Come in here," she says. "I'm going to give you this gun."

"Aw, don't do that."

"Yes, I'm going to give it to you."

"I can't shoot no dove."

"You're a good shot, Roosevelt. Your dad told me."

"It ain't that. It's just that I ain't Mr. Harry's company."

Miss Frankie lays her gun down on the bench with a clunk and opens the door of the blind and comes out and sits down next to him on the ground. "Let me see that book," she says. He gives her the book. She flips through it and hands it back to him and says, "Read me 'Troubled Woman' again." She leans her head back against the blind. He doesn't look at her but he can see her anyway, her long white neck coming up out of the hunting jacket and her face still and her long hair loose around her shoulders. He'd like to touch it. At school he touched a white girl's hair. He'll touch it again if she'll let him. He reads Miss Frankie the poem. Over where his uncle's at he hears four shots, *boom boom ba-boom boom,* and farther away another two shots, then a third. Miss Frankie lifts her head and says, "Doesn't it sound like a fucking war?"

COLE JONES

1969

Summoned by the Matriarch, Cole had no choice but to call halt to half a dozen earthmovers and their men, close up the office for the day, and take the long pretty ride out to Longbrow Plantation. He called Karen to tell her he didn't know when he'd be home. It was their nineteenth wedding anniversary and her disappointment carried with it an accusation he guessed he might deserve.

He tried to put this out of his mind as he settled behind the wheel of the Buick. Gunmetal gray exterior, white leather seats. He should have told her he'd take her out tomorrow night. Go to the Sandy Knickers for surf 'n' turf. She liked the catfish there. He didn't like catfish anywhere. He liked scallops though, almost any kind of shellfish. He couldn't figure out why anyone would want to eat a bottom-feeding fish out of a muddy river when they could eat a nice clean white-fleshed scallop out of the sea. They're flown in, she said. Well, that might be true but flown in or not they kept their mouths or valves or ports or whatever they sucked with out of the human filth at the bottom of a river. There's plenty of human filth in the sea, she said, ain't there? He didn't like it when she used *ain't* and she knew he didn't like it.

When she used *ain't* he felt it as a match struck close to the pile of wood chips and paper and plywood on which he stood, which made him the tall man he was.

Cole Jones set his mind to the road out of Thomasville—not because he couldn't drive it unconscious. He could and had proved it dozens of times as a wild drinking boy back before he met Karen. His wild oats had taken him many a time out this way when two sisters named Saralee and Charity Stringer used to command his attention and every other young man's this side of the Florida line. In those days, same as now, Thomas County was dry and the way to have a party was to know someone whose daddy had a still. Jax Liquors the other side of the line ran a good business but the Georgia Staties ran an equally good one if you were fool enough to try and bring it over. So just about no one did. That left the need to make the acquaintance of a pretty girl from a bootlegging family. And in the Stringer family there happened to be two.

Whatever happened to those girls? It came into his head that they had met an early and violent death. He shook his head to clear it of such a thought and then because he was passing the pecan grove that used to represent the city limits of Thomasville, a grove whose very existence had in the time before Karen made him feel wild and free, he looked up into the rearview, which shrank the town to a negotiable rectangle, and nudged the accelerator. For a full ten seconds the winner of the Masonic Lodge Most Cautious Driver Award went flying along the flat clay road that connected the house he was born in—the house his mother still got up in every morning—with the property he'd give his eye teeth to own, going sixty-two miles per hour at three in the afternoon.

Gosh, it was pretty. The world could look so pretty or it could look so mean. The winter sun fairly bounced off the trunks of the pecan trees, bringing a warm nutty smell to him through his open window. Past the grove a grown-over lane with a crippled mailbox that used to say Stringer. Cole was tempted for a second to turn down it but then the afternoon seemed too fine to lose on lost memories. And besides that, there was the Matriarch. He'd do better to get to her before her speech got thick. With her husband flat in the bed he didn't blame her. How many years now? He knew he'd been summoned for company, though she always found a task to justify his time. Long ago he'd determined to give her that time. Have one glass of whatever she saw fit to fix for him—Hankey Bannister Scotch whiskey it turned out—and sit quiet and listen. He was a bourbon man but it had been fair sacrifice. He'd made his money in board feet of listening.

His own father had died swiftly in his sleep, died dreaming, Cole liked to think. Though dreams could be terrible things—could cause death, he imagined. Not his father's dreams which were neither potent nor unmet, simply scrawny by anyone else's standards. He was a part-time druggist who married a schoolteacher and had five kids who strained their finances considerably but not direly enough to convince Cole's father to work a full week like other men did. He didn't gamble and he didn't drink and he was a poor eater as well. In other words, he wasn't an expensive man to keep, and this in the end balanced out his scant earnings.

Just ahead the Tallahassee Road staggered on south to Florida while the Old Magnolia Road left-forked out toward the great plantations: Pebble Hill, Sunny Hill, Horseshoe, Foshalee, Tall Pine, Longpine, Melrose, Suwannee. And Longbrow. Cole set his blinker and slowed considerably as he always did to make the turn though it was an easy left—a shift of his weight in the seat might have accomplished it. He'd gotten himself in the ditch here once, stone sober after a two-day rain slicked the road to where you were skating on clay or bogged down in it, one or the other. On his right he passed the new radio station, a mustard-colored block building decorated for Christmas, set next to a high, slim antenna. A white child barely out of diapers poked a stick at a hound too old and feeble to get up and cause a fuss. On his left the Slater place planted in winter wheat, fences a disgrace. Beyond that on both sides of the road some sorry shacks Cole knew to be home to a large colored family by the name of Washington. Bare dirt yards covered with thin chickens and thinner hounds and a few teenage girls tub-washing the clothes and hanging them up in the shade. A clothesline on every porch, it didn't make sense to Cole. Why not put a line out there in the sun from one of the houses to that skinny loblolly by the road? Or a freestanding pole, the kind Karen used before he bought her the Maytag set? She still used that old thing in the summer, which he could tolerate, though all winter it looked poor and ugly in its unemployment. There were things she didn't notice, blights she didn't see, and Cole didn't know how to make her see them or make himself not see them.

Now he came to upright fences strung with barbwire on the left and pines that grew right up to the fences and would have kept growing right on through the ditch and up to the road if not for the long scything blades of the county road crew. Faded white signs on the trees that said POSTED and in smaller letters he couldn't read but knew by heart said:

H. A. Detroit
No Hunting or Fishing
Violators Will Be Prosecuted

He'd suggested to the Matriarch that she post a fine as well. Nothing deterred poachers like the promise of a fine. She'd raised her glass and laughed. "A toast to you, Cole. The last of God's honest men. But nothing I know deters a poacher like quailshot in the pants. Put that on your sign: We Reserve the Right to Shoot You. Or Shoot *at* You. That's honest. I couldn't trust myself anymore to hit the Aswan Dam if it were coming at me. And Henry." She inclined her head toward the bedroom. "Henry's not likely to hit anything ever again."

"He was a great shot," Cole had said, knowing it was an exaggeration.

"He was a fair shot. The only great shots I know were not bred by me and Henry. You're one of them and Annie Oakley Quinn Valentine's the other."

A mile and a quarter of good fence and posted land, then a sudden shock of lush Kentucky bluegrass like a flag of cool enticement touching the red road. The Detroits' driveway took off there, lined with grass across the culvert that bridged the ditch, working straight on and businesslike back through the first line of pines, a plain board fence and a stock gate painted white. Three neat green clapboard houses set three feet high on cinder blocks too close to the drive, each with a solid porch and four wide steps down to a shared grassless yard. Smoke rising from one of them, Dosha Mae Hill with her kids home from school. Is it possible she cooked on a woodstove still? Had to be as it was a warm afternoon. Cole felt pleased with these houses which were not shacks, but regretted as he always did the grassless yard which looked sullen and neglected, not even a toy in sight. It was poor advertisement for Longbrow, right here at the mouth of her hospitality. He had hoped Henry's son Harry would see it the way he did and set the houses back in the pines, not spilling their private misfortune out onto the road. If you couldn't grow grass and kids in the same yard, wasn't that your own business? Why should it catch the eye of every visitor to this great plantation?

But Harry had not seen it. Because he liked too well to glorify the colored man. Well, he could have done the colored man a favor and given him the plantation house, Cole thought. Instead he set him up to fail as a showpiece at the gateway to a rich man's land. It didn't make sense. None of it made sense. The way Yankees treated the colored was a mystery to him. Men Harry's age in particular, but even old Henry, H.A., had had an odd notion or two, like housing the colored help under his own roof, up on the third floor of the old plantation house back in town, before they moved out here to the land. In the twenties he did such a thing. Other men, Yankees among them, had seen the old slave shacks behind the great houses fit quarters for their help, and the help too seemed to find them fit for they'd lived without complaint. A rat or a weasel might get in, might bite a child, or a snake looking for warmth. But as for illness, it spread just as quickly up on Henry Detroit's third floor as it did down on the ground. The damp brought more fever but the open-air living brought a quicker cure.

Cole balanced these thoughts and confirmed his belief in them as he drove. Half a mile and the wooden boards of the bridge over Bully Creek rang a hollow note under his tires. He had liked that sound from the minute he heard it six years ago, when the bridge and the house were new. He stopped there, looked down at the creek that was little more than a muddy trickle, and up into the tangled world of green needle and leaf and gray Spanish moss above him, a world that closed him in yet did not make him feel closed in or alone. The hot creosote smell of the bridge, the filtered weak light of late afternoon, the rank smell of the creek and the faint sound of it like a girl pouring wash water slow and steady from a tub. It all made him feel good. It restored him to the person he thought he truly was. He spent too much time inside, pulling numbers apart and putting them back together. Or he spent time with Karen or with his daughters. Always with someone. And often with the sense that they did better without him, that his presence chastened them.

The moss hung ghostly. Oh, if he could but rise up into it. Not to disappear—the force of his life felt too strong for that. He was no weak old man willing to die in a dream. But to float up from his flaws and failings and leave his carnal body a husk on the planks of the bridge. Cole tapped on the windshield as if to ask *Is this really my prison?* The answer came *Yessir, it is.* He squeezed his eyes shut and opened them, the closest thing he could think of to a fresh start.

He inched the car forward plank by plank and was soon across, the pines thinning immediately as he climbed up out of the bottom. A strong curve to the right, the road flanked by a dove field that for its own good reasons all but weakened his resolve to be better, try harder. Just beyond that the last hill and the sight of Ray Luken's sorry white pickup parked halfway up it at the kennels. Ray himself in a pen with two liver pointers whose names Cole should know but didn't. The two men exchanged a wave and the dogs could never let a car go by, even at feeding time. H.A.'s chocolate Lab in the corner pen nearest the road started it and the other two dozen took to baying in bursts between muzzlefuls of food. Nothing could keep a dog from barking, thought Cole. Not food, not weather, not illness, not pain. Maybe snakebite. Maybe quailshot. Maybe death. He drove on up over the hill and there was the house, low, wood, and modern with its short gravel drive. A turnaround and island thick with grass and a failing live oak tree. There was nothing majestic in this sight and Cole knew it and liked it. The new house failed to strike awe in you as the old one had, for it did not intend to. Its nature was good-hearted. Its sense of cool was simple shade, not distance. He parked right in front of the house as he always did when Harry wasn't there. He saw it as the place of the protector. He got out and smoothed his tie, tucked his shirt, took off his cap and held it down on his thigh as he walked to the door. Crossed a narrow veranda not burdened by columns and out of habit touched the bell. Then remembered she hated the bell, and consequently it wasn't wired. He was meant to let himself in and call from the hallway. Another odd Yankeeism. But this time she herself opened the door, a possibility he hadn't imagined. This close to her he felt foolish as a boy. He went to speak but couldn't, too aware he had whiled away long useless moments at the bridge while she paced here like a cat. She said, "You and the ice age, Cole. Come in." By which he understood she was cold sober and in no mood to let where she was displace who she was. Where she happened to be was where her husband had brought her, but that didn't mean she'd drop every punctual bone in her body and take up the Southern custom of ease.

ROWENA DETROIT

1969

Rowena Detroit was a small human being who expanded with excitement and shrank with displeasure. She stood there at just under five feet, a good inch less than content. Pearls at her throat, an open cashmere sweater that did not try to hide the age of her neck which had once been more like a turkey neck but had with Scotch and time got pouchy. Pale blue eyes almost gray. Short straight white hair with bangs. A Roman nose she'd passed to her sons and a good figure still she'd kept for herself. Today she had on jodhpurs that might have fit her when she was a girl.

She was seventy-four years old and did not doubt she would live to see ninety. A good thing as long as she was doomed to deal with Cole Jones and his molassesine timetable. She liked Cole but could not understand what in the world time meant to him. Well, the whole South went by a different clock as far as she was concerned. That's what Henry had always loved and what she had only managed to put up with.

Cole looked cool as a cucumber getting out of that car. His face was boyish and handsome behind a misfortune of acne scars. A face like soft rock upon which every hailstorm and passing animal left its print. He had evenly thin dark blond hair, thin brown lips, and a mouth that ran flat and slow downhill to the left where it ended in a lazy curl. Trump card of a mouth. Narrow eyes that looked not suspect but languidly sleepy. He wore a Tyrolean cap all winter and a suit and tie of hunter's green. On a cool day a dun-colored raincoat.

He could talk a snake out of its skin, thought Rowena. He could talk the teeth off a comb and the red apple roundness from a baby's cheek. He could talk deep sorrowful sighs from any woman out-of-doors. Except his wife. His wife was an indoor wife who came perfumed and spider thin into a room like a dancing skeleton. Had she never been fed? Not recently by Cole. Her gauzy blond beehive hummed and hovered above her head, slim evidence of an active mind. But an anxious spirit, Rowena knew, a quivering uncertainty as to the staying power of the man she'd married.

She let Cole in directly. He stood inside with his hat to his chest as if shielding his heart from whatever sorry news must have brought her to the door. "Henry's failing," she said, sounding calmer than she felt. She'd lived with the words for two days—longer than that for he'd been sinking six years. Now there was little left of the afternoon. It was after four o'clock. She would fix them both a drink then send him on his mission, there was no hurry.

"The doctor's come and gone," she added. They passed into the high-ceilinged living room where Osee Davis had laid and lit the fire. "He came yesterday before breakfast. Sit, Cole. There's no need to say anything. We've all expected this for some time."

Cole in fact seemed unable to speak. She put him in Henry's red leather chair to the side of the fire and went herself to mix his hemlock. With a drink in his hand, the sound of the ice, the cool of the glass, the warmth of the fire, he seemed to reclaim himself. "You could have called me first thing, Mrs. Detroit," he said. "I'm awake at five."

"I don't believe in bad news over the telephone." Though God knows she'd spent the day before doing that very thing, tracking down her two boys. "Harry's on his way. His train's delayed."

She sat facing the fire on the green-and-white-striped sofa, her right leg folded under her like a wing. Her customary position with Scotch in hand, company close, the long day's hours in back of her at last and ahead of her a muddy future. Not so muddy in fact. But the feel of it was brown and slow and sunken, like a muskrat drowned in a trap. Lacking the light and air she loved. She said to Cole, "Did I ever tell you how we met?"

"No ma'am, you never did."

"Cigarette?"

"No thank you."

She slid a Lucky Strike from the pack and Cole half rose to light it for her but she waved him away. "We met at the Nassau County air show on Long Island, the hot summer of 1931. I was a flapper. There was a depression going on and we'd lost our cook, Billy and I. Billy's father had left us by then and we were just as happy. He wasn't much of a man. So I took my son out to see the planes. We rode the train from the city all the way out to Long Island, which felt like sheer country to us. It was then too. I don't know if you've ever been to New York, Cole, but it's a nonstop city. It goes and goes. It's city all the way north into Connecticut and before I die it'll go all the way to Maine. Well, not if Boston can help it. You ought to make it up to where we live. See the sights. See what we put up with. It's funny, I could never talk about all that in the past tense, even if I haven't seen it for six years. Even if I never see it again. Though I will." She pulled the ashtray to her. "I will. I tell him not to hurry but he doesn't listen. They don't make his kind anymore, Cole."

"No, they don't."

"Would you like more in that glass?"

"Thank you."

"You get it for both of us."

When he came back and sat down she said, "That wasn't much of a story. I got off track."

"You said it was hot," said Cole. "You said the cook left."

"The cook didn't leave, she just stopped cooking. I stopped paying her when she stopped cooking but money didn't mean that much, there was nothing to buy. She was content to live under our roof and eat our food. What could you do? You couldn't put someone out on the street to starve. She kept her room clean and when Henry and I began our courtship she looked after Billy in the evenings. She was company for him. What was that woman's name? I thought I'd never forget her name. There are things I never in my life believed I'd forget and I have."

"What kind of air show was it?"

"Kind? I don't know what kind. What are my choices?"

"Well, I mean was it military planes or civilian?"

"That I couldn't tell you. Billy could tell you. We'll ask him. When he was a little boy he knew all his planes. Seth had the same thing for cars. You remember Seth? Billy's son Seth? At four he could tell you every car in a New York City block. I don't understand that kind of memory, do you? Maybe you do."

Cole nodded. "I had it for guns."

"I have it now for dogs but as a child I could barely remember my own name. I can tell you every dog in this kennel as of today—every one that's ever been with us, old Longbrow or new.

It's useless. Who needs to remember all that? I don't know why my mind wastes itself on things like that. I guess we don't have much say about what our minds do, do we?"

Cole looked at her curiously. "Yes ma'am, I believe we do. I *hope* we do."

Hope is the best defense of the young, she thought. In the end she didn't have the energy to dishearten him.

The story never got itself told. Which left her and Henry yet unmet on the green turf of Long Island under a white wing-filled sky. Billy by her side. Her second son Harry a year away from his own beginning. But the telephone rang and the mysteries of space and time collided to produce Harry's voice thirty-eight years later, like clear hot grease congealing, making clouds as it cools. He called to say he just stepped off the train in Nahunta—a grueling eight hours late. His wife Kate with him and two of their three daughters. Rowena with tears of relief put the phone down and turned to Cole. "You see what I need?"

He did and he nodded.

"Billy's family's coming in too. At nine in Tallahassee. Quinn and the boys. Billy can't get away until the weekend. So there's two ways to go. Whoever you want to get you get and I'll send Osee after the others. God bless you, Cole. Frankie," she added, "is on her own as usual."

She came over to where he was sitting and he quickly went to rise but she said, "Sit there and think about it a minute. You'd be an angel to drive all the way to Nahunta." She clutched his shoulder, gave it a squeeze. "When you decide, call your wife and tell her. I'm going back in to lie down with Henry."

At the door she said, "I never knew what we'd do when the time finally came down to a matter of days. You think it will never be over, and then it threatens to be, and then it is. It isn't yet. It's still only threatening. But I feel like I used to when the boys were small. Any harm that came at them by accident or intention was mine to ward off. I had to be with them, to look out for them until they were grown.

"Henry's growing. He's growing into his last farewell. He's not been much these months but my life's full of him. He's all over this house and this land. He's a huge man. He's going to empty this place right out when he goes. A whole way of life. You can't think these thoughts though. Not when it's your husband and there's an end to it and the end's not even over there anymore but right here. I didn't know what I'd do or how I'd feel but now I know the end is like the beginning in so many ways. I want to spend all my time lying next to him and holding him and not letting him get away for any reason. And if he goes, wanting to go with him. Like he was just getting up to open the window.

"I used to get up with him. We'd talk in the night. I talk to him all the time now. I can almost count the words we have left. It's a surprising feeling. Maybe we've even got a week or two. Still, the end comes up like a blindfold."

It was longer than she intended to speak but not more than she intended to say. She left him to his thinking then. The world now belonged more to Cole and her children than to herself and Henry. They'd soon learn to fill it with their thoughts and deeds, and leave behind the young vanity of their hopes.

COLE JONES

1969

Cole drove. He drove in a defeated straight line toward the train, away from Tallahassee and what his heart wanted, and what every instinct in his body told him he should not have. A vivid picture leapt to mind: Quinn's long back, buttocks, the stark white bottoms of her feet. He shook his head, snapped it from side to side as if to fling all that away from him, outside the car, onto the singing asphalt.

There was no time to stop but he had to eat, and to eat he had to work his disappointment down to the size of something he could swallow or spit out. As it was it closed his throat. He got it down to the size of a plug of tobacco and let it sit there oozing its tar poison. It came to him then for the first time: Henry Detroit was going. The thought shot across his vision like an actual band of light. A light that divided the windshield north and south and was gone with two words to Cole he would never forget: *Use me!*

A minute later he passed a turquoise trailer with a clean sign that said ETTA's hanging on a new pole in the yard. A cardboard Santa and sleigh without reindeer leaned up against the pole. There were dogs in the yard, he counted nine healthy-looking flop-eared hounds long of leg with a blue tint to their skin. They barked in succession as he parked next to a black Mustang and came out of the Buick and walked toward the open door of the trailer. He stopped outside the door and figured if his life kept going this way he might as well let it—waiting outside a door for a woman to let him in.

"We got company," came a girl's voice from inside. "Can I wait on him? I think it's a him." A laugh, then a feeling of eyes on him. "It's a him."

A woman called back, "He ain't company till he crosses the threshold, tell him. Tell him the food ain't free but he don't need no invitation to try it. We ain't killed no one yet."

"We ain't been open a day," said the girl.

"I guess you never seen anyone die of ptomaine," said the woman. "It can kill 'em quick as a bullet. They lean over their dinner, cough a bit of blood, and expire. It's over before they can reach in their pocket and pay their bill."

Cole was thankful for the information. It could have kept him from crossing the threshold. But his hunger finally forced him inside. A new yellow Formica counter half filled the place. Round red stools covered in plastic leather. The girl about sixteen and pale in a brown pullover sweater and jeans stood waiting for him, her hair dark, straight, and shiny like a wet winter road. She asked him to sit down anywhere and he said stupidly without thinking, "Is there a booth?"

"What if he wants a booth?" the girl called.

How the other woman could be any distance away in that tin-sided coffin proved to be an architectural enigma, but her voice came faint and muffled and Cole realized she must be inside a closet or a walk-in cooler. "If he wants a booth, give him a booth," she yelled.

The girl looked around her then yelled back, "We ain't got a booth." She shook her head and whispered to Cole, "She knows that. She's just proud of that counter."

The woman, apparently struggling with something that took her breath, called hoarsely, "Help me with this, Linda, will you?"

Linda looked alarmed. "But we got company."

"Company'll have to wait. He ain't company anyways. He's a gentleman come to eat at a booth we ain't got. We don't know him good enough for company, and he don't know if he's coming or going. He's going somewheres. I can feel that about him. He wishes he was going somewheres else. I can stand here all night and prophesy for nothing, but I give up that work to start a café. And you're the one I hired to help me. Now come on."

Linda shrugged and said she'd be right back, and Cole sat down on a stool to think. Thought came too easily. He knew every minute he took was a minute more Harry and his wife and girls had to wait. Cole's two daughters were the age of Harry's youngest who was nine, whose name Cole couldn't remember. Karen would know it. He made a deal with himself: If he didn't have it by the time he got to Waycross he'd stop and call Karen. Say goodnight to his girls while he was at it. But he better eat now. His whole head was sinking. The Matriarch's Scotch had worn off and he was down to the bone of his hunger. He wished he could go out and bury it in the yard, dig it up later, but he could not. An awful lot of dogs out there anyway.

Linda came back followed closely by a woman her height but twice as wide. She was wearing what Cole had heard called a shift, and over that an untied apron spotted with large grease stains and yellow mustard stains and stains the color of blood dried and washed. She wore a long black braid down her back. A little gray hair stood out at her temples. Her face was paste white and round as a kettle pot. She said, "We've had some trouble here. We didn't go asking for it, it just fell upon us. We plan to feed you. We can do that I guess. But there's a body in that walk-in and it's lying on top of a big box of steaks. If you want steaks we're gonna have to move the fellow, and me and Linda we can't do it alone."

"We just tried it," said Linda. "Whoever he is he's fa-at."

"Sunk all my money in that cooler just to have a stranger move in," said the woman.

"He *ain't* moving in," said Linda firmly.

"Well, he ain't moving out. He weighs more than you and me together."

"We'll get him out," said Linda.

"I'm Byrdine," said the woman. "Byrdine Dean. They call me Deedee. This here's Linda." She laughed. "And you can quit looking for Etta."

"There ain't no Etta," said Linda. "It's just a name she come up with."

"Messing with the word *eats,*" said Byrdine. "Eats, Eta's, Etta's. It don't take no Frankenstein to figure that one out. You want a cup of coffee?"

"He's *my* customer," said Linda.

"Well, ask him if he wants a cup of coffee. Body or no body, we can give him coffee." She went back into the kitchen a few steps away.

"She wants to know if you want a cup of coffee," said Linda. Cole without knowing he did so nodded.

"Ask him if he wants steak," said Byrdine.

"You want steak?" asked Linda.

Byrdine said, "We got steak with complications."

"No steak," said Cole. "No thank you. Just a sandwich of some kind. And coffee."

"You already told me the coffee," said Linda. "I can hear. Now what do you like on that sandwich? Meat or cheese? Mustard?" She made a face. "I hate mustard. Miracle Whip? Mmm, that's good. It goes good with everything. Sandwich comes with a quarter dill pickle and potato chips, and you can get it on toast or plain bread, white, wheat, or rye. We don't make our own bread yet, we buy it from the store. I like it better from the store. It's light. We only been open a day," she added. "We ain't even decorated yet."

"Just a cheese sandwich," said Cole.

"Plain?" said the girl.

"Lettuce and tomato if you have it."

She shook her head. "We're out of vegetables. All's we got is ketchup."

"No ketchup."

"I can grill it."

"Do that."

"A grill cheese sandwich," she said proudly. "And I didn't even give you a menu. Grill cheese!" she called to Byrdine in the kitchen. "Give him white bread I guess and I'll get him his coffee. He looks like he's about to flop on the floor."

The food when it came brought him upright and the coffee set him on his feet again. He ate quickly and the women let him be. He paid and said his thanks to them—he meant for their silence, finally, as much as for the meal. He said he hoped their complications worked themselves out. They seemed to have forgotten the body in the cooler—they both drew blanks. It had gotten dark. The girl scattered the dogs with a clap of her hands and Cole crossed the yard to his car. It was predictable what she said but he liked it: "Come back now!" A man *was* his manners—and a woman too, a girl. It didn't take any Frankenstein to figure that one out. He smiled for the first time that day.

By Waycross he remembered the child's name: It was Lucy. He had made good time and decided to call home anyway, say good-night to the twins and build a fast bridge to Karen. Twice already today he'd talked to her but three times wouldn't hurt. Next year would mark twenty years together and he wondered now about all these bridges. A man threw them up like it was second nature, like it was nothing at all to connect two places nature intended to set apart. He built and built, each one made of its own peculiar moment and materials handy. Each design intending to be better and stronger than what came before it but seldom succeeding. What Cole didn't know was did a man ever get to cross over what his mind's intelligence had joined with his hands to make? Did he ever get to use his work, use all these quilt pieces of arch and sky and strut and pure space that flew so easily upward from the ground and were handsome to look at, even beautiful, yet weightless themselves held no weight? Pretty things in the sky. Heavenward glory. But of pale substance he feared. It occurred to him as he pulled into an Esso station with a phone booth outdoors that his bridges were made of hope and duty, the strongest stuff he knew. But maybe there was something else, something he'd have to know soon. Something of another kind of strength that could support two people's cautious tread as they approached each other from opposite ends of the same marriage.

The girls were in bed—they slept in the same twin bed though each had her own. "Twin beds are for twins!" was

Cherry's thought. She thought the world generous while Debby saw it as a frosty place, so together they found a balance unachievable alone. A good marriage, though Cole worried they'd never find it elsewhere in their lives. Few did. They climbed out of their bed to say a sleepy goodnight, then Karen got on. He found himself telling her about the body, shocked now by the strangeness of it. Hadn't he found it spooky? Karen asked. Hadn't it troubled him? He'd been able to eat a sandwich in a café with a corpse in the cooler? She caught herself then and inside he thanked her for not going on.

She asked where he was calling from and he told her street and cross street to settle any geographical disbelief and to anchor them both in the same wild sea. As they were closing she said, "I hope to trust you soon, Cole. It's Christmas."

"Alright," he said. "Whenever you like."

"No. Don't say that. Only say right now what's true. You don't owe us anything. Just love and fatherhood but you know how to give that with your eyes closed. You know how to do the right thing and you do it, but you leave us behind sometimes. You're a good man. You mind your own business until it kills you. You never ask how a dead man comes to be locked up in a cooler, like you never ask me how I feel about you. An unpleasantness behind a cold door is who I am to you. I ain't angry, Cole. I have been. Now I'm just sorry."

She started to cry and Cole pressed the phone close to his ear to be close to her. He wanted to tell her the man wasn't locked in the cooler, he was just in there. After a while he said, "Don't cry now. I don't want to leave you crying."

"You better go," she said.

"Yeah, I got to."

"I'll see you tonight then."

"Yeah, late tonight."

"Why late?" she asked, the edge in her voice again.

"Well, later. It won't be before ten."

He was sorry to keep a woman at that edge. There was a sure chasm between trust and not and to live so close to it was bound to bring her harm. Bring them all harm. He gassed up the Buick and pulled out onto the road forgetting his headlights for a moment until the next passing car almost blinded him. Blew its horn for a full few seconds, a loud violent note trailing away into something mournful.

ROWENA DETROIT

1969

In her possession were the letters he wrote to his wife, her grandmother, Ellen Boyle Ewing Sherman, and to these she now turned without quite knowing why. It was not the first time, certainly. For years she had laid down her route through his indecipherable cursive until it was by now familiar country through which she traveled—at a good clip, unless she slowed to reread something that newly called to her in his descriptions or offended her in his opinions. The way he dragged his pen (it had a flawed nib all through Georgia) and the haste with which the words were assembled during the dreadful autumn of 1864. Familiar. A companion somehow. She could not explain it.

She had begun her acquaintance with her grandfather half a century after his death, in 1941, when generals once again walked the earth, and some were good and some were bad and the flavor of her own family history eluded her like a food she had never developed a taste for.

It's not a matter of taste, said Henry, but taste buds. You lack nothing but the will to know.

Yet still there was no need to know until Billy, her own son Billy, Ensign William Valentine of the U.S. Navy, stood at the docks in New York harbor and flashed the smile he'd learned to smile when he was scared or in love, and Rowena walked home from the bottom of Manhattan and opened the drawer that had always contained the letters, a neat yellowed packet tied with thin brown twine, and she threw herself at them, into them, asking of her grandfather, What is this? What is war? and at that moment he came alive in her hands, leaping from one century to the next with the effortless grace of a ghost fulfilled.

The days and nights stretch on endlessly in the wake of Atlanta. The men can taste the end, the taste of the last blood, and I confess I do little to hold them back. They would plunder, they would burn, they would avenge the atrocious deaths they have witnessed and grant themselves amnesty for the ones they have inflicted. It is war, Ellen. In places even the women are left with nothing to eat and no roof over their heads. The men defy orders and destroy everything that might mean something to those feminine hearts, even their books.

Even their books. Destroyed, as were their sons and husbands, fathers and brothers. And their homes, the crops in their fields. There was precious little left. The slaves had run to her grandfather's army. The land itself remained, bare-boned, fleshless. Did they look upon it as curse or salvation, those hungry homeless widows? The land that brought the slaves that brought the war that brought her grandfather.

The amputations are worse than death, and for most, death follows soon after. Surgeons wielding filthy knives. Behind the hospital tent a pile of limbs the height of a man, and peg-leg men on crutches sent to dig the hole to bury them. To bury their own bodies! Times I've seen a soldier still on the operating table gape in despair at the place his arm used to be, and beg the surgeon bring it to him, pick it up off the floor and lay it on his chest where he holds it like a babe.

Like a babe! And had he held his own so, Grandfather Sherman? Had he held Rowena's mother in his arms? There was no comfort in the grisly facts he wrote about, the loss of limb and life. It was his voice, the man made eternal by his own scribblings. Not what he spoke of, but the fact that he spoke at all. After death he spoke. A man's death was not the end of him.

This failed to soothe her as her son's convoy cut north to Newfoundland and east. How simply and cruelly he put it: It is war, Rowena.

But he's my son!

I lost my sons. Every one of them. One to the priesthood, the others to early death.

But not to war.

It makes no difference. They're gone now. And their sisters. All of them gone.

She remembered with a sudden dizziness her own blond ringlets, a sailor suit with a smart little sailor cap, a foggy day. She sat by the window and pretended she was high up the mast of a pirate ship. *Ahoy! Ahoy!* The fog brushed up and down the flanks of the island, swept across the stony promontory of its single skyscraper. Manhattan. She knew the word and liked the sound of it on her tongue. *Manhattan*. Outside, the view of fibrous white nothing. Inside, the chocolaty scent of her father's leather shoes. The sour, ashy smell of her mother's skin. A father's smells had to do with what he wore, but a mother, a woman, smelled of her body.

December 7th, 1864

Dear Ellen,

For the first time today I am hopeful of reaching our goal by Christmas. We meet little resistance, except the mud, and the damn Rebel cavalry. Four days ago the crossing at Ebenezer Creek. Great loss of life, but we have rid ourselves at last of the many useless mouths to feed, those refugees who cling to this army for salvation. Hundreds of Negro women and children perished, I am told. Clearly it was preferable to die freemen rather than live as slaves, for such a stampede into those icy waters I could never have imagined. The creek, which lies between the Ogeechee and Savannah rivers, was running high and unfordable. Our engineers hurried to lay down the pontoon bridges and the army crossed. Jeff Davis at the rear of Slocum's wing has borne the burden of the ragtag Negroes who follow in numbers greater than five thousand, perhaps twice that, begging for food our soldiers don't have. I can only assume he acted on behalf of his men and this army when he gave the order to take up the bridges, leaving all but the able-bodied Negroes to their fate. And knowing, perhaps, that soon the Rebels would be upon them from the rear, those pitiful stranded souls ran like cattle into the bone-chilling water where, unable to swim and at the mercy of the swift current, they disappeared. Some of our brave men swam out after them, but it was useless. There will be an inquiry, of course. Davis will not stand up well to close examination as he is known to have killed a major general over an insult.

Affectionately,
Cump

Affectionately. Affection at the distance required by war, and on war's terms. But to whom did he tell his heart? *Great loss of life.*

Hundreds of Negro women and children perished. We have rid ourselves at last of the many useless mouths. Did he feel nothing? Regret nothing? Desire nothing? Was he a man of flesh or steel?

Rowena took the matter to her pragmatic husband who reminded her that early in the war her grandfather Sherman had released himself from duty and gone home to plant a garden and live beside his wife and children. For this he was considered mad.

He redeemed himself, she said.

Redemption, said Henry, of a most subjective kind. He's as good as the devil in Georgia.

She wondered at the intersection of history and chance. That she might be the commanding general of a house in which the descendants of those who perished at Ebenezer Creek now lay down their own bridges made of flour and sugar and bread and butter. Made of orange cake and the smell of ironing and the sound of a knife hitting wood, hitting a cutting board, and the smell of fatback and the sound of water being poured from a pitcher and a shirt snapped in the air and the telephone and one of them laughing—Pearly, Pearly laughing—and the soft shuffling of feet and blue milk in a glass and the sound of a fly at the window and the smell of chicken and soup. From their side of the creek to hers they lay them down, bridges of folded clothes like Christmas packages. And soft-boiled eggs, and oatmeal fixed the way she liked it with salt and sugar and butter and cream. There seemed no end to it, to their desire to cross the river and meet on the other side. Rutha sang about it. Heaven, of course. But in this life too.

She folded the letters and put them away. She went in to Henry who was sleeping. She leaned to kiss him and his cheek was smooth and he smelled of soap and the clean starched smell of his pajamas. She slipped in beside him on her side of the bed. She laid her hand against the cloth of his pajamas but it wasn't enough and she lifted the cloth and found his skin and let her hand soften against the hard ridges of his ribs. She thought of her grandmother Ellen Sherman and wondered if she understood that the general who sent his affection to her, who sat with pen and paper in the dim flickering candlelight after a day of war, was a man like any other, a man of flesh, and when the guns stopped and the night became clear and dark and filled with the steady sound of horses chewing and soldiers crying or talking in their sleep, he desired her. He desired to converse with her, to share her civilized company, to touch her, surely.

FRANKIE DETROIT

1969

Frankie left her bed and stepped out into moonlight blinding as the Resurrection, dropped to her knees in order to remember what green felt like at night. Ran down the lawn to the wading pool, shucked her nightgown, slipped in, and sat with the backs of her legs along the rough concrete bottom, arms outstretched along the edge of the pool. Head thrown back, neck taut to the humming moon. Before her the statue of a putto looking down at his little dick as he peed pool water. The difference between boy and angel is a matter of wings, she thought. This one was entirely caught up in human wonder.

The breeze came and she sucked it in, took it between her teeth like a peppermint until her mouth felt like winter. How did they live in heat like this, those who did? They just did, the same way she lived in cold. Back home the hip-high snow and subzero mornings on her way to work. Lane, the girl she carpooled with, unable to brake on streets of sheet ice. She loathed those mornings, yet there was something about the cruelty of the world at that hour that seemed honest and alive. She no longer looked at winter as a dead space between the carnage of fall and spring's manic flowering. It was the oldest season, wizened and white-haired. It began at the bottom of the year and carried the light upward and sent people out onto the frozen lakes which were nothing but hardened light reflecting light, and out onto the bone-white snow-encrusted golf courses, and even onto the frozen river which at night divided light from light, twin from twin, Minneapolis from the city of St. Paul. Then spring came, Easter, and laid claim to all that light, when it was winter's light carried in on winter's back in small loads the size of minutes.

She paddled her feet underwater, watched a rose petal surf to the shore of her breasts. Hardened nipples, floating islands in a cool sea. Hello, body. Overdressed, underused body. She felt sexy and shimmery in the water. The warm air hummed like a swarm of bees. The breeze came again. An owl called. Something far away screeched like a frightened girl. A heron? She didn't know squat about birds. Or anything in nature. Her life had taken her from one cold climate to another, where people hurried through tunnels and never knew the sounds the world made, the unholy sounds, the inhuman ones.

The putto looked up from his appendage and winked—winked at *her*—and she remembered the time she took her mother's nail polish and painted his little dick red. Well, he deserved it, infatuated narcissist. Not long after, she'd been caught filching fags from her grandmother, Mars. Luckies! Sheer desperation! Yet Mars had stood in the bow of her moral rowboat, like Washington crossing the Delaware, and proclaimed her—*Who me? Frankie?*—a petty thief. Declared war and victory in the same breath, sent Papa out to set the terms of surrender. Grant at Appomattox. Or Sherman handing Joe Johnston the deal of a lifetime, the Fuller Brush man of peace. *See, Mars, I know a thing or two about the old gentleman, which is more than you can say for your darling Seth, who believes the blood in his veins comes directly from Adam without the messy interlude of rape, pillage, villainy, and civil war. And glory too. Happiness contradicted by misery. Oh it's all in us, and at the same time back behind us. Who would claim such a past if they didn't have to? I would, Mars. Me.*

Night after night, for hours at a time, the baby cried. Rowena claimed not to hear it, and indeed slept soundly. It wasn't hers, she reminded Henry, nor his. Kate and Harry were young, too young, but they had made this little girl and could care for her—had to, it was as simple as that.

But why would an infant feel such sorrow?

Sorrow! laughed Rowena. You're hopeless, Henry. Don't you remember Harry fussing and squawking half the night? It isn't sorrow in a baby, it's colic or prickly heat or hunger or gas. It wants to nurse. It's teething. It has a dirty diaper. Now go to sleep. It will grow up soon.

But at three years old the girl still moaned and cried, punctuated by a few high-pitched howls. Henry lay rigid in bed, imagining little Frankie's lungs, the pink health of them and their elastic strength—two vegetable-like flaps expanding at an alarming rate. Sometimes he thought of her as a garden of root crops, her organs every variety of potato. Harry and Kate seemed undisturbed by the racket, or had found no solution to it and given up. Rowena seemed determined to ignore it and warned against coddling. But Henry's distress grew each night until finally, seeking quiet, he slipped out of bed and into his clothes and followed the road to the barn.

Miss Belle Walker, Rowena's old mare, stood at the pasture gate. Henry cupped her head against his shoulder. Want to come out, old girl? She nudged him, lightly stamped her foot. She was a dapple gray, snow white around the muzzle. Her back sagged and her ribs protruded. Her fine thin legs were rickety as sticks. And yet he didn't have it in him to put her down. Not yet. There seemed no reason. She pulled away from him and whinnied and the others crossed the pasture to the gate. Henry held out his hand to Cotton, the new chocolate-brown gelding, and the horse came close and sniffed and stood back again.

From the tack room he brought Midas's old bridle and saddle and set them outside on the hitching post. He went out into the pasture and led Cotton in and tacked him up. There was plenty of moonlight and he took him out onto the dirt road that led back to the house. They circled the house, stopped on the lawn, and Henry told the horse he was a good horse, that Midas before him had been a good horse but wild at heart, not a horse for a man's old age. Inside he could hear the child crying and it saddened him to think of her alone in her bed, crying through the night. He rode around to the front of the house and hitched the horse to a live oak and waited a moment to see if Cotton would reach up and take the Spanish moss and drag it down as Midas used to, with long comical lips like a camel's. But Cotton only stood and watched him.

Upstairs the little girl's room striped with moonlight. Henry stood at the door and called to her softly, not to scare her. She seemed to be waiting for him and stopped her crying and sat up in bed, pushing her tangled hair out of her face, rubbing her eyes with the back of her hand. Papa, she said. Going?

He came and sat on her bed. Where would you like to go?

Outside?

Let's go outside, he said.

Let's whisper.

Good idea, he whispered. How about clothes?

I have them! I have clothes!

Good. I'll help you get dressed then. Or do you dress yourself?

She seemed suddenly prim. I dress myself, she said. Like a grown-up. But you can help me.

They got her into a warm shirt and overalls and her brown shoes. Only one sock could be found so she went without socks and that seemed an adventure in itself. Would you like me to carry you? he asked.

Where?

Outside.

I can go myself.

Down the stairs slowly, holding her grandfather's hand, then out into the flooding moonlight, across the gravel.

What's that? she cried, pulling back on his hand, seeing only the dark shape of the horse.

That's Cotton.

Oh, *Cotton*. Is he coming with us?

We're going with him.

He unhitched the horse, boosted Frankie into the saddle and instructed her to hold on, then swung up behind her. He wondered if she would be afraid, but she buried her hands in Cotton's mane and leaned and put her cheek on his neck. I like him, she said. Do we still have to whisper?

What do you think?

I think we can talk like people.

Henry turned the horse and they started across the noisy gravel which made the girl laugh. It's so crunchy!

It's crunchy and munchy, he said.

Not munchy.

No?

It sounds like toast.

They walked on down the road, laughing as the Spanish moss swept their faces. Henry pulled some down and made himself a beard but it frightened her. Take it off! Take it off! she insisted. You don't look like Papa.

They rode back through the old slave quarters where a few of the shacks still stood. Who lives here? asked the girl.

Nobody lives here.

Why does nobody live here?

The people have all gone away.

They're dead? asked the girl.

A long time ago they died.

Before you were born?

After.

Was Cotton born then?

No, he's a young fellow.

Can he understand us? she whispered.

I don't think so, said Henry.

I don't think horses have a language, said the girl.

You don't?

She shook her head no.

They rode out to the barn and turned around. Belle and the other horses and the mules lined the fence, whinnying softly. On the way home he asked her if she still thought horses didn't have a language, or if she'd changed her mind. But she was asleep. He tucked her in against him and in front of the house he asked Cotton to stand and he dismounted and lifted the girl off the saddle. He carried her upstairs and into her room and pulled her shoes off and loosened the overalls and pulled them off in case she got up later to go to the bathroom. He left the shirt on and pulled the blankets up and kissed her on the nose though his lips felt big and awkward.

The next morning she came down to breakfast with her mother and the first thing she said was, There's Papa! She had to sit next to him, had to have her eggs scrambled just like his, had to have the same two pieces of bacon and a drop of coffee in her milk. Rowena looked up from her own poached egg and said, Papa's very popular this morning.

Henry frowned at her over the top of his glasses. He helped the girl load a spoonful of eggs.

Kate said, Frankie had the strangest dream—

It wasn't a dream, Mama.

About a wild horse that lifted her up and carried her away. And when she woke up she had changed out of her pajamas.

I was wearing my shirt!

Your shirt? asked her grandmother.

This shirt, Mars! This hot shirt!

That hot shirt?

And overalls and shoes but no socks. Ask Papa.

Henry? said Rowena. Henry. As fascinating as the silverware may be, consider joining us for a moment. Someone here seems to think you can shed light on the strange events of last evening. Is this true, dearie?

There were no socks. That much is true.

Tell them, Papa! cried the girl. You took me out on the horse, and we went to the barn, and we came back again, and I fell asleep.

And I carried you in, and I took off your overalls and shoes, and I put you in bed under the covers, and you slept until morning.

The end.

That's right, said Henry, folding his napkin and placing it on the table beside his plate. Frankie did the same.

It was expected after that that he would carry her out on the horse in the evening and in this way she would fall sleep. There was good moonlight, and then the next time she came to visit the nights were black. She was scared of the dark at first, but the breath of the horse and his steady movement seemed to comfort her, and Henry held her close against him so she was pressed between two animals. He could tell by her breathing and by other almost imperceptible changes in her body exactly when she crossed the line. He thought of it as a line, a line made of spiderwebs and hair, the shimmery crossing between wake and sleep. On Cotton's back she flew across without effort. In her bed she struggled like a tiger. Why? he wondered, but the why didn't matter. What mattered was that Rowena was right, of course. She would outgrow this time, as children outgrow everything. They shed like snakes, and sometimes when she came down from her nap he felt a change in her, as if a dullness or dearness had sloughed off her, and if he went upstairs to her room he might find a milky, crepey essence left behind on her pillow. Once when he sat reading the paper she called from the doorway and came in and he patted his lap for her to come sit. She liked to sit on his lap and play with his glasses. She came halfway to him and stopped and looked at him in confusion, and he felt he was looking in the window of a train, watching a stranger.

She became a young lady. She smelled of something dug from the earth, something she splashed on, called patchouli. The horse still knew her, would come to her though he was otherwise a one-man horse and it had been a decade since he carried her on his back. Rowena did poorly with young ladies and with Frankie in particular—they were too alike. She caught the girl stealing cigarettes and sent Henry out to crack the whip.

He met her at the wading pool. The house was still new and around the pool the grass had come in poorly. He took note of the many raccoon tracks and the not surprising fact that nineteen of Rowena's prized goldfish had disappeared overnight, leaving eleven doomed swimmers. Frankie came and stood beside him. She was almost as tall as he. She was barefoot, wearing a T-shirt and ragged cutoffs. He had on his white linen Sunday suit with a white shirt and a paisley tie she'd given him. A pair of wingtips. Straw hat with a red hatband.

Mars'll have a cow, said the girl.

Your grandmother wouldn't know what to do with a cow.

She should've gotten catfish, like Cole said.

Catfish! said Henry crossly. Catfish like garbage and mud, as Cole knows.

She moved around the pool until she stood across from him. She glanced up. You're wearing your tie.

Of course I am. It's my mod tie.

He saw the fleeting pleasure it gave her. Young ladies were old hands at fleeting pleasure.

She looked down at the surface of the water. We're going to lose the rest tonight.

We could post a guard, he suggested. Cole's the best shot we have.

No, Aunt Quinn is.

Could she kill a raccoon?

Sure. She can hit a turkey right in the eye. She can hit a duck in the dark.

She shouldn't be shooting ducks in the dark.

Well, she doesn't. But she could.

I couldn't shoot a raccoon. I wouldn't hit it anyway, but I couldn't even aim my gun at one.

Why not?

They're furry. And they have those inquisitive faces. And their hands are practically human.

Frankie snorted. I don't think Aunt Quinn'll have any problem with their hands.

No, he agreed. Probably not. They walked through the rose garden that formed a crescent below the wading pool at the bottom of the lawn, a fragrant island toward which the surrounding pines and high quail-concealing grasses seemed to swim. He wondered if she knew he was ill. He hoped she didn't. They stopped and sat on a stone bench and he pointed to a golden-yellow rose with a white tag marked Marechal Niel.

See that? That's what you get when you cross Charleston, South Carolina, with the best of France. Look at it. It's marvelous, isn't it?

You're much more like a woman than a man, Papa.

He laughed. Why do you say that?

Because you like flowers. And you don't like to shoot things.

No, he corrected her, I'm a bad shot. That's different.

The women in this family are the hunters.

That's true, Frances. And they have hearts of steel.

Stone.

No no, not stone. It may seem that way because they're sharpshooters. And good fast talkers. They're doers. My mother was, and Caroline, and Quinn is. Caroline was my—

I know who she was.

One thing I always liked about your grandmother was she didn't care too much for shooting and she wasn't much of a shot. But she's tough in other ways, isn't she? A steel heart is not a stone heart. It's strong but it can warm up and bend.

The girl looked doubtful.

Let me tell you something. One time, long before you were born, Geneva—she wasn't our cook then, Rachel was—she fell down in the kitchen and started bleeding until we thought she would bleed to death. We didn't know where the blood was coming from, and there was so much of it all of a sudden. By the time Rutha came and got us, Geneva was pale.

Geneva couldn't *be* pale.

She was. She was as pale as Geneva can be. She was lying on the floor in a pool of blood and no one knew what to do.

Call a doctor!

We did that. We called the doctor, but this was in the old days when it took some time to get anywhere. Sometimes there wasn't a car and sometimes there was, and sometimes the doctor knew how to drive it and sometimes he didn't. So we weren't counting on him. We couldn't. But Rachel and Aunt Annie—

I've heard of Aunt Annie.

—they were both doctors in their way, and your grandmother knew it and she also knew as long as I was in the room no one would do anything for poor Geneva—

Why?

Out of respect. It was my house. I was the boss. In the boss's house you use the boss's medicine, even if there is no medicine, even if the medicine can't get there on time. So your grandmother told me to go out and check the horses. She said she thought Belle was limping and she wanted me to go check on her.

I thought she was crazy, but I went. And after I went the ladies went to work.

Mars too?

Yes. Mars too.

And what was the matter with Geneva?

Miscarriage.

A miscarriage!

Do you know what that means?

Of course I do.

She had many of them and that was the last.

How do you know that, Papa?

Your grandmother knew all about things like that.

How did they save Geneva's life?

Now that's a question for your grandmother.

Frankie sighed and said, I know what we're supposed to talk about, Papa. I won't bum any more cigarettes from her. She doesn't have to worry.

It's the smoking that worries her, not the bumming. I'm supposed to tell you that smoking causes lung cancer. In rats at least. Why do we care so much about rats?

In people too.

In people too? So you've taken on the habit in full knowledge of its ill effects. That's good. Is it a habit?

The girl looked at her hands. You start because . . . I don't know. Dumb reasons.

Because you want to be liked.

I guess. Then you can't stop.

A habit, he nodded. That's the way I used to feel about tennis. You did it because the next fellow did it, whether you liked it or not. Then one morning you woke up feeling you couldn't live without it.

Tennis is different.

Why is it different?

It's not bad for you. It won't kill you.

It killed Warren Hardy. Doctor Hardy. He dropped at the net and never got up again. I saw it too. I was on the next court.

Papa. You can ask anyone if tennis is like smoking and they'll tell you it's not. If it was you'd still be playing tennis. Every day. Ten times a day. That's like half a pack. A small habit.

He laughed, gave her the point. Have you figured out how you're going to buy these cigarettes? A lifetime of cigarettes, Frances. You could have a horse and a good saddle for that.

I don't want a horse and a good saddle, Papa. I guess I'm lucky.

Ah, lucky, he nodded sadly. What everyone your age wishes to be.

What do you mean?

He turned to her, gripped her elbow, surprised them both. There was a time, dear girl, when you loved to ride, when you lived all day to get to the night. You don't remember it.

I do!

Maybe you do. I hope you do. Some of my fondest memories.

ROOSEVELT DAVIS

1965

No matter how hard he tried to put his mind elsewhere, Miss Frankie Detroit's long brown ponytail distracted him. She had just learned to drive the old green open-topped jeep and she drove them to a place near the Cocroft dove field where three red plantation roads came together in a Y. She was fourteen years old, Roosevelt was eleven, and his sister Charlene eight. It was a cold day in December.

Charlene had stiff hair straightened with an iron on her mother's ironing board. It hung in short black sheets around her face. She was so chubby she filled out her overalls. Kids didn't like her because she acted like a little man. At the Y in the road she said, "Lemme drive, okay?" She sat in the passenger seat which was ripped open with its foam spilling out. Roosevelt sat behind Frankie on the spare tire in the open back of the jeep. He said, "Shush Charlene, you ain't driving."

"She can drive," said Frankie.

"Naw, don't do that," said Roosevelt.

"I can drive," said Charlene. "She said I could."

"She's just being nice, Charlene. She don't want you driving."

"But she *said*. Anyhow you don't own the place. This ain't your jeep."

"It's not mine either," said Frankie.

"It's Mr. Billy's," said Roosevelt.

"No, it's my dad's," said Frankie.

"This old thing belong to Mr. Harry?" said Charlene.

"He bought it used," said Frankie. "It doesn't matter whose it is. You can both drive."

"I ain't allowed to drive," said Roosevelt.

"I'm not either," said Frankie.

"You ain't?" said Charlene.

"I wasn't supposed to learn."

"You ain't learning no more," said Charlene, "you driving. You ain't doing nothing you ain't allowed to do."

Roosevelt laughed.

They drove on into the dove field, lurched across it to the open middle. At the far end a flock of dove burst forth out of the benne. He knew their sound. They wheezed like his daddy.

"This sure is a heap," said Charlene, "this thing we're riding in. My head's coming off at the stalk. Let's go back to that smooth road, I like that better."

"I thought you wanted to drive," said Frankie. "This is where you learn to drive, out in the middle."

"Forget that. I don't need no middle. I want to drive on the road. There's plenty a road."

"There's plenty of road and plenty of ditch," said Frankie.

"I'll drive," said Roosevelt. "I would like to drive."

"You ain't allowed," said Charlene.

"Shut up, Charlene."

"Well, you ain't."

She moved into the back, moving slow as a glacier, and Frankie moved into her seat and Roosevelt climbed behind the wheel. He wasn't tall like Frankie was, and he was slight in his frame, plain skinny really. He gripped the wheel so hard his brown knuckles turned pale.

"Don't let it stall out or it might not start up again," said Frankie. "The gears are sticky and the brakes don't work too well, okay? Just don't try and stop fast. You won't need to. That's why we're out here."

"That's not why I'm out here," said Charlene.

Roosevelt relaxed his hold on the wheel. "Shut up, Charlene."

"Shut up yourself."

"Why are you out here, Charlene?" asked Frankie.

"Roosevelt drug me out. Said if he come out with you I gotta come too. Said it ain't right he be driving alone with a white girl. You ain't but a couple years older."

"I'm more than a couple," said Frankie. She yawned and covered her mouth. "You guys smoke?"

"Unh-*unh,*" said Charlene. "No *thank* you. That's all my brother Dallas do is smoke. And look like now he come home to join the Army. He gonna go to war."

"Why does he want to do that?"

Charlene shrugged. "I don't know."

"Well, ask him. I've got to have a cigarette."

"You go right ahead."

"Smoking keeps you skinny," said Frankie.

"Skinny as him?" Charlene pointed at her brother.

"Maybe not that skinny."

"Ain't no one that skinny."

Roosevelt's head hung low. His hands had fallen from the wheel and rested upwards on his thighs. He waited to feel the feeling of a fit coming on him, but all he felt was the jeep chugging impatiently in neutral and then a sudden lurch as it died. He raised his head and looked at Frankie in panic.

"You done it now," said Charlene. "We be walking home." She dangled one leg over the side of the jeep, half in half out. "Bet we miss Christmas."

"Your sister's a pain in the neck," said Frankie. Roosevelt said nothing, looked again at his lap. "Try starting it. Don't give it any gas, just turn the key. It'll start."

"Get your leg in, Charlene," said Roosevelt. She pulled her leg in and he turned the key and the engine caught and idled roughly and died again. Quick he turned the key again, this time playing the accelerator lightly. It started and stalled, he did it again, it started and stalled, and once more he did it and it held. A look came on his face, a small part relief and the rest wonder at what he'd done. Driving wasn't steering as he had thought, it was something else altogether. He drove them easily around that field, finding each gear at its moment, going so smooth it was as if the humps of the rows lay down as he came along. Frankie didn't teach him how to do it, he just did it. Charlene stayed quiet and proud in the back, her smart mouth resting.

"You go on and drive us home," Frankie told him.

"Naw," he said. "It ain't mine to be driving."

"Take us part of the way home. Try it out on the road. You can get up some speed on the road."

"Naw. I don't need to drive nowhere."

"You drove somewheres already," said Charlene. "Drive some more."

He did. He drove to the duck pond a few miles from the plantation house where he and Frankie changed seats and she drove them home. Their house was another mile beyond the big house.

It was green clapboard set up on cinder blocks to let the cool air circulate in the hottest weather. Three like houses sat back there, one belonging to Osee and Pearly Mae Davis, the second to Pearly's brother Robert and his wife Dosha Mae Hill, and the third to Lewis Brown and his wife Rutha who was cousin to the Hills somehow through her mother's line. Roosevelt and Charlene got out and Charlene came and shook Frankie's hand and said, "I'll never be as skinny as he is and that's just the way it is." Roosevelt walked to the front of the jeep as if to go directly into the house without a word, but he turned and put his hand on the hood and nodded and said, "We'll be seeing you." He patted the hood twice, then he said Frankie's name aloud and nodded again and turned to follow his sister across the clay yard that had not a blade of grass on it and no ornamentation but the human marks of coming in and going out, and one rusted red tricycle almost colorless under the cool of the house.

ROOSEVELT DAVIS

1967

It was a heavy-warm spring day. His mother ironed a white shirt for him to put on fresh after church. He walked the mile from his house along the long driveway, going as slow as he could in those hot clothes. He walked by the kennel and every dog in there stood up and howled, telling him to turn around and go back. He stopped in the shade of the kennel shed until the iron smell of shit sent him up the last hill.

He went in through the kitchen out of habit. Mrs. Detroit still in her nightclothes, trying to get the gas stove lit. High-heeled slippers and a light-blue quilted bathrobe, same as his Aunt Rutha had, the same pearly buttons and lace collar.

He started to back out, head down, saying, "'Scuse me ma'am. I guess I'll come back another time."

"Roosevelt!" she cried, and she did seem happy to see him. "You're the one I need. Come help me, will you? You've got eyes. I never can light this damn thing." She sighed loudly. "You don't know how I hate Sundays. There should be a little light in there that lights the burner."

"Yes ma'am," he said, approaching her. "This one don't stay lit. Miss Geneva, she use a match."

"A match! That makes life simple."

"Yes ma'am." Was she making fun of him? "It sure do."

"Where does she keep her matches?"

He pulled out the drawer beside the stove and showed her. She asked him to light it for her and he did and settled the kettle so it wouldn't rock, like he'd seen Miss Geneva do. That made her happy, to have the water going, and she sat down at the kitchen table where his mother usually sat and pulled a cigarette from the pocket of her bathrobe. He thought she might ask him to light that for her too. He hoped she wouldn't. She might have read his mind because she pulled a silver lighter from the other pocket and said, "Don't worry. I've seen a man so drunk he didn't know his own wife, but he could pour himself another drink and never spill a drop." She laughed. "That's desperate, Roosevelt. Our bad habits make us desperate."

She lit up, sucked in the smoke like he'd watched his mother do, hungrylike. She coughed a little as she exhaled, then picked a speck of tobacco off her tongue with the same hand that held the cigarette. He was standing too close to her but he didn't feel like he could back up. He was only an arm's length away.

"Don't ever smoke," she told him.

"No ma'am. I won't."

"You will. You'll try it. You all do."

"Yes ma'am."

"Just don't go any deeper into it than that."

"No ma'am. I don't intend to."

"You will, though. You will."

"Yes ma'am."

"How's our water doing?"

He turned to look at the stove and got away from her that way. "It ain't quite there."

"It's not?"

"No ma'am. A little while yet."

"You know Frances?" she asked, but he knew no Frances. "My granddaughter, Frankie?"

"Yes ma'am. Miss Frankie."

"She smokes. She started smoking at your age. How old are you, Roosevelt?"

"Twelve."

"She was twelve. Talk to her now. She'd like to stop, she's tried to stop, but she can't. I smoke because I like it. She does it because she can't stop herself."

She stubbed out her cigarette in the same ashtray his mother used. Steam poured out the nose of the kettle and Roosevelt turned the water off. "Ma'am? Your water's boiled."

"Just leave it," she said, passing her hand over her eyes. He didn't know what to do then, so he stood there. Finally she said, "Do you want something, Roosevelt?"

"Mr. Detroit, he asked me to come."

"I mean do you want a soda or something? Coffee? You're too young for coffee. How about a ginger ale?"

He wished she'd said a Co-Cola. An icy Co-Cola would taste just right and cool his hot throat. He didn't much like ginger ale. He said, "Thank you ma'am. I don't need nothing to drink." Then he took courage. "I reckon if Mr. Detroit's too busy today I can come back some other time. Sometime after school."

"Now, Roosevelt. You've gotten yourself all dressed up, and probably for the second time today as clean as that shirt looks, and you've walked all the way up that endless driveway to see a man who doesn't have the common courtesy to keep an appointment. Well, I'll be damned if you're going to have to go through the same rigmarole twice. Your time's as valuable as his is." She pushed herself out of the chair. "You wait here and I'll go get him."

She tilted off across the kitchen and disappeared into the front of the house, calling out "Hennery! Hennery, dear!" And what was he supposed to do? He'd lit her stove, boiled her water, agreed never to try tobacco, and refused her ginger ale. He was hungry all of a sudden. He hadn't eaten more than a biscuit for breakfast and nothing yet for dinner. Miss Geneva kept a cookie jar next to the bread box. It was only a few steps away and he thought hard about going to it and took his first step toward it and stopped. He listened to the sounds of the house and when he knew no one was coming he went a couple of steps more and grabbed a peanut butter cookie and a chocolate chip cookie out of the jar. He pushed them into his mouth, one after the other, without even tasting them. He'd seen dogs do that, take a whole piece of meat and swallow it like a snake eating a frog. But he couldn't swallow. The cookies were dry and they filled his mouth. He couldn't chew. He heard her coming back again, talking as she came. They were walking on bricks, through the gun room. The kitchen was next. Her slippers went smack, smack, smack. He whirled around and slipped open the screen door and ran to the side of the house and emptied his mouth onto the ground. He stood out there wiping at his mouth as they came into the kitchen.

Mrs. Detroit said, "Where on earth did that boy go?"

Mr. Detroit laughed and said, "Maybe he wasn't here."

"Of course he was here. He boiled my water for me."

"He what?"

"He got the stove going, the kettle."

"Which one is this again?"

"Roosevelt," said Mrs. Detroit. "You're getting very bad, Henry."

"I thought he was the one who went to war."

"That's Dallas."

"Like Texas," said Mr. Detroit.

"No, like Dallas."

"What happened to him?"

"Nothing happened to him. He's coming home."

"Home? Where's he been?"

"The war, Henry."

"What war?"

"Our present war."

"I don't remember that war."

"It doesn't matter. Let's get you sitting down. He's here somewhere. Maybe he's in the john."

"If he's in the john, leave him, Rowena. Don't go knocking. You'll only embarrass him."

"I wasn't thinking of going in after him. Good heavens, Henry. We'll just wait. He waited for you, you can wait for him. I can make some coffee."

"Does the boy drink coffee?"

"He likes ginger ale."

"I'll take a ginger ale too."

"You hate ginger ale."

"I'll have one anyway."

"Don't be stupid," said Mrs. Detroit. "I'm making you coffee."

"Will he drink coffee?"

"He's too young for coffee. He's the epileptic."

"Epileptic? Am I an epileptic?"

"No, dearie. No, you're not."

"Then what's the matter with me?"

"You're forgetful. That's what's the matter with you. You have good days and bad ones."

"There must be more to it than that."

"But there isn't."

"There must be. There's no point keeping it from me, Rowena. Even on a bad day, I'm not a child."

"Of course you're not a child."

"You think of me as a child."

"Henry, please! I think nothing of the sort. You know yourself, the doctor has told you, there's no name for this . . . this *thing* that seems to make you forgetful and feeble sometimes."

"Ill."

"That's right, ill. Not yourself."

"A man who's lost at cards all his life. You shouldn't put up with me."

"Don't be silly."

"You shouldn't fuss so much. You should go away more, take a trip."

"Now, don't be ridiculous. Where would I go? I don't want to go anywhere."

"Visit somebody."

"Who would I visit?" laughed Mrs. Detroit.

"Your grandfather."

"My grandfather? Grandfather Sherman?"

"Uncle Billy. That's what his men used to call him."

"How on earth do you know that?"

"He tells me things, Rowena."

"Does he?"

"He steals a horse and comes to visit, looking for you, but you're always away. I entertain him as best I can, feed and water the animal and listen to his tales of reckless bravado. Last time I caught him in the act, stealing old Alabama out from under our noses. He seemed desperate and I let him have her. For a price."

"I'm sure you did," said Mrs. Detroit. "But I didn't realize Alabama was still with us."

"Gone now."

"She was Caroline's mare."

"They come and go. Which reminds me," Mr. Detroit lowered his voice, "did they find the body?"

"The body? What body?"

"The boy's body?"

"Which boy is this?"

"The one the war killed."

"I didn't say killed, I said he's coming home."

"Did we send someone?"

"Send someone where, darling?"

"You know."

"I don't know."

"Stop fussing!"

"I'm hardly fussing, Henry. I'm trying to talk to you."

"I don't know why."

"Well, I don't either sometimes. It's difficult."

"Is there some reason I'm sitting here?"

"We're waiting for Roosevelt to come out of the john."

"Oh?" asked Mr. Detroit. "He's here for a visit, is he?"

"A job, I think."

"A job! Hasn't he got his hands full being president?"

"Oh, Henry," said Mrs. Detroit. "I don't know when to laugh and when to cry anymore."

"Laugh in the morning, cry in the afternoon. That's the rule."

"It sounds like a good rule. You look tired, dear."

"I am. I'm tuckered out."

"You've been up too long."

"I'm tired as a rat in a package."

"Go on back to bed."

"A small rat. A blackish rat."

"Go on now. I'll bring you your coffee."

Roosevelt heard him get up, heard his chair squeal along the floor and the kitchen table creak as he leaned against it. "We never did find him, did we?"

"Who, darling?"

"That youngster. Osee's boy. The one who isn't the one who fought the war."

"You mean Roosevelt."

"The one in the john."

"That's Roosevelt. You had some business with him."

"Truth is, I want to give him a job with Ray." He started to cough and Mrs. Detroit said something Roosevelt couldn't hear. Mr. Detroit said, "I'm alright, I'm alright. For the love of Pete, stop *fussing,* Rowena. If you see him, tell him I'm under the weather, will you? Tell him I'm under the sea. Tell him whatever you want. He can start tomorrow. Tell him he's a bright boy and I'm glad to have him. And tell him . . . tell him if he can put up with Ray he can have my job."

He knocked on the table twice and Roosevelt heard him leave the kitchen. He heard Mrs. Detroit getting the coffee things ready, just like his mother did every other day but Sunday.

CHARLENE DAVIS

1967

Charlene stepped into his room, only it was Roosevelt's room now, and saw him like he was, with the window behind him and all the light in the world just trying to set down on his skin, like he was the honey tree. But his skin said no to it and it stood off him, close, like a shadow of light all around his man's body. Right before she saw what he'd done to himself she saw he was a man now, Dallas was a man just in time to die.

That day in school they learned the moon makes the tide work. She thought of the moon as a big man sucking up oceans with a straw, sucking them up and spitting them back. She'd never seen tide, only pictures of the ocean, and she saw the water walling up when the tide rose, rising straight up like it did in a glass. It hung above the beaches. Only the bravest people went out. When the tide went out it was like someone stood on top of the wall and threw bricks down.

She knew he had girlfriends who weren't colored. One of them gave him all her teeth. He called them gooks. He said that's what everyone called them. They were Orientals. They lived in the mud in stick houses. They were poor. They ate dogs. He said they hated him, but that girl gave him all her teeth. He wore them on a necklace made out of another one's hair. He had some gook children but no pictures of them. He didn't want pictures of them. Some day they'd come walking up the road looking for him and he didn't want anything around that said they were right, that said he was the right man.

In school they learned about rivers. She came home and fixed herself bread and butter and got herself a pop and went into his room where he always was in the afternoon, lying on his bed with everything on, even his boots. He was smoking. He always smoked. She knew it was marijuana because that's what he said it was. If his brother Curtis was there they were both smoking. That's what he called Curtis after they came home from the war, his brother. There weren't any friends anymore, just brothers, and the only brother who came by was Curtis because he was in the same trouble Dallas was, which they explained to her was the trouble of coming home from hell. Hell comes with you. That's all they said. The rest of the time they smoked and she told them about her day and they said umm-hmm and let their eyes close and she thought she might be helping them, like a mother reading her children to sleep.

He said, School never taught me nothing. It was a day when Curtis wasn't there. He said, You want to see a river, you got to lay eyes on the Mekong. All kinds of shit in there, bodies without no heads coming down by the hundreds, live gooks hanging on to dead ones. You like animals, Charlene. You oughtta seen those animals, big old water buffaloes trying to get the hell out of the river, pigs all ballooned up, rotting dogs, chickens in cages, one old bastard still crowing, and people, delta people, so hungry they send a kid out in a boat to get it and the kid gets shot. So they send another kid. That kid gets shot. They go through the whole family trying to get one rooster. Finally the old grandfather goes out and gets it and he has it all to himself. He's the only one left. You believe it?

No.

It's the truth.

Other stuff he told her came in fits like hard rain. Like someone got up after a long time asleep and went out and filled a bucket and poured it on the bed. She was the only one who knew him. She was there when a story came out. All he was now was sleep and stories, smoke and sleep and stories, and in the day when everyone was out of the house he watched TV. He got them a TV and he watched it. If he wasn't watching it no one was. At night the rest of them watched over at Auntie's like they always had.

He got up out of his bed and went outside in the dark. Since he came home he couldn't be out at night. Too quiet. He could feel the enemy moving behind his back. He walked across the yard with his head down and went up Aunt Rutha's steps and went inside. Charlene was in there with the others. She was eating a piece of chocolate cake. He said, Something the matter with the TV we got at home?

She was sitting on the floor and she put her plate down on the floor and said, Nothing I know of.

I got that TV for y'all to watch it.

Nothing on I want to look at.

Aunt Rutha said, Dallas. Honey, come sit with us. She told Roosevelt, Get your brother a chair.

Osee and Pearly Mae looked at him like he had dragged a dead dog in through the door. Uncle Lewis nodded at him and went back to watching his TV.

What're you looking at here, Charlene, you don't want to look at across the yard?

I ain't looking at nothing. I'm eating my cake. Over there we ain't got cake. Sit down. He got you a chair.

I can't sit down.

Aunt Rutha came with his cake and he stood and held the plate as long as he could, until they all got settled again, then he let it go and it fell straight down and blew apart, the dark icing rolling up like mud.

She had a list of spelling words. Estuary? she said. What's this mean?

Curtis laughed. Sound like some kind a problem a girl get in her pussy.

Don't say that shit, said Dallas.

What shit?

Don't talk that shit.

She gotta know what pussy mean.

Dallas looked like he didn't know what he was doing. He pulled the gun out from under the mattress, it was a shotgun and the barrel made a kind of cold bridge between him and Curtis. He pushed the gun against Curtis's belly and the flesh tightened up. Whoa, man, said Curtis. I won't say nothing about nothing, alright? He got up and left the room and Dallas never saw him again.

It was like he couldn't get the sight of it, of hell, out of his head unless he opened a window in his head, and he did that. She liked to think at least it was out of his body now. It was loose in the world but at least he'd freed himself.

DALLAS DAVIS

1967

The funeral of Leroy Dallas Davis took place at the Reverend Cordell Walker's Mount Hebron Baptist Church in Boston, Georgia, on the day after Thanksgiving. The parents of the deceased, Osee and Pearly Mae Davis, his four surviving brothers, Clarence, Bernard, Roosevelt, and Daniel, and his two sisters, Eunice and Charlene, occupied the first row of benches in that little church. Clarence and Bernard both wore the uniform of the United States Army, the weight of the cloth visible to all, the way it bent their young backs to an ancient stoop.

Behind them sat Eunice's husband and their twin boys, dressed up smartly in new Sunday clothes. Clarence's pregnant wife Patrice beside them. Then a row of Miss Pearly Mae's kin, her brother Robert and his wife, her seven sisters all in brand-new hats, Lewis and Rutha Brown, and Osee's two brothers dressed in dark suits they had grown too small for. A few more rows of miscellaneous relatives, some of them from out of state—Maryland, New York, and New Jersey by their license plates. Then a strange sight: a solitary white girl, a child of perhaps sixteen (though Reverend Walker was no judge), sitting up tall and straight in a row all by herself. She wore a shapeless blue dress. What looked like a bomber jacket hung off her shoulders. She had a long brown ponytail which she kept twisting and stroking like she was some kind of snake handler.

Missing, to the reverend's eye, were the people who might have called themselves Leroy Dallas Davis's friends. There was not one visible man or woman who fit that description, unless it was that white girl somehow. Where were they all? Dead, or just unable to set foot inside a house of God, given the sparse comfort God had granted His own son Dallas? Unable or unwilling? On a day like this it amounted to the same load of disrespect.

Missing too, for all known reasons, was Dallas's half brother Julian, his mother's child by a marooned sailor, a white man she'd met up in Norfolk in 1943. The story went that he was a Moultrie boy, sick to death of Virginia, homesick for south Georgia. Either drink had blurred his vision or the stark violence in Europe had turned him away from his own kind. Pure speculation. He'd picked an honest beauty, no matter what color he was schooled in. (Without even looking her way, Reverend Walker could call up Pearly Mae's good looks, the startled doe's face, fine-boned and clear-eyed to this day. Something her sisters must envy still and punish her for—yes, he finally understood those brand-new fancy feathered hats in the wake of her loss. The finery sat atop those seven heads like vultures.)

In all this time she had never told her side of the story, her reasons for such a union, or if in fact she had consented to it. She never breathed the sailor's name, not to anyone. He took shape only in her son, and so was buried with her son in May of 1965 out of this same church where they were gathered now to bury the next one. She would never look again upon the face of her miscalculation—or her misfortune, which it surely was, no matter how wrong or right, how desperate or destined that foolishness had been.

Her boy Julian had died of drowning, though he could swim the legs off a frog. He had not been a drinker and was brought up Christian till the day he left home at fifteen. But he was haunted sometimes, heard voices others didn't hear (like Our Lord), and tried to do their bidding (Jesus again), even if it meant offering himself open-armed and naked to a lake called Winnepasaukee, no language he even understood. He borrowed a boat, more likely stole it, and it came home without him, bumped the shore in mid-December. This was up in cold country, the state of New Hampshire. One week later the ice healed up and sealed him in till spring, a long cool rest.

Reverend Walker had done that funeral, his first funeral in what even he thought of now as "this little church." A church much like his old beagle dog, Bake, short in the leg and harmless looking, but with a spirit you couldn't reach with a ladder. He liked his work here and knew it would be his last post. He had another twenty-five good years in him, the same as the parents of the boys he'd buried, this boy he was burying now. He hadn't known Dallas, hadn't known any of these soldiers or the war they fought. They'd been off fighting it ever since he'd taken hold here. But he could see by their deaths that it was not the war of their fathers, men his own age who mostly believed in their own heroism, though it was ignored and exploited by a white race as blind as anything out of Germany. Back then there had been an enemy at least, an aggressor that added up, right or wrong, to a country. Then more countries lined up on the side of evil and it was clear as day, if you were not with them you were against them, and good.

This war though. It was an American war against an idea that had not yet shown itself to be more harmful than the harm we would inflict in fighting it. And the people we fought it for were not us. They were not our kin, our friends, our allies, or our neighbors. They were faraway strangers. How could our young boys, our sons, fight such a war and win it if they could not fight it and believe in it? If it meant they came home only to die? Reverend Walker had just one child, a daughter, and thanked God every day for that, no matter what mess she threw at him just to show him she could. The sons of Boston, Georgia, were being mown down without mercy, and he doubted not one minute this was but the beginning of bloodshed.

"Let us pray," he said at last, rising out of his plain wooden chair behind the altar. Coming to his full height—he was five feet, five inches tall—was still, after all these preaching years, an exercise in humility. Stretching out his arms like Our Savior on the cross, he said to the earnest gathering, "Let us pray, brothers and sisters, for our dearly departed son and brother, Leroy Dallas Davis, who died a soldier in the war beyond wars and is born again now into the life beyond life, the true life of the Resurrection."

From the middle rows came a few *Amens*. A few heads nodded. No one else seemed to be listening. You agreed not to speak the truth at a funeral and what happened? Nobody listened. That or they listened too hard, wanted too much, drank in one man's limited vision as if he'd signed a covenant to save them. As if he knew them. Which this man did not. He knew their appearances, their habits only, and drew no conclusions. He mistrusted conclusions, preached against them often, and yet he was called upon over and over again to eulogize, to judge the lives of those unknown to him in order to satisfy the grief they left behind. It made this particular fire and brimstone around Dallas Davis's sanctified body a pile of cold ashes, a trap set for fools.

He made himself look at Pearly Mae Davis's form, her pretty face lowered, her shoulders pressed forward, making the front of her dark dress shapeless. A woman so lost herself to her child, to her son, that when he left he took her body. He took the place in her that had nourished him. He took the best of her. It angered Reverend Walker suddenly, the waste of death, of this death in particular. Everything surrounding the boy seemed shrouded in the same loose cloth that hung on his mother.

He went on, "We thank you, Jesus, for the life of this man, for the short time he walked among us, and for all he leaves behind. His family, his friends," *his little half-breed Oriental children,* "his love of hunting," *and poaching,* "his love of fast cars," *and unreliable women, and marijuana. That he was high on drugs, Lord Jesus, we have no doubt, and that it led him through a terrible suffering to an unspeakable death*. "We ask forgiveness for our own sin of blindness, and we ask that the horrors of the war he and others have come home from be lifted from all these brave boys who survive to become men. For it is not the horror, not ordinary blood, but the blood of the Resurrection by which true nations are made.

"A special prayer for Charlene Davis, Lord, for the cleansing of her heart and mind, for an end to her nightmares, her visions of darkness and death," *which no child ought to witness, damn him.* "His sickness is healed and his wounds have closed over. May such a resurrection come to his family and to all who remember him as he lived." *And again, Lord, may the one who saw his death fresh, who walked in his still-flowing blood and tried with her ten-year-old hands to save him, to keep him from spilling his own life onto the floor, may she not go blind in her need never to see such suffering again, and may the gun he raised against himself die with him, a full death. May it close this sorrowful chapter here forever.*

FRANKIE DETROIT

1967

Frankie's shoes pinched. Her dress was too big and too blue, an A-line she'd found on sale at Wade's at the last minute. A-line? It looked like an O on her. Well, she wasn't in jeans at least. She could have come in a tutu or a hula skirt as far as Mars was concerned. Anything but jeans. "You're representing the family, Frances." Now she sat and wondered why the family hadn't put on their own uncomfortable clothes and come and represented themselves.

The preacher was a little man, a square man with a big voice. But what he didn't say was even louder. He didn't know Dallas, and what killed Dallas seemed equally a mystery to him. You don't put a shotgun to your head and pull the trigger in a not quite empty house unless you're sufficiently fucked up by something, and if you're just back from Vietnam, thirteen months dragging your ass through the jungle and dragging your buddies' bodies out wounded or dead, and pointing a heavy gun at frightened yellow women the size of your leg, with their sick and screaming terrified children which half-belong to you or people like you, and choppers falling out of the sky and napalm burning and the enemy popping up from underground like immortal moles, and your own feet rotting out from under you along with every other thing you used to call important, and a good meal meaning rice and dog, then you're probably fucked up enough to do anything to anyone and an act of mercy is to do the bad thing to yourself. Why couldn't he understand that, this little preacher? Praise him where it counted? Forget the hunting and fast cars bullshit. Blowing his brains out might have been the most merciful thing Dallas Davis ever did.

She hadn't seen him since he got home but she'd heard he looked like a corpse that got up in the afternoon. Pearly Mae fussed about how long he slept, how little he ate, how much he swore at her and Osee. Lots of bad language he'd picked up in the Army. Hands that shook and a green fungus covering his feet and ankles. Any thunderstorm you'd find him under the kitchen table. Other times, when he wasn't in bed, he was out walking the road looking for work. He fixed a few lawn mowers, got a few cars running for friends. He was a good mechanic and Frankie asked her grandfather to hire him for small repairs on the jeep. Papa said he'd think about it. He guessed the jeep would be alright, but he wasn't about to turn him loose on the Mercedes. Then a few days before Thanksgiving Dallas decided things for himself, and now Frankie would think about him every time she tried to keep the old Willy's idling at a stop sign.

The little preacher was working himself up again, with real enthusiasm this time, pacing back and forth in front of the altar. She disagreed with him. It *was* ordinary blood—and guts and blown brains and bodily fluids—plenty of it, which made nations. Didn't he own a TV? The altar was a square wooden table the size of a card table. Its legs were painted sky blue and it was decorated with a white plaster cross and a tin vase of yellow roses. She looked around her. There were more roses and pots of chrysanthemums on the floor. A few pictures hung on the whitewashed walls. The one above her head looked like it had been cut out of a magazine and framed. It showed the boy Jesus sawing a piece of wood at His workbench. He was brown-skinned and dark-haired and His body emanated light. She'd forgotten He was a carpenter. Was there anything He couldn't do?

The front door of the church stood open and she could see the corner of a grass yard and beyond that the dead-end street. She thought she heard a sheep or a goat bleating, complaining of the bitterness of all that grew on old Methodist graves. Four tall windows let in a depressing gray-blue light. One pair faced the parking lot and the other the cemetery where the white folks, whose church this once had been, even after death kept strict rules about who could join them there in their everlasting sleep. Which didn't, of course, include Dallas. He'd be buried in what everyone called "the Negro graveyard," an acre of untended ground out on the Moynihan plantation, muddy in any rainstorm, the headstones mossy and canted like sinking ships. One day, when old Mrs. Moynihan turned a hundred and was closing in on her own everlasting snooze, her sons or grandsons or great-grandsons would carry her out there, covered in blankets on her chaise lounge, and she'd offer up some crap about the value of such a landmark and the deep disgrace of its neglect, and then she'd disinter everybody, generations of Davises, Browns, Hills, Washingtons, Jeffersons, and Nixons, and sell off the spot to her highest-bidding boy who would build a brick Tara on any leftover bones. This was not prophecy, just the likely outcome of personality dressed in circumstance.

Mrs. Moynihan was deaf as a post, and before her grandfather got sick, Frankie spent more than one evening watching her chain-smoke Parliaments and listening to the old boot shout about her great sums of money and the greed of her children and how she wished to outlive them all. Finally she could keep her mouth shut no longer.

"Why would you want to do that?" she asked.

"You're mumbling!" cried Mrs. Moynihan.

"I said, why would you want to do that? Outlive your kids?"

"Oh, I know! Aren't I wicked!"

"Frances, dear, get Mrs. Moynihan an ashtray," said Mars.

"Too late!" hooted the old dame, rubbing the rug with the toe of her riding boot. It was as ridiculous as Mars in her jodhpurs, this one with the riding boots. Why didn't she carry a crop and wear that velvet bucket on her head while she was at it? Spurs! A lasso! What were they supposed to think, that she arrived for cocktails *à cheval*? Mrs. Moynihan hadn't graced the backside of a *cheval* for quite some time, was Frankie's guess. She mentioned this to her grandfather after the great ship sailed, which was how he referred to her in private, H.M.S. *Moynihan*.

"One doesn't grace the backside of a horse, my dear. The rump sits aft of the saddle. But the rest is true, sadly. She used to be too blotto to ride, back in the days when she rode. She'd have a better shot at it now. I don't know why she doesn't."

"You're saying she isn't blotto? Are we talking about the same Mrs. Moynihan?"

"Stone sober."

"She drinks like a fish!"

"True," said her grandfather. "I should know. I mix her drinks."

"Then what are you saying?"

"There's nothing in them, Frances. Nothing but flat Coca-Cola, water, and ice. A twist of lemon. The appearance of a cocktail, with none of its bite." He was sitting down, the Atlanta paper open in his lap. He was still able to read then. He leaned toward her. “Appearances are very important aboard the *Moynihan,* and many other great ships we know. It’s an elaborate charade. Which is why we don’t go out much anymore, your grandmother and I. We stay put like a pair of old shoes and read our books and talk to our children and grandchildren on the telephone. We aren’t bored and we don’t envy the revelers, but we don’t disapprove of them either. Don’t you disapprove of them. People your age disapprove of everything and it shows off a terrible ignorance on your part. Unsolicited advice,” he added. “Sorry.”

“Why did she stop drinking?”

“She killed her husband.”

Frankie stared at him.

“She was driving drunk and he was with her.”

“Oh, Papa.”

“She’s made of iron. A crusty old rusty piece of iron. Nothing soft about her. That’s what you don’t like.”

“No. I don’t like the way she calls black people darkies and orders them around like they aren’t human beings.”

“I don’t like that either.”

“Why does she do it?”

“Because she can.”

“That’s not an answer.”

“I know it’s not, but it’s the only one I have.”

“She’s a racist,” Frankie shrugged. “That’s the answer.”

“Rubbish. That’s no more of an answer than mine. It describes actions and behaviors but it tells me nothing about what makes a person that way.”

“All whites are racists, Papa.”

He looked at her severely. “If that’s what you think, then you had your answer before you asked the question. Leave that to the lawyers, Frances. True inquiry is the search for understanding. You're using it only to build a case."

"That's not true. I'm searching for understanding. But my understanding and yours are different, they're very different. This isn't your world anymore, Papa. True inquiry means you have to keep updating your understanding all the time. You can't just say it was or it wasn't this or that, and that's the way it will always be, because it changes, it's changing. People used to think it was okay to buy and sell other human beings. Inquiry at that time led to that conclusion—"

"Many people did not conclude that. *Many.* The world is not just political, Frances. Politics makes a big noise but we are and always have been definable by other things, by small worthy acts that catch the eye of no one, yet they shout of our humanity, our goodwill. Or at least our efforts in those directions. I'm a hypocrite. Sooner or later you'll have to call me that. I make money—and therefore you do too—off the hard labor of human beings who aren't paid well enough, who risk their lives to feed their children, who have no choices, or few, who hate their job, their life, and me. Whose anger ruins their children and slowly kills their wives. I confess. I have done little to alleviate this situation and much to exploit it. And the fruits of their labor will send you to college where you, in the security of academia, among others just like you, can destroy all that brought you there, destroy it with your mind. And not remake it, Frances. That's the tragedy. Build yourselves something, all of you, build like we did. You can scratch and claw at the old world all you want, but if you build nothing you have nothing, you're standing only on our grave."

He was pale and breathing hard, his hands gripping the arms of his chair. "It's okay, Papa," she said.

"You haven't even heard me."

"I have heard you."

"No. No, you'd like me to stop, and I will stop. I'll just say one more thing. It's not my world anymore, you're right. But I don't want it. I want you to have it. All of you. Every last one of you. Take hold of it, for God's sake. Do what What's-his-name did. What's the man's name, Frankie? The one with the screw?"

"The one with the screw?"

"The Greek."

She started to laugh. "The Greek with the screw? I don't know a Greek with a screw. Is this someone you've met, Papa?"

"No! Years ago!"

"You met him years ago?"

"No! Oh, you're hopeless, child. Get Mars. Bring her to me. Bring her! Bring her!"

By the time Frankie found her grandmother and brought her, the name of the Greek had already been retrieved from the files of her grandfather's memory. He was an old Greek indeed.

"Oh, Rowena." Papa held out his hands. "I'm in too deep. I'm drowning the girl. Come help me."

"You're not drowning her," said Mars. "You're boring her to death. Who's this Greek? I don't remember any Greek."

"Archimedes!"

"Good lord. What is your mind made of?"

"Stuff."

"Stuff?"

Frankie said, "Papa. What am I supposed to do that Archimedes did? You said, Take hold. Do what What's-his-name did. Well, he already did it."

"Do it again."

"What do you mean, do it again?"

"Do it again."

"That doesn't help."

"Exactly. Get your hands wet and move water uphill, if that will help someone. Defy gravity, the laws of nature, fixed ideas. Run against the stream in which you live."

"I don't shave my armpits. Does that count?"

"Oh, Frankie. That's rebellion. It has nothing to do with it." He looked directly at her, almost through her. "Help someone. For God's sake. Be of use!"

Is that what she was here for, then, in this little church? To be of use? She couldn't stand those shoes another second. She slipped them off, heard them clunk to the floor. Of use to whom? Not to Papa. His mind was going from stuff to feathers and there was not one thing she could do to stop it. And not to Dallas. Not anymore. The word *useful* never would have crossed her mind or his. Too cool and calculating, when the plain truth was: He gave her something, and she gave him something back. He had the best grass she'd ever smoked anywhere, and in that frame of mind he liked to talk and she liked to listen.

The first time she got high she was smoking Dallas's amazing dope. She'd smoked a few times up north. In Newton there was plenty of pot going around her Catholic country day school, right under the noses of the Madames. But her friends were either cheap or poor, or just didn't know better, so there was a lot of funky homegrown, mixed with tobacco or tarragon. Frankie kept trying to find the right grass to take her to the right place, but it didn't happen until she went south for Christmas and taught herself to drive the Willy's, and that rusty old jeep, held together by green paint and a stubborn nature, brought her, one day, to Dallas.

She liked to drive all the way out to Lake Walter on the plantation road. Sometimes she took Man with her, her grandfather's chocolate Lab. He rode shotgun with his square head tilted back, his muzzle to the wind, ears flapping. She'd park at the lake (or stall out there) and he'd hop out and run and hurl himself in the water. He was a big, powerful dog, all instinct, without brilliance or imagination. She often thought what a good soldier he'd make.

No one she knew ever went to Lake Walter in the winter. The shooting wasn't any good because the lake was too small for ducks and the land around it was too swampy for quail. There was fishing, but people didn't fish much in the winter. Dallas, it turned out, fished summer or winter, whenever he was home. He went out there like she did, to get away from people telling him what he should and shouldn't do with his life.

He sat on the dock and she could tell before she even shut the engine off that he was stoned. She knew right away who he was because he looked so much like his mother and his brother Roosevelt. He had the long thin face that dominated looks in the Hill family. Pearly Mae's brother Robert was one of the most handsome men Frankie had ever laid eyes on.

She got out of the jeep and went over and stood on the shore by the dock. Man nosed around, lifted his leg on the front tire, and came and stood behind her. "If we come out there, are we going to scare your fish?" she asked.

Dallas finally looked up. "They ain't my fish."

She went halfway out the dock and sat down. The dog stayed behind on the shore, whining and digging a nervous little hole.

"How come he don't come out?"

"I guess he doesn't feel like it."

"He got to feel like it."

"Why?"

She took her shoes off and put her feet in the water, even though she was scared of snapping turtles.

"You watch out them cottonmouths don't get you," he said. He was a few years older than she was. She remembered Charlene had told her he was going to Vietnam.

"Can I have some of that stuff you're smoking?"

He looked at her and laughed.

"You're Dallas," she said.

"That's right."

"I'm Frankie."

"What's his name?"

"Who?"

"The dog."

"Man."

"He's afraid a me, Mister Man."

"He's not afraid of you."

"He act like he is."

"He just doesn't know you."

"I think he's afraid a me." He laid his rod on the dock. "You ever smoke before?"

"Sure." She flipped her hair back. "A lot."

The minute she inhaled she knew she was in a different space. They passed the joint back and forth and she pulled her feet out of the water and let them air-dry. Everything seemed bouncy to her all of a sudden. Bendable. She felt like she was as awake as she'd ever be, and at the same time asleep.

She lit a cigarette and pushed one over to him and he took it and put it in his shirt pocket. "Man and Man's best friend," he said. He went back to his fishing. He held the rod with both hands and the line went straight down into Lake Walter. She kept thinking, *What are we going to do if he catches something? Oh my God.* But in the times they were out there she never saw a single fish. Once they saw a water moccasin. She didn't know what it was but he did and he trapped it against the dock with a stick and started beating it until he'd beaten it to death.

That first day he told her, "Don't bring the dog no more."

"Why not?"

"He's afraid a me."

"Stop it. He's not."

But the next time she tried to get Man to come with her he slunk away and hid in the hedge.

He told her the story of a brother of his who was crazy, who thought he was Jesus. Frankie said, "Plenty of people thought Jesus was crazy."

"Yeah, but the man had a way of following through. Julian, he didn't work no miracles."

"Do you believe in Jesus?"

"I believe in the man."

"All these people who say 'I've got Jesus on my side,' and then they go out and throw a brick at someone."

"Jesus ain't nowhere near that crowd."

"But that crowd believes he is. It's the same crowd that's got His picture hung up on the wall, opposite the TV, or in their car. You've seen those pictures, Dallas. He's a white man. He's got all this golden hair and blue eyes. He's Mr. White Man."

"They got to have a picture."

"But they believe in it. They make up an image and use it against others. That's why I don't believe in Jesus."

"Sounds like you don't believe in how they use Him. They ought to make themselves a big old cross—"

"Are you kidding? Stick it on your lawn and set it on fire?"

"A big old cross made out of a living tree, just like the one they hung Him on. Let people go to it and touch it and climb on it and carve their name in it and whatever all they want. A tree right out in the yard. Something alive that grow and give shade and ain't just to look at and wonder is it white or colored. Call it Jesus. A plain old tree."

Even if she didn't understand him, she listened. She sat on the dock or lay on the dock and listened. And then one day she was out there and he wasn't, and the next day he still wasn't, and she realized he'd gone off to war and that was the one thing he hadn't talked about, that he was going away to a place that was heating up hour by hour and would become, in the months he was there, hallowed ground for most of the men he knew. And she realized it wasn't possible for him to talk about it because he was scared and uncertain. He didn't know if he believed in his own sacrifice, didn't know if a sane man went to war. He didn't like the thought of being crazy. Like his brother. Like his brother who believed he was Jesus and died because he wasn't. Believed he could cross the water on his own two feet, walk miles on the living water and be delivered to a living shore. Crazy, like Jesus Himself. Because who was Jesus, anyway, but a madman who envisioned a world worth dying for? Dallas had no such vision.

RAY LUKEN JR.

1968

Sometimes he thought he would kill Rosemary. There was not a gun in the house that did not seem a fit tool. Like he told his little girl, his little Brenda, when old Torpedo went and got himself all caught up in that goddamn nigger's trap, he told her: A thing can't be released then it gotta be destroyed.

There was not a gun in the house unclean or unready to do what he would have it do. His old deer rifle. His twelve-gauge shotgun. The 410 he used for training dogs. A couple of pistols, one dating back to the Confederacy, though who it came from and how it got there he couldn't remember. Must've gone back through Rosemary's side to her granddaddy or great-granddaddy, one of them who rode with the patrols. They roughed up deserters, caught and returned runaway property, and later set so-called freedmen on the right path, the path to freedom, a noose around the neck. So you'd have to say one of those guns was the rightful possession of his wife who had never laid a hand on anything more quick and easy than an electric mixer, or more destructive than a lawn mower—if you didn't count Ray himself.

Sometimes he thought he'd kill his mama's husband, his daddy, the man whose name he was given, first and last, and whose blood, Ray liked to think, purified itself in him, the son. It came to him all messed up and he took it and cleaned it, just as he had that one time and never again taken and cleaned his daddy's gun. What else could he do? He could say Yessir or be put out the house. His mama didn't say Yessir to his daddy, she said, Raymond, how come if you hate the niggers so bad you gotta go find yourself a nigger woman to mess with? Raymond, plenty a white gals to mess with, if you won't mess with me. You always did like your nigger pussy, just like it run in your veins. His daddy didn't put her out the house. He took his things and went himself. Come back a few days later and she'd laugh at him and call him boy.

Sometimes Ray went and took his gun and killed anything that crossed his path. He never aimed that he didn't kill. Maybe a high, fast one, a dove at the end of the day. He'd go out of his way to shoot a snake and sometimes he'd hit a gopher tortoise just to see the shot bounce off the shell. Brenda liked for him to bring home a gopher. She'd sit on it and try and get it to poke its head out so she could feed it, but it wouldn't ever eat for her or drink nothing and soon it'd die and she'd just walk around it in the yard like it wasn't there at all. Then Rosemary'd be on him to take it somewhere and he'd take it down to the kennel and tie it up by the neck, let the dogs jump for it.

Whenever he had a little time his daddy'd ride out in the swamp and hunt gator. Or poach gator. His mama cooked up a lot of gator tail. Whenever he had a little time his daddy'd ride out at night and set a nigger house on fire. Or a nigger school. Or nigger land. The smell of gasoline would come home with him and the smell of burnt wood and sometimes the smell of roasted meat. His mama'd cry. She'd be a different kind of mama than the one he knew. She'd lose her smart mouth and cry and more than once she took the boy off with her and they'd be gone a few days just driving around, maybe go down into Florida or into Alabama. She could drive as good as his daddy. She could drive better. And she wouldn't let him miss a day of his lessons. She taught him how to multiply and divide in his head. And they'd stop to eat, she'd make him read the menu, and he'd say, Mama, I can't read that, but she'd tell him, Go ahead. He'd say, Well, I guess we got pie and we got hamburger and we got coleslaw, like we had everywhere else, and she'd always say thank you and what a smart boy he was and she'd order the same thing every time, a plain hamburger with a side of coleslaw and a piece of chocolate cream pie.

He'd look at his daddy sometimes and see the nigger in him. His hair was wavy, it wouldn't lie flat, and his nose was broad and his lips were too full to be a white man's lips. He'd look at his mama and she was pretty, and he'd look at himself and wonder if it showed in him like it showed in his daddy and he decided it did not, he decided he was a white man. His mama called his daddy a Clorox nigger. She called him boy. And one day when Ray was down by the creek oiling a trap she called his daddy the last thing she ever called anyone, and his daddy came and got him and told him go in and clean that gun, he was done with it.

Sometimes Rosemary does not know when to stop with that tongue of hers and he cannot abide the whipping she gives him. Even with her silence she gives it to him, and he goes somewhere where there is neither silence nor talk, just the dumb indifference of animals.

BRENDA LUKEN

1968

Brenda Luken spit-shines her shoes. Mama is out in the yard, hanging Daddy on the line. Wind comes up and Daddy kicks Mama and punches her and gets himself free. Mama chases him past the doghouse. Old Torpedo's gone to heaven. She chases him past the barbecue pit and her little flower garden. Brenda helps Mama in the garden when the weather is nice. Nothing in it now but a bunch of old stickers and burrs. Mama chases him to the swing set where he gets into the swing and Brenda can hear him laughing as the wind blows. That's where Mama grabs him and sticks him over her shoulder and hauls him back to the line. She pins him quick, then the wind comes up again and he tries to get her but she's fast.

Now he's doing the backstroke, just like he taught his little girl. He don't like to put his face in the pool. It's a public pool and he don't like to put his face nowhere niggers have been. They don't swim with the niggers. The niggers swim one time, the whites swim another. But it's the same water. Daddy says niggers spit and do their business in the water and Brenda says why would they do that when there's a restroom they can do their business in. Daddy says that's the way niggers are and Brenda says well, maybe they can't help it.

They're her good party shoes, black patent leather with a purse to match. Brenda picks out a ribbon from her pink music box with the ballerina in it. Open the box and the ballerina pops up and twirls. Brenda's almost seven years old and her hair is brown. She picks a green ribbon to go with her eyes. She tries to tie her hair back in a nice ponytail but Mama always does that for her and the ribbon won't stay. Is it time to put on her dress? She laughs out loud. Stupid! Put on your dress, *then* fix your hair. She isn't used to the exact order of things. Mama's in charge of that. But Mama's out in the yard, pinning up the clothes, pinning up Brenda's own underpants and undershirts and her little blouses she wears so nice to school. Mama moves the basket along the ground, she kicks it a little so it's always where it's supposed to be, right under the empty place on the line she's about to fill up. It's like writing in a book. Mama writes and writes until she comes to the end of the line. If she has a few words left in her basket she'll get out the rack and put them there. The words on the rack aren't as easy to read as the words on the line. When Brenda writes in the dark in her pink diary, some of the words go on top of other words, whole lines go on top of other lines, and in the morning she goes to read what she wrote and it isn't there. All those marks, they don't mean a thing. Words are marks too, but they're marks with a certain meaning. She remembers the first time a mark turned into a word, right in front of her eyes, right on the page of a book Mama was reading her. The book was about a little girl the Indians carried away. They carried her away on a horse. The mark that turned into a word was *up*. Brenda looks out at the yard to see if the word *up* is hanging on the line. She sees Daddy kicking and kicking though Mama is all the way at the other end of the line about to be done with the clothes. Brenda kneels on her bed which is next to the window. She thinks Mama is so beautiful. She likes to look at her. Sometimes she says, Mama, will I be beautiful like you? But Mama always says, Shoot higher, darling. She looks sad when she says it. If Daddy is there he says, Your mama made one mistake, sugarplum. Don't you go and make that mistake. Brenda knows what the mistake is but she always says, What mistake, Daddy? and he says, She went blind for a minute or two and thought she was marrying a rich man. Then he laughs. Mama shrugs her shoulders. Brenda feels a powerful yearning to suck her thumb. She sucks the back of her hand instead and thinks about what could cause such a moment of blindness. Soap in the eyes? Looking at the sun? Too much reading in the dark? Every time she opens a book, takes a bath, or sits outside, she is sure she is one step closer to marrying a man like Daddy.

By her bed is a brand-new Mickey Mouse clock Daddy gave her for Christmas. Mickey's long hand is on the three, his short hand on the one. She has until two o'clock. She moves away from the window and goes to pick out her dress. Then something occurs to her, something so clear and right it is like a star falling into a lake up high in the mountains, a lake made of ice: She will wear panty hose. She will wear her pink dress and black shoes and panty hose. Like an older girl. She'll look grown up and pretty like Mama, and they'll never forget to invite her again, and they won't ever mention and she won't either that she's come on her own, to fix a mistake, the mistake of inviting all the other boys and girls except her. Maybe Mama has panty hose. She tiptoes into Mama's room and there, thrown across the foot of the bed, waiting for her, are Mama's stockings. Two of them. One for each leg. She opens Mama's drawers and there are more stockings, some with a dark line down the back, some the color of dirt. She takes a pair with a dark seam. These are the ones Mama wears most, though she doesn't wear them to church. But how do they stay up? They have to look smooth, like panty hose. Brenda looks on the bed, she looks in a little pile of Mama's clothes on the floor. She finds it there and grabs it up and even then it feels wrong, too stiff and bony, like something you would cook and eat. But she knows this is it, she's seen Mama in it, she's watched her lean over and snap her stockings to it. She runs back to her room and looks at the clock. She has to go! Soon the children will be there. Cherry and Debby. She doesn't know them. They go to the all-white school. Daniel. She loves Daniel. Except he's colored. Mama's still in the yard, airing the blankets now. She'll say this is the beautiful day she's been waiting all December for. But Brenda has no time for Mama. She throws the stockings on the bed. She won't even have time for her hair! She slips on the girdle but it doesn't stay. It hangs loose around her, even when she pushes out her belly. No time! She sits on the bed and pulls the stockings on, puts a run in each of them with her long toenails. Shoot! She clips them to the girdle. They're too long and baggy. She throws her pink dress over her head and stuffs her feet into her shoes, first tugging at the toes of the stockings to get them to smooth out, which makes the girdle drop. She pulls it up and orders it to stay. She brushes her hair, two rough strokes down each side and one in back. She has a little lipstick from dress-up and she puts that on as best she can and doesn't worry that it smears and her lips look twice their size. She's ready. How to get around Mama? Oh, and her little purse. It's two o'clock, a little after, and Mama's having quite a time out there in the sun. Go away, Mama. Go around the house, Mama. Less than a minute is all I need.

But Mama was busy taking Daddy off the line. He wasn't Daddy anymore, he was just a pair of old long johns. She took Daddy off, then she took the other things off, then she took all the clothes off the rack and folded them and got set to carry them inside. She erased everything. She took all the words and put them one on top of the other and carried the pile of them toward the house like she was carrying the dictionary A to Z. Then a terrible thing happened. Daddy drove up. He parked in the carport and got out of his white truck and Daniel Davis got out the other side of his white truck and said, "Thank you, sir," and waved and started walking the last little bit up to the big house. Daddy came over to Mama and said, "You know where that little nigger's going? He's going to a party. You know who's having the party? That Detroit girl, the one Brenda's age, her and her fat-assed little boy cousin. They got the niggers coming, they got Cole's kids, I'm asking you, what in the hell passed through their minds? All these years I worked for them and they give us this house to live in like we're neighbors. And our Brenda here's not invited? Well, that ain't neighborly. What in the *hell* is wrong with those people? They reach out to the colored but they ain't got the decency to reach out to their own."

Mama said, "We ain't their own, Ray."

"I know that," said Daddy. He looked at Mama like he didn't know where she'd come from, like it wasn't her own yard she was standing in. "You think I don't know that? You look at me and sometimes I think you see a pile of steaming dog shit."

"Ray, don't talk that way."

"You see a snake so stupid it bit itself in its own behind. You see a worm. You see the ground and me in it, like a worm, like a maggot. You see my corpse, Rosemary. You see me eating off a my own corpse. And you count the days."

Daddy was getting red in the face and Mama was taking tiny steps backward, steps too small to notice. But she got herself to the corner of the house and dropped the clothes and ran for the door. She came in and closed the door, though she didn't lock it which meant she didn't think he was drunk. She went into Brenda's room but Brenda wasn't there.

Brenda runs into the den and crouches down behind Daddy's La-Z-Boy and waits for Mama to come into the house. Mama comes in, then Daddy comes in after her. Brenda goes out the door to the carport. It's warm under there but she's shivering in her pink dress. She waits until she hears the fighting. Mama can curse as good as Daddy, but Daddy can't scream the way Mama does. The fighting's Brenda's magic coat, it makes her invisible. She wears it all the way up to the big house.

She doesn't know but she might still be wearing it when the lady opens the door. She's a white lady, shriveled like a prune, and her hair is all white and she's short, shorter than Daddy. She takes a long while before she says, "Yes?" Brenda doesn't have a tongue just yet. That's what happens to her after she gets invisible. Finally she asks, "Is this the front door?" The lady nods and says, "You must be here for the party." "I am!" cries Brenda, feeling happy again, loved. Then the lady does a surprising thing. Instead of letting Brenda in, she steps out and closes the door behind her. She takes Brenda's hand which is sweaty and smudged with lipstick. She says, "And what's your name? I bet it's Brenda." "It *is* Brenda! What's yours?" "I'm Rowena," says the lady. She leads her around the house to the door Brenda knows is the kitchen door and they go inside. Daniel's mama is there. She's skinny. She's not as pretty as Mama. Well, how could she be? A big fat colored lady is icing the cake for the party, and another fat one is ironing a pair of underpants that look just like Brenda's. The white lady makes an announcement, "Brenda's here for the party," and Brenda feels proud. The white lady says, "Maybe we can get her some of Lucy's things to wear. And the face," she says to Daniel's mama. Daniel's mama comes over to Brenda and says, "Honey, come on with me. We gonna get you looking like a princess. How you liking school this year?" and off they go, into the restroom right there off the kitchen. Brenda says, "This is the first time I ever been in a colored restroom." "Zat right?" says Daniel's mama. She stands her next to the sink and scrubs her face until it feels all raw and new. She starts to put Brenda's hair in two braids. "I don't want braids. I want to look more grown up." Daniel's mama keeps on braiding. "I don't want braids!" Daniel's mama says, "Braids is what you get. I like your purse." Brenda is holding the little black shiny purse in front of her. She never lets go of it. "There's nothing in it," she says, "not one red cent." "Not one red cent?" says Daniel's mama. "Here," and she pulls a stick of gum out of her own pocket and gives it to Brenda. "Thank you," says Brenda.

Lucy Detroit is a bigger girl and her dress comes down below Brenda's knees. Besides, it's yellow. Brenda hates yellow. Daniel's mama fixes it up with pins and finds her a green sash to wear, and a pair of little yellow socks. "Why can't I keep my pink dress on? I love pink. I hate yellow." Daniel's mama says, "That dress got lipstick all over it. You don't want to go to no party all covered in lipstick. The other children'll laugh at you." "Not Daniel," says Brenda. "He wouldn't laugh." "Daniel's a good boy," says his mama. "He would never be cruel to no child." "Are there other nigger children here?" asks Brenda. The fat lady at the ironing board is using something out of a bottle to get the lipstick off Brenda's dress. She says, "Daniel, he's a colored boy. He don't like to be called nigger." "That's what my daddy calls him," says Brenda. The fat lady nods and rubs a little at Brenda's dress. "Everything your daddy call your mama, that what she like to be called?" She holds the dress up and finds another red spot and lays the dress down and rubs it again.

She remembers one thing about the party: A boy held out her chair when they sat down for ice cream and cake, and she knew he was going to pull it away like the boys did at school. She stood there. He was a fat stupid boy and she could stand there forever. The other children started to laugh, but they were laughing at him not her. He ducked his head and went back to his own seat at the end of the table. His name was Leo.

The other children have a mother or father who comes for them. Brenda watches them go. She counts the ones left, subtracts herself and Daniel and Lucy and Leo, and soon there are two, and then one, and then that one is gone. Leo and Daniel are looking at human skin through Leo's microscope and Lucy has run away upstairs, telling Brenda, "Don't follow me!" Then a terrible thing happens. A terrible and wonderful thing. Daniel's mama comes out of the kitchen and says Mama is waiting for her. Mama is in the kitchen. She has a scarf over her head, tied under her chin, and she's holding a paper bag with Brenda's things in it, all clean and ironed. The scarf is Mama's magic coat but it's not as good as Brenda's magic coat. She stands by the door, looking out the door, and everyone else is so busy they don't even notice her. "Mama," says Brenda. Mama whispers, "Little Miss High-And-Mighty! I oughtta give you a whipping right here!" Daniel's mama says, "Don't forget your purse now. That's such a pretty little purse," and the washing and ironing lady says, "You tell your mama what good manners you got. You tell her let you come and see us again. Alright?"

Later Brenda lies in bed and looks out the window and sees moonlight slick as soapy water washing the yard. Daddy's truck is gone. Nights like this he'll drive it till it runs out of gas, then he'll sleep right there where it stops. Sometimes, Brenda knows, he sleeps down at the kennel. He'll get in a pen and curl up right in the doghouse, sleep with the dogs. She knows her daddy is not a bad man because no animal would tolerate a bad man's company.

RUTHA BROWN

1969

Seemed like Roosevelt turned fifteen all of a sudden and decided it was time his old Aunt Rutha learned to read and write. She had one day off, it was Sunday, and after church and getting dinner ready and eaten and washed up she sat down with the boy in front of an empty piece of paper. He wrote his name on it. That was easy to read. It must have said Roosevelt. He made her name and she watched him close. Then she held the pencil and he put his hand over hers and they made her name together starting with an R, same as his name. She wrote it again and again while he watched her and finished off a pan of cornbread.

"You want some milk with that?"

"No ma'am. But I would take coffee."

"Coffee! Since when you started drinking coffee?"

"I don't know. I liked it for a long time."

"It stunt your growth."

"Something else must've did that already."

He was a small boy, Roosevelt. Five feet tall and skinny so people thought he was a child. Then he opened his mouth and they knew he wasn't. He'd fill out someday. He was handsome anyway.

The next week he came and ate another pan of cornbread and a couple pieces of chocolate cake while she wrote Rutha Rutha Rutha Rutha till her whole arm ached. Of all the letters in the world she could claim five of them now, could form them in her own hand and find them too. Her nephew wrote out the word *truth* and sure enough, it was most of her name.

"Brown's your name too," he told her.

"Naw. That belong to Lewis."

"When you married him you took his name."

"I know all that."

"It's only four more letters. You already got your R."

"Them letters don't make no difference to me. All my life I just put a little scratch like this and that worked just as good as all these other scratches that's supposed to mean Rutha Brown."

"The more letters you know, the more words you can read."

"I read all I need to read."

"If you mean your Bible, you open it up and hear it in your head. That ain't reading."

"What I got to learn to read for?"

"The world's changing, Auntie."

"It's always changing. It never has stood still. It feels like it sometimes, but it never has stopped. It don't know how to stop."

"No, it don't stop. It just go backwards."

"'Splain that one to me."

"Aw, you don't want to hear it."

"If I don't want to hear it, why am I asking you to 'splain it?"

"You asking so you can tell me I get my head stuffed full a strange ideas at school."

"It ain't school. It's all them books you read."

"It ain't only books. It's the newspaper and the TV. You don't want to look at no newspaper."

"Can't read, can I?"

"No, 'cause you don't want to look at the way it is. I got to live in this world, Auntie, and it's a world where every time a black boy like me gets up to complain in front of a white man, to say he'd like some water with his bread, you can be sure he won't see no bread or water tomorrow and maybe not the next day neither."

"Hold on now."

"That's the world going backwards."

"Hold on. Now listen to me. Maybe you got to wait a day, maybe you got to wait two. But the day after that, you going to get your water. It come raining from the sky, don't it? Nothing can stop that rain. And you going to get your bread, it come growing up from the ground. Hot loaves of bread and plates of biscuits—"

"That's Bible talk."

"Bible's one book you ought to read and remember. Bread and biscuits, pans of cornbread. You may have to wait for it, son, but you going to get it. That's what's kept us alive all these years, don't you know that?"

He didn't know it and he didn't believe it. He believed another way. He was teaching her that way all the time and she only understood this because at night when she could sit with herself and think, what she thought about was him.

ROOSEVELT DAVIS

1969

Mouth and anus packed in fifty pounds of flesh. That's what a dog was. You poured in food and scraped up shit all day long. And piss. You couldn't clean the piss stink out of those pens no matter how good you hosed them down. Ray Luken had him down on all fours, doglike, scrubbing, raw bleach stinging his eyes, burning his hands. Called him a Clorox nigger. Until one day Roosevelt stood up and said, "Nosir, I ain't nobody's nigger." Walked away and wouldn't have gone back again.

But his Aunt Rutha said, "So tell me again why I gotta learn to read?"

"To live in the world, Auntie."

"To live in the world? To live in what world? Ain't it the same world you got to live in? And ain't it the same world Mr. Luken, he got to live in? And ain't it the only world we got? And how's this world ever gonna change if we walk away from it? How's it ever gonna go forward? Man call us a name? That's the same name he call himself. He call you it 'cause he can't tolerate it no more inside him, and he got to get it out and he get it out at you. Same as you used to call Daniel a crybaby, hide the tears in your own eyes. Now go on, Roosevelt. Go on back. This man be your deliverance."

"He ain't *my* deliverance."

"We all be deliverance for one another."

The spring warmed up until it was too hot to run dogs. The pups in the new litter were all named for planets, and Roosevelt favored Earth, a little liver-and-white pointer bitch with green eyes. She was Mr. Detroit's favorite as well. Mrs. Detroit drove him down—he was all wrapped up in a blanket, even in that heat. She parked by the pen and he sat in the car and watched the puppies play for a while. He pointed at Earth and said to Roosevelt, "There's your dog."

"Yessir," said Roosevelt. "She's quite a dog."

Mrs. Detroit said, "Are you giving Roosevelt that dog, Henry?"

Mr. Detroit looked confused. "Who does it belong to?"

"It belongs to you. They all belong to you. Everything belongs to you."

His face lit up. "I'm giving it to Roosevelt."

Roosevelt said, "Thank you, Mr. Detroit, sir. But I couldn't take that dog. But I'll take good care of her. I will."

Mr. Detroit said, "My best dog."

"I know, sir. Thank you."

"It's yours."

"Thank you, sir."

Luken came over and Mr. Detroit nodded and said, "Ray."

"Mr. Detroit. Mrs. Detroit," said Luken. He also nodded. He was wearing a black cap with the word *Purina* on it. He took it off. His hair lay mashed against his sweaty head.

"I've given Roosevelt this dog," said Mr. Detroit.

Luken looked around. "Which dog?"

"It's the best dog I've got, Ray."

"Yessir. Which dog is that?"

Mr. Detroit pointed. "Old beauty there."

"That little bitch with the green eyes?"

"That's the one."

"That's the one we call Earth. She's worth something, sir. She's the best of the litter."

"Earth is her name?"

"She's definitely worth something. She'll amount to something. We could get a good price for her, that's what I been thinking. Breed her, then sell her. She could pay for some of these others around here, the ones don't pull their weight."

"I don't think you're interested in selling little Earth, are you, Henry?" asked Mrs. Detroit.

"Selling? I've just given her to Roosevelt. He can do what he wants with her. He can sell her."

"Sir, if I may say so," said Luken, "that little bitch is worth one-and-a-half two hundred dollars. *Un*trained."

Mr. Detroit turned to Roosevelt. "Hear that? If I were you I'd sell her. Train her and sell her. Put that money in your piggy bank."

"Sir—" Luken began, but a strange look passed over Mr. Detroit's face and he closed his eyes as if he were concentrating hard. Suddenly he cried, "Rowena! Oh, Rowena, I've crapped in my pants!"

Roosevelt turned away quickly. He went into the shed and sat down between two big bags of dog food. When he came out again Luken was watching the dust settle on the driveway. He had his cap back on and he was shaking his head. "That's one sorry old fool. That's one carcass waiting to die. Shit. Give you that dog. Just between you and me, boy, you think that little bitch belong to you somehow, you better think again. She's worth something.

I can train her up so she's worth more than any three of these slackers put together. Now see that Ur*a*nus over there. Sorry name for a sorry dog. I think we'll give him to you, Roosevelt. Come here, dumb-fuck," called Luken, and the dog came. "See, ain't he smart enough to know his name? We'll give him to you."

In the middle of the summer hookworm went around the kennel, taking four of the seven puppies. That left only Venus, Uranus, and Earth. "Dumb-fuck" as Luken called him, was turning into a real bird dog. He was more nervous than the other two, but he had a good nose and he wanted to please Luken. He became his favorite and worked hard for him, though it wouldn't be for a couple of months that the hard work really began. The weather was too hot and humid to work the puppies much, and the hookworm had weakened all of them.

One day when Roosevelt was done with the feeding and watering, after he'd hosed the dog shit to the back of the pens and shoveled it up, he was dumping the last load on the compost pile, upturning the wheelbarrow, when he felt a fit coming on, a lift in his chest like the beginning of a sneeze, and a second later he was writhing and twisting on the ground. It was a bad one, and when he came out of it his arms and face and clothes were covered with dog shit, and his body ached like he'd jumped from a moving train. He was dry-mouthed and cotton-headed for a few days after that. If Luken noticed, he said nothing, just rode him a little harder than usual.

It began to cool off in October, but instead of getting stronger and friskier, the puppies seemed to slow down. One morning Roosevelt noticed that Earth was off her feed. All she wanted to do was sleep. She got up and sniffed her bowl and turned around and went back into the doghouse. Venus and Uranus ate, then stood leaning against the chain-link fence of the puppy pen with their heads and tails down, their eyes fixed on the ground.

Roosevelt stopped in the middle of his chores and went up to Luken's house to find him. Mrs. Luken answered the door, her face lit up in a false smile. "How *nice* to see you, Roosevelt. Oh, I'd ask you in but the house is kinda disorderly at the moment. Is there something I can do for you, Roosevelt? I'm kinda in the middle of things here. I'm afraid there just isn't enough hours in the day. Well, sometimes there isn't, and sometimes there seem to be *too* many." She laughed at that and Roosevelt suddenly saw what a sad woman she was, like a plate with a crack in it.

"Yes ma'am," he said. "I know what you mean. Some days go along so slow and others they just run away from you."

"That's it!" she cried.

"I know what you mean," he said again. "And I don't mean to bother you, ma'am, but I'm looking for Mr. Luken. We got some sick dogs down there and he ain't come in yet."

"Oh, no, Roosevelt." The false smile returned. "No, you must be mistaken. Ray got up early—he got up in the dark, Roosevelt—to go feed those dogs. Then he had something else to do. Come to think of it, I'm surprised to see you up and about after what you've been through."

"Ma'am?"

"Well, I heard you had a little upset the other day." She leaned closer and whispered, "A little fit. Ray told me about it, said he was letting you take a few mornings off just to get yourself back on the ground. Now he would know what that all's like, since he had fits himself. Had a good whack on the head about . . . let's see . . . fifteen years ago. Kicked and kicked good by that mean old horse belong to Mr. Detroit. That Cotton."

"Yes ma'am," said Roosevelt, not knowing what else to say. Then he said, "That fit I had was back in July."

"You don't have to make up stories, Roosevelt. And I'm sure you don't have to worry about sick dogs, either. You had sick dogs, Ray would've called Dr. Irons or taken care of them himself. Now I gotta get busy. I got a bunch a dishes to do and I gotta do my hair and then I got to get some groceries and wait for Brenda to get home, and by then," she clapped her hands, "this whole day will've disappeared. This is one of the ones that's gonna fly by, I tell you." She barked a little laugh and closed the door.

A few hours later Luken came back from wherever he'd been and Roosevelt called him over to the puppy pen. All three pups looked a little better and by the end of the day Earth took an interest in her food. But the next morning it was the same, except this time none of them was eating and they all lay down against the chain-link and slept. By the evening they were better and they ate, then the next morning they were bad again.

On the fourth day, when Roosevelt got there just before light, Uranus lay up against the fence and couldn't move. He couldn't even raise his head. There was no point going up to Luken's house again, so Roosevelt called Dr. Irons himself, asked him to get there quick, they had a dog down and two others doing poorly. The vet said, "Who am I talking to? Is that you, Roosevelt?"

"Yessir, it is."

"Where's Ray Luken at? Isn't he your dog man there or did you get yourself a promotion?"

"I don't know, sir. No, I didn't get no promotion. I don't know where he's at."

The vet said, "I bet his wife doesn't either."

By the time he came, Uranus had started to improve and the other two were also moving around better. Dr. Irons said, "You feed them this morning?"

"Nosir. They didn't look fit enough."

"That's good. Don't feed them. If they're hungry later on, make up some rice and ground beef and feed them that." He nodded toward the big house. "Mrs. Nixon still cooking up there?"

"Yessir."

"Are you in good favor up there?"

"Well, yessir, I hope so."

"Good. Then you're the one to ask Mrs. Nixon can she cook up some dog food today along with everything else she's got to do. How's that sound?"

"It sounds good. But I got to go to school. I just work the morning and evening and then on the weekends."

"You've got to go to school now?"

"I'm late already."

"I'll take you," said Dr. Irons. "We'll let Ray figure out the dog food. That's his job. Your job is to go to school."

Luken was down at the kennel early the next morning, waiting. He sat in his white pickup with the window rolled up and Roosevelt walked by like he had his own window rolled up. But Luken got out and caught him by the arm and Roosevelt turned in surprise. He looked right at him and said, "You'd do better not to touch me, Mr. Luken." Luken was working his jaw hard and his face was all bunched up and suddenly he spun away from Roosevelt and punched the door of his truck. Left a dent. Roosevelt thought of Mrs. Luken then and feared what her face looked like this morning.

Luken took his cap off and put it on again and said, "Dumbfuck's dead."

"Dead?"

"He's dead," Luken repeated, then he said it again, "He's dead."

Uranus was lying in the middle of the puppy pen, laid out on his side. There was blood and vomit all around him. Earth and Venus were inside the doghouse. Roosevelt could hear the thud of their limbs on the wooden floor as they shifted around nervously. Luken stood looking down at the dead dog, shaking his head, and Roosevelt told him, "Get the other two out of here. Put them in the heat pen." Then he dragged Uranus to Luken's pickup and lifted him into the bed. The dog was stiff and he balanced him awkwardly, like a heavy board. He guessed he'd been dead most of the night. He covered him with a burlap sack. He went back and found Luken inside the heat pen, trying to work the gate. He was sliding the bolt back and forth, pushing at the gate when he should have pulled it. Roosevelt let him out and said, "Go on home, Ray."

"Can't go on home."

"I'll take the dog in."

"What's the point of that? Dog's dead."

"Gotta find out what killed him."

"You oughtta know what killed him." He eyed Roosevelt. "You got Irons out here yesterday, make it look like I can't do my own job."

"You want to do your job? You go ahead and do your job, Ray. Take that dog in. I gotta feed and water the rest of these animals. I got my own job."

Luken walked to the truck and got in. Then he got out again and came back and stood in the door of the shed and said to

Roosevelt, "Now one thing I can't tolerate too good is a colored boy messing with my wife. I heard you come up and paid her a visit. I heard about it. She told me. I meant to tell you first thing but that goddamn dog threw me off. I don't want you near her again, you hear me?"

Roosevelt had his back to Luken. He was scooping up puppy food. He put enough in for three and had to take one away—that was the measurable side of death. He kept his back to him. He didn't want to look at the man, he didn't want to see him. He was not a man worth turning around for, deliverance or no deliverance. He was an unclean man, a man whose foulness, whose rottenness, seeped out of him and infected the world around him. It had infected his wife, his child, and now this dog dead in the back of his truck. Roosevelt looked at the wall and said to the man, "It's a new world, Ray. It's not your world no more. It's not mine either, not yet, but it's getting to be."

"Getting to be?"

"It's going that way. We're moving it that way, we're not waiting no more, we're not waiting on you, we're not waiting on anyone. It take a long time to move the world. It take a long time and a lot of us. A lot of sweat it take. I go to these meetings. All kinds of people at these meetings. Church meetings. People interested in moving the world from this place to that place. Old people, young people. Black people, Ray. You seen us going in and out of the church."

"I seen it. We all seen it."

"Go in tired and hungry, go in from a world that don't often respect us, and come out like we just eaten a powerful meal. What is that, Ray? Don't you wish you knew what that was, that make us strong?"

"I know what it is."

"Lot of people talk about the Lord," Roosevelt went on, "but I don't talk about Him. I talk about books. I talk about reading. I talk about sitting in school and learning what we got to learn. We don't learn it, we ain't gonna move the world. Any old thing come at us, we gonna believe it. Unless we trust ourselves. And the way we trust ourselves is we find ourselves. We find out who we are in books." He turned around and faced Luken and said, "Who I am ain't 'boy.' Who I am ain't 'nigger.' Who I am ain't 'coon' or 'darky' or a man gonna mess with your wife, and she know it and you know it. That's from the old world, Ray. That's shit from the old world. In that old world I'd be afraid a you, the way you're afraid a me. But it ain't so. Look here, Ray. Look at my hand. See? It ain't shaking. It ain't shaking at all."

Luken had his cap off and he was crushing it between his hands. He said, "Maybe you ain't as smart as you think you are. Afraid a you?" He spat out a laugh. "I ain't afraid a you. You and your books and your schools. That don't mean nothing to me. My daddy, he used to get so busy burning down nigger schools, he hardly had time on a Sunday to burn out a nigger church." He went and got in his truck but he got out a second time and came back and said, "You gonna do your job right, put them supplements in with the puppy chow. You got a new bag of food there. Mix them right into the new bag."

"What supplements?" asked Roosevelt.

"Just mix them in. Four five cups for the fifty-pound bag. That's about all you got left, four five cups."

Roosevelt looked at the shelf above the dog food. "I don't see no supplements."

Luken laughed. "You're the one does all the reading. It must be making you blind." He reached past Roosevelt and grabbed a sack of powdered bleach and dumped it into the puppy food. "Just mix it in good."

Roosevelt stared at him.

"What're you looking at me like that for? Just mix it in."

"You know what this is?"

"It's something supposed to grow their bones. It must've been here since the last pups. I seen it and I remember it worked good for them, thought I'd try it on these ones here."

"But this ain't that."

"You telling me they take the same sack and put something different in it?"

"I'm telling you this ain't the same thing. This ain't got the same name. All they got in common is the sack look the same." He shook his head in confusion, then it came to him and he said, "What's the name of these supplements?"

Luken looked at the sack. "I don't know. Don't matter what it's called. It's supplements. You want to know what it's called, here it is, you read it."

"You were giving him a little extra," said Roosevelt, nodding toward the back of the truck. "You were feeding him a little extra."

"Well, yeah. Just this last day or two I give him extra. That ain't a crime, far as I know. I figured the size that dog was he could use extra. I figured on him being the best we had, the best we'd maybe ever have. He could've been that," said Luken, looking down at the ground. "You think he could've been that?"

Roosevelt nodded, though he didn't mean yes by it. He had no opinion on what that dog might have become. He knew only one thing: The dog in his present state was worth nothing, and he would never be worth anything again. He nodded not in answer to the man's question but the way he'd seen his Aunt Rutha nod when she was reading along, reading the newspaper or her Bible and her finger hit a word she'd never seen before, and she couldn't make the word talk to her until letter by letter she sounded it out and suddenly it came to her, *machine! government! elastic!* the word a cause of joy to her, her new understanding a cause of joy. His understanding of Luken, of this man all bunched up inside his own illiteracy, this man who clung to his ignorance to the point of destruction, this was not a joyful understanding, and it was not a pretty understanding, but it made the man at least no mystery to Roosevelt because he could see him now. He could see him the way you looked down into the muddy water of Bully Creek and saw the mud moving, unsettling, saw it fanning this way and that almost dainty-like, and a few bubbles of air coming out of it to break right in front of your fishing line, and you knew it meant catfish. A hidden man, a man who lived in the dark and ate off the bottom and knew his river was dying, that the new world was killing it. Because this new world brought destruction, it had to, before it could bring creation. Roosevelt knew that, and the man was beginning to understand it, though he fought it hard, was still fighting it, and was willing to die for the old world, as Roosevelt was willing to die for the new. He walked back to the truck and Roosevelt watched him go, and he pitied this man, knowing he'd soon have to hear the news that he'd poisoned his own hopes.

BYRDINE DEAN

1969

Byrdine Dean ran the Hoover across the tattered beige wall-to-wall and thought to herself, That man'll be back. Thought to herself, I ought to tear up this crappy carpet and put down some nice linoleum, something bright that'll clean up good and pick up the yellow of the counter. "Linda!" she called, the Hoover sucking up her voice. Linda came. "This old piece of rat fur's been down too long, let's tug it up."

Linda cupped her hand to her ear and shouted, "*What?*"

"*I said help me take the carpet up!*"

The girl came and switched the Hoover off. "If it's something more about the . . . the thing in the cooler, I don't want to hear it."

"I said the carpet. The darn thing's rotten right through, there's no sense in Hoovering it."

"Then why are you?"

The girl could be blunt, that's what Byrdine liked and didn't like about her. She had a habit of snapping her gum while waiting on a customer but besides that she was a good, eager girl, neat and clean and starry-eyed. She could take direction. She'd do. A little work on her sums and she'd shape up just fine. It hadn't been an easy week either. The day they opened, Bog White's brother Leon drives up and unloads a body in broad daylight, customers number twelve and thirteen. "I can explain everything," he says to Byrdine.

"I expect you can."

"But I ain't got time just yet. Let me get him on ice."

"This ain't a *morgue,* Leon. It's a café open for business. Or are you blind?"

"Aw, Deedee. I'll sit down and eat something soon as I'm through."

"You miss the point."

"Look, I got a man here. He ain't getting no fresher. You got that big old brand-new cooler—"

"It ain't brand-new. It's reconditioned."

"Deedee," he says, actually dropping to one knee in the yard. "I will pay you ten dollars rent for one night accommodations for a quiet cold nigger name of Willie Hadley. If that ain't enough, name your price."

She draws her breath in quick, glances at the back of the truck where the dogs have gathered sniffing the tailgate. Inside, a long lump covered with canvas. "That's not Willie," she says.

"Ma'am?"

"Willie Hadley's eating griddle cakes and bacon inside at this moment."

Leon's face does a somersault and somehow comes out right side up. "Hell. They said it was Willie." He raises himself and walks to the truck and flips the canvas aside. Byrdine looks the other way. "It's a white man," he says. "Bare-assed."

"You know him?"

"Not like this I don't. Maybe with clothes on."

"Well, get some clothes on him. You can't bring him in without clothes. I got a girl here would faint at the sight of a man naked."

"He ain't a man, Deedee. He's a corpse."

"She'd faint twice."

"Where am I going to find clothes?"

"You're wearing some I see," she says. It is for this reason Leon White is remembered as the husky young fellow who on Etta's opening day arrived in a red plaid hunting jacket, period. Some say he wore his underwear beneath but others swear he was bare as the day he was born. Among the latter was the doctor who delivered him, Dr. Armistead Graves, who happened to be customer number nine.

All week Byrdine has asked herself over and over again why she agreed to shelter a body and whose body is it anyway? True to his word, Leon had been willing to explain everything, but everything turned out to be next to nothing. His brother Bog knew more. Leon wasn't the brightest light on the Christmas tree. The biggest but not the brightest. Bog told Leon to deliver the lump called Willie Hadley to Byrdine's door, no questions asked. Bog would be by in a day or two to take the package away.

But a day or two had turned to four and "the thing in the cooler" as Linda called it was still with them. Out of the way of their coming and going but still hard to ignore. The girl was holding up well in spite of it. Byrdine in a moment of intuitive understanding knew that her reasons for hiring Linda and admitting a cold white corpse to her inner—what did they call it, the sacred place, the room inside all the others where a person was safe to sit alone and think or carry on a love affair? Her chamber. Her sanctuary, that was it. The reasons for the two were the same. Leon had gotten down on the ground and offered her money he didn't even have. He was in trouble bigger than he knew but he let her know it by falling to his knee. And Linda. Linda was her best friend Terry's daughter, only Terry hadn't taken to motherhood and somehow expected the girl to grow up on her own. Hunt and gather and toilet train herself, bring herself a cup of warm milk after a nightmare. Which is pretty much the way it had gone. Byrdine took her for months at a time whenever Terry met a new traveling man whose body she couldn't live without. They were in one of those times now, though Linda was grown up and lived almost the way she wanted to, without her mother or her mother's men in the house.

Her own mother had been like that, she'd had the wanderlust, but along with it the good sense to marry a man who owned a junkyard and could keep her in tires. Until he died young, then Byrdine and her brother Floyd tagged around after her like a pair of ugly ducklings, a few months here, a few months there. They'd settled in just about every town in south Georgia. Some of them twice. Which is why she'd always taken in the strays, tried to make life easier for the downtrodden. In her old line of business she'd worn herself out worrying about every bad hand that came to rest on her table. How to say without saying it, *Here's a break in the lifeline that means sudden or violent death*. You couldn't deliver that news to a human being, even if it meant they'd mend their ways and live the life they'd wish they had if they hadn't. She often tried to disbelieve what she saw but her gift was not shallow, did not offer such rest. Rest came from the part of her that truly knew prophecy couldn't cure or kill, that reading the flesh meant nothing next to the little things lived daily.

By the time they got the rug up it was after eight o'clock and Linda yawned three times long and loud before Byrdine caught on and told her, "Go on. Go on home." They'd uncovered a plywood floor in fair condition. The girl thought it would look nice painted turquoise. “Can’t clean a plywood floor,” Byrdine reminded her. “The health department’d shut us down.”

“What health department?”

“The state’s got rules. If you’re feeding people you got to go by the rules.”

“Rules!” Linda snorted. “I guess we got a big old rule-breaker right there in the cooler.”

Byrdine said nothing but after the girl got her hat and coat and said goodnight she sat down on a stool at the counter and watched the black Mustang pull out of the yard. She was a cautious driver at least. Not like her mother. Nothing about her like her mother. In temperament she was more Byrdine’s child. And she was right. They did have themselves a big old rule-breaker on the premises. Thirteen, as she called him. The thirteenth customer.

Byrdine began in a tired but orderly fashion to address the problem of him in her mind, but just as her wheels began to turn a set of headlights near blinded her. A car slowed on the road and headed into the yard. She recognized its shape in the dark. She wondered how he’d found her again in the black of night with no light on the sign. She patted her hair, smoothed her braid down the back, and wished her dress were cleaner, wished she were prettier. She hadn’t had that thought in about twenty years.

He hesitated at the threshold like he had the time before, then came in blinking. She was at the machine making a fresh pot of coffee. “It’s cold out,” she said. “And just the other night it was too warm to breathe.” He smiled and she told herself, Stop chattering for Pete’s sake and let the man get anchored. “Have a seat,” she added. “We still ain’t got a booth.”

“Oh,” he said. “Yes, I remember.”

"We tore up the rug tonight too just in case this place was beginning to look too settled. Too moved into I mean. Linda— you remember Linda. She just now went home."

"You're not even open then."

"If I'm here we're open."

"Well." He held his hat in his hand and seemed ready to put it back on. "You would tell me if you were closed?"

"I would, sir. I would say those words in fact. But I'm open. You take your coffee black, is that right?"

"Black, yes. Though in the morning I take milk in it."

It was an intimate detail in this man's life. Not a word of it escaped Byrdine's attention. He sat down at the counter and she poured two coffees and stood where she was, guessing twenty-one inches of yellow Formica between them was what he needed to feel safe. "It's only two nights till Christmas Eve," she said conversationally.

"My girls won't let me forget it."

"How nice you got girls."

"Twins."

"Twins! How old?"

"Nine last August."

"That's a nice age. Not quite young and not quite grown."

"Young one minute and grown up the next."

"It's always a surprise."

"I love them when they're," he held his hands a foot apart, "this big."

"You were worried you wouldn't love them as they grew."

He looked at her strangely. "That's true."

"But you did. You do. More coffee?" She filled his cup and reminded herself to keep his thoughts to herself, he wasn't ready.

Not even the purpose of his visit was clear to him, which is why the threshold stopped him both times. "I hate entering a room," she said.

"Ma'am?"

"Even if it's full of friends. The reason they make a doorway small is because that's the size you got to squeeze down to in order to fit into the way everybody sees you. You got to shrink your personal self smaller than the heighth and width of the room."

He laughed at that. "But a doorway's bigger than we'll ever be."

"Not as big as you think. Not as big as we could be."

"You're an optimist then."

"A practicing optimist. It's my religion."

He looked in his coffee as if searching for the words to use next, or for something he'd lost, or both. "I gave up on God."

"On religion maybe."

"More than that. The old man with the beard. He's gone."

"That's just Santa Claus and he goes when he ought to, when we grow up. God don't have no beard 'cause he don't have no face. His face is so vast and complicated you couldn't call it a face as we know it. You could call it a feeling, a connecting sort of feeling. Mostly I call it nothing." She laughed. "But mostly I don't have these kinds of talks."

"Me neither."

"Now that's the kind of thing a nine-year-old would say. That's just how they'd say it. It's good you got 'em. They get inside you."

She came around the counter and sat down three stools away. He swiveled toward her. "How old are your children?"

"Linda's sweet sixteen but we're not related. She's the only child I got."

"Never married?"

"No."

"It's none of my business, but why did you pass it by?"

She laughed. "You're a gentleman, sir. It passed me by, but thank you."

"If you're content, you came out ahead."

"I am. And known to be happy."

A silence came over them then, like an angel's thick and downy wing muffling thought and speech. Along with it the old urge she'd learned to suppress—it almost got the best of her this time. She felt the ache in her hand, like a hunger pain, the desire to reach out and draw his hand to her and turn it to read the writing in his palm. His hands were a cross between money and love, hard work and soft, ambition and guilt, she could see all that in the blunt line and shredded cuticles of his fingers and thumbs, yet the skin was silky. And the way he joined his hands together, laced his fingers in front of him in his lap or on the counter, there was a quality there like a closed door, yet a reaching, a desire to reconcile. She could not be blind to these things. It was all there to be seen whether they gave you their palm or not. The palm was pointless really, an elucidation or a comfort, like a saddle on a horse. But it was warm and it was flesh and to touch the one whose self you are pursuing and into whose inner sanctuary you have been invited gives you something which not touching cannot. It gives you the face of God, thought Byrdine. If only she could tell this man that.

He'd never taken his coat off, a raincoat. He'd unbuttoned it though and now he stood up slowly as an old man and did up the first three buttons from the bottom. He must have gotten what he came for, she thought. I wonder if he knows what that was. She herself was happy to rid her mind of Thirteen for an hour, but it all crashed in when he said, "I meant to ask about your complications." She waved it away, hiding her disappointment poorly.

"I shouldn't have spoken," he said.

"No, you spoke just right. Our complications are still complicated. I sat down this evening to come up with a plan."

He looked shaken. "And I interrupted you!"

"I thank you for it. Someone needed to. I do plan best in my sleep. I'll go out with you now, lock the place up. I'll have my solution by morning."

In the yard he noticed she had no car and insisted he take her home. She didn't refuse, though she liked the night walk. It got her mind clear and her limbs relaxed. She was only a quarter mile down the road. They fell to silence again as he drove. She knew that would be the way at the end. She said two words, a warm "thank you," and meant it. Like a gentleman he waited for her house to let her in and close around her before he backed out and made his slow way somewhere else.

ROWENA DETROIT

1969

"It's primitive," said Harry. "He wants the horse killed why? So he can ride it into the afterlife?"

"No," said Rowena wearily. "No."

"Yes," said her son. "Yes. It's very Greek, Mother. Very Hector. Hector was the one who wanted to be buried with his horse, wasn't he, Lize? Liza?"

Eliza looked up from her book. "It was Alexander the Great, Dad. And Hector was a Trojan. Don't be dense."

"I will not have that language in here," said Rowena sternly.

"Dense?" laughed Eliza. "It's not a swear." She went back to her book, her smelly feet up on the coffee table where she knew they weren't meant to be. Then in came trouble, in from what they all seemed to call "a jog." Frances, her new short hair sticking out from her head like Mrs. Tiggywinkle's. She planted herself right smack in the middle of the living room, stretching, or unstretching, whatever it was.

Her sister said to her, "They're putting Cotton to sleep."

The stretching stopped. The girl straightened up to her full height—she had grown past Harry. *"What?"*

"I kid you not."

"Whose idea was that?"

"Papa's."

"No it wasn't."

"Frances," said Rowena, "this is a large house and there are plenty of other places for you to do your exercises."

The girl ignored her. "He'd never do that."

"Well, now he would like it done," said Rowena. "If he had his druthers he'd do it himself."

"Gross," said Eliza. "I could never kill anything. I mean, big. Like a horse."

"He's always done it himself."

"Get Luken to do it," said Harry.

"Ray wouldn't go near that horse. Not even to kill it."

The girl said, "It's not going to happen."

"Frances, dear, it's his wish," said Rowena. "Why deny him his wish? He doesn't want the animal to suffer. There's so little else he can control." Her son with his back to the room was unmistakably pouring himself a drink. "Whatever you're having there, Harry, I'll have one too."

"It's not quite time yet, Mother. It's only quarter to."

"I don't give a good goddamn *what* time it is. While you're a guest in my house, drinking my Scotch—a guest in our house, mine and your father's—you and your children will treat me with respect, with the same respect you would this old horse you're all so fond of. Grant me what you would so freely give to Cotton." She glared at all of them. "This is all I ask."

A silent minute went by. Finally Harry said, "Fine," and poured her drink. The older girl sighed huffily and took her sweaty body off to her own room and, hopefully, a bath. The younger one resumed her reading with those great big feet of hers gracing the coffee table. Her mother's feet, they had to be. They certainly weren't Detroit feet, or Sherman feet. The Sherman women were well known for their diminutive feet. Not so tiny as to look footbound, but agreeably well proportioned. Rowena's grandmother wore a size four-and-a-half shoe and was herself just over five feet tall and reasonably slim. Of her own grandchildren, only Billy's boy Seth had the true Sherman stature, small and quick and light. Though it was generally thought wasted on a boy.

"Shall I light the fire?" asked Harry.

"It's chilly," said Rowena, "isn't it?"

Harry's youngest child, Lucy, came running into the room, bathed and scrubbed, in her nightclothes. Eliza emerged from the page just long enough to say, "Why are you wearing your pajamas? It's still light out."

"Me and Mom took a bath."

"So?"

"I like my pajamas."

Rowena patted the sofa. "Come sit here, Lucy Goosey."

Lucy sat. "Mars, why do you always sit on your leg like that?"

"Because it's comfortable."

"Not for me."Then she was up again. "Let me light the match, Dad! Let *me!*"

It was all such a tumble, such a jumble and tumble of activity and rivalry, drawn swords and shouts and challenges. While in the next room, dreaming his own dreams, lay the last chapter of the same book, a man at the end of the game, a man no longer interested in lighting the match, a man no longer able to. Yet set in his desire to put his old horse down, and hoarding his energy to that purpose. The spark belonged to the living, yes it did, but in the hands of the dying lay the brightest coal. She said to Lucy, "Think of him every time you strike a match. Every time, think of him."

"Who?" said the child. Even Eliza looked up.

"Papa," said Rowena.

"Alright. That's who I thought."

COLE JONES

1969

One thing puzzled Cole: How could a man go missing at Christmas and have not one warm soul searching under every bush and upturning stones to find him? As much as he tried he could not shake from his mind the unclaimed body in Etta's cooler—though her name wasn't Etta, was it? What *was* that woman's name? He stood dressing himself for church, pulling on clothes that were meant to make him a different man for an hour or two. Karen feeding the girls their supper in the kitchen, Cherry in a nightgown and Debby in pajamas, the beginning of the end of twinness. He tried to imagine life without all of them in it and was thankful he couldn't.

His sister Celine arrived to sit the kids while he was in the bathroom going over his rubbled face with a razor. He slapped aftershave on though it was sweeter than he liked to smell. He could hear Karen making irritable small talk and decided to take his time. It was hard to leave the girls on Christmas Eve. They'd got the stockings hung and Cherry'd left a plate of cookies for Santa by the back door where she was convinced he came in because it was way too dirty going down a whole lot of folks' chimneys. Karen had grown up Catholic and liked to go to midnight Mass, liked that one ritual once a year. Next year when the twins were ten they'd take them. They'd fall asleep and he'd carry them out to the car one by one. They'd weigh a whole year more then, look a whole year different. Even now they spoke of ten as the age at which life began.

His sister stood inside the front door with her arms tight at her sides and her feet together. She was short and roly-poly and her hair was dyed a deep rusty color with an old permanent lingering at the ends. "Hullo, Celine," he said and came and kissed her. "Merry Christmas."

He got between her and Karen, and Karen let her snarl go slack and said, "I got to get the girls dessert."

"You go," said Cole. "We'll be right in." Cherry and Debby had come from the kitchen and he said, "Tell your Aunt Celine hello before you disappear."

"Hello," they said in chorus, then followed the wake of their mother's silence out of the room.

Karen didn't know the effect her likes and dislikes had on them. Never before had this troubled him for himself. "Let me take your coat, Celine."

"It's nothing but a jacket."

"We'll hang it up anyway. It's quite a jacket."

"Mickey's ball team gives 'em out. They say they're made of real silk and sewn by hand all the way in China."

"It's pretty enough." Cole looked at the tag. "It says here 'Made in Taiwan.'"

"Them liars," Celine pouted. "They told me pure silk made in China."

"Oh, it's China. There's two different Chinas. One of them's called Taiwan."

She frowned. "That I never heard. How do they do that?"

He laughed. "They just do it."

"And everybody goes along with it?"

"Everybody except China—the other China. And Russia. And Cuba. Places like that."

"Dang, Cole, you know too much."

He took her into the kitchen, took her hand and led her like a boy with his baby sister, though she was older by a year and a half and he was no boy. There wasn't anything to worry about with her. She would entertain the girls—or let them entertain her—and they would be safe. Her judgments were sound if her knowledge was incomplete. If the house caught fire she'd have them out quick with their coats and shoes on. He trusted her. They seemed to also, and liked her too when their mother wasn't around. Karen could not be convinced that Celine could care for children—pour their milk and boil their frankfurters, read to them and tuck the covers up to their chin. Celine loved animals and ran a kennel where good people going on fancy vacations brought their dogs and took them home again whole and cared for, groomed and mostly flea-free. Cole in a useless moment of exasperation had once faced down Karen with the words, "What we've got here is just a two-dog kennel. At home she handles up to fourteen."

"Your own kin living like crackers," was her reply, and though it hurt him to hear it he'd felt it often enough himself, finding his sister's shit-stained bare dirt barking back yard depressing to the point of tears.

Celine lowered her head in the bright fluorescence of the kitchen and Cole said, "Debby, honey, get that light, will you?" Debby took her time but went and flicked off the overhead light.

Cherry said, "Ooh, spooky! Come and sit with us, Aunt Celine." Bless that child, thought Cole and gave his sister an imperceptible push, like getting a ball rolling on flat ground. She was near-lost without her glasses, the lenses thick as Coca-Cola bottles, but they magnified the most ordinary light to a blinding level and he always forgot. She toddled molelike to the table. Karen got up and got busy at the sink. She still rarely used the dishwasher he'd bought her but he'd save that gripe for another time.

"Y'all eat so late," said Celine.

"We don't always," said Cherry. "And they didn't even eat yet, they're going out."

"Don't it give you bad dreams, eating so late?"

Cherry shrugged and Debby said, "What gives me bad dreams is okra."

"Okra?"

"Ew, I hate okra."

"Everyone hates okra."

"I don't hate it," said Cherry.

"You got to cook it right," said Celine.

"Mama cooks it good."

"I don't care how they cook it," said Debby, "I still hate it."

"It's kinda like eating something pulled from your own throat," said Celine.

"Ew," Debby made a face, then she laughed, "That's just right!"

Cole looked at Karen. She was scrubbing a frypan furiously. "We better go if we're going," he said. He went and kissed the girls and Celine too on the top of her head.

"Mickey brought me," she said. "He said call him and he'll come and pick me up."

"We'll be late," said Cole. "I'll take you home. Mickey ought to come in sometime. Stick his head in and say hello to the girls."

"He had bowling, he said to tell you."

"Christmas Eve *night?*" said Karen.

Celine looked embarrassed and Cole said, "Maybe it's a Jewish league." He laughed to let her know he was kidding but the feeling in the room stayed raw until Cherry said, "Me and Debby, we been bowling. We like to bowl."

"Mickey could take you sometime," said Celine.

"The part I don't like is the shoes," said Debby. "Putting your foot in that shoe where everybody else in the world has put their foot." She frowned and shook her head.

"We got to go," Cole said again. "Be good, girls. We'll see you bright and early in the morning."

"We'll see you on Christmas!" cried Cherry.

"Bye Mama," said Debby.

Karen came and kissed them both and said, "If you get hungry, Celine, we got some leftover Jell-O."

"And a whole big jar of Christmas cookies!" Cherry reminded her.

"Well, we're saving them for tomorrow, sweetheart."

Outside the front door she said, "I just pray they'll be okay."

"We've never had to rely on prayer before," said Cole. "Don't see why we would tonight."

They rode in silence to the Sandy Knickers. He'd intended to take her out on their anniversary but Henry Detroit and his family had begged his time, time he was noticeably glad to give them. He should have known better than to say what he next said but he wasn't seeing things through her eyes, just letting himself talk, and the subject honestly seemed neutral to him, one they could put their heads together over and it might help them smooth out their differences.

"It's a hell of a time for a man to be dying, Karen."

She turned her head away, looked out the window. "I feel like Christmas didn't happen this year. At least it didn't happen to us. I haven't felt that way in a long time."

"It'll happen tomorrow, right on time, I promise."

She ignored this. "It's funny to look out and see other people having Christmas. They got their lights up and their crèches out and their kids have gone and sat on Santa's lap at the shopping center."

"I'm sorry."

"I haven't seen any of it until this moment." She laughed sharply. "I've been blind to the light."

"We got a tree up," Cole offered. "Got it decorated. The girls wouldn't ever let us forget about Christmas."

"There's no Christmas if there's no spirit."

"There's spirit," he said softly.

"Sure there is, but it's not in our house. You're having your Christmas somewhere else, with other people."

"That's not true, Karen."

"Not strictly true, no. You'll grace our table tomorrow and play with the girls and give me a gift I won't forget, like that dishwasher. But where are *you,* Cole? The man is dying, I know that. Well, we're dying too. We talk around this every time we talk. Which ain't much these days."

He pulled into the parking lot of the restaurant, placed himself between two white lines, and turned the engine off. "It's not crowded," he said. "I thought it might be."

"People eat at home tonight."

"Look," he turned to her. "He can't go too much longer. This is something that'll happen only once, then never again. I can't say no to them, Karen. They pay me to say yes and right now to say no would change our future, yours and mine. The thing's shaking up. I need to be inside the door. I don't want that door closed in my face, you can understand that, I know you can." He stopped himself. Don't patronize her. Just get her to see. He put his arm across her shoulder and felt her melt a degree and made his own gesture softer and more real. "The son's a different man than his father."

"I know that, Cole. I've been married to you half my life."

He let it go, let her misunderstand him. He was afraid if he spoke again it would lead them to the place they wanted most to be done with, though for his part he knew now with certainty he was not. Inside they ate a decent meal and he had the genuine pleasure of her public company. She was a good-looking woman and eyes went to her and then to him with a kind of envy he'd learned to like. The pleasure too of being in charge of things, their booth a little boat in the river and he leaning over the side to haul a fish to her plate. Then paying the bill and laying down a good tip besides, providing for her in a way he could and letting go for an hour all the ways he could not.

Halfway through she surprised him and said, "What'll the Lord think of me if I have a glass of wine?"

"Have one," he said. "It's Christmas."

She smiled. "I don't want to be giggling through the Mass. You know what wine does to me."

She drank so seldom alcohol went right to her head and she got kittenish.

"You've got some food in you. You won't get giggly. Try some of this, it's a Chablis."

He passed her his wine and she sipped and nodded and said, "You help me if I can't finish it."

"You don't have to finish it. Keep that glass and I'll order another one for me."

"What is the name of a flavor like this?"

"It's called Chablis."

"I mean what exactly does it taste like, that's what I'm trying to figure out. It tastes kind of like fruit and kind of like dirt. Oh," she laughed. "I mean that in a good way."

"Well, the fruit would be the grape and the grape's grown in dirt, so you might be exactly right about the taste of a good dry white wine. They ought to put that on the bottle, 'Tastes like fruit and dirt.' You think it would sell?"

"People read the bottle?"

"Sure they do. They want to know the taste they're buying. Not every Chablis tastes like every other. It depends on where it's grown and the growing stock."

Their waitress came with Cole's wine and he toasted his wife with a simple "To your eyes." It was an old toast for them but he hadn't uttered those words in more than a year, since their eighteenth anniversary. It felt good to say it. She did have the bluest eyes.

She picked at her fish some more then said, "Your daddy never took your mama out I bet." He shook his head, cleaned the last scallop from his plate, dipped it in tartar sauce. She reached across the table and he gave her his hand. "You've done more than make up for him, Cole. Most days I know I'm a lucky woman."

"Most days?"

"I lose sight of you sometimes."

"I'm right here, Karen."

She nodded solemnly. "Sitting in my booth. I hope you'll always come back to my booth, always and forever."

So she expected him to wander. He gripped her hand, grateful to her for freeing them both. "I will," he said. He could keep that promise, he hoped.

COLE JONES

1969

Through the open doors of St. Claire's he could hear the choir's angels straining to magnify the Lord on notes too high for human voice. Once across the threshold in the flickering dark Karen stopped to light a candle while he looked up as he did every year and considered himself within the maw of Christmas. He was neither doubter nor follower, would not have found a place at Christ's table but felt himself embodied by the innkeeper at the birth, an early practitioner of the law of complementary resources. Earn a buck, house a messiah. To Karen he whispered, "Light one for us."

"I did. I always do."

He was a step behind her as she steered down the side aisle to a pew up front. That close he could see the sweat on the back of the priest's hand if he chose. He stopped himself from pulling Karen near and wondered what was right about a religion that kept the flesh imprisoned. The priest there, he was a man of flesh surely. Cole had never wondered at the vow of chastity but he wondered now. And to his amazement found that he could sympathize with whatever it was that took a man there. It wasn't all denial of nature but a channeling of smaller events to larger purposes. If one could call such things events and call them small. An older man could. Not a boy whose every thought and deed was aligned with physical necessity. A boy's religion was sensation. Cole in his youthful prayers had always begged for a state beyond that, a state of grace if he'd known the words then, where he lived free of urgency. Not pure. Purity meant little to him. But a free agent.

The priest gave forth a great gust of Latin and Cole basked in the solemn noise of that language. The incense gave him a headache but he liked the smell of it just the same, and more than that believed in ritual, the continuity of action across centuries of changing faces, borders in flux, new and potent technologies, and the rumor of a dying planet. Christ Himself had smelled this smell, the raw smoke of frankincense. And before Him all the rest though Cole couldn't name them except for Moses. He would read the Bible someday, read it aloud to his girls if they'd listen. His own parents had never thrown that book at him or any other and his mother still refused even the social comfort of a congregation. The Ladies of the Foraging Moose, or whatever, got not a hoof in the door without her barking at them to give up their lies and lures. Prayer Didn't Work. She could prove it too. Hadn't she prayed for her own child Celine and felt her prayers all fall flat? Flat as that girl's own shufflefoot walk, feet pointed ten o'clock two o'clock? From then on she'd taken laughter as her personal savior.

Karen leaned to him and whispered, "I'm worried about the girls."

"They're okay." He patted her hand. "We'll be home soon."

"I feel like there's some kind of trouble. It's that kind of feeling. It's strong."

He looked at her and could see the trouble in her face, hoped that's where it lay and not in the house. "You sure?"

She nodded. It didn't happen often anymore that she got such a feeling, though after the girls were born she was like human radar.

"Tell you what. I'll go find a phone and call Celine, how's that sound?"

"Okay," she said softly, on the verge of tears.

"You sit here and I'll be right back."

"Okay. Cole?" He brought his face close to hers. "There wouldn't be trouble on this night, would there, when we're starting to feel . . ." She didn't finish.

"No," he whispered. "I don't think so." He patted her hand again and slipped out of the pew.

It was raining out, a thin little rain that smelled of dust and slicked the street to a black shine, then quit. He walked three blocks east past Wade's department store with its windows lit up red and green and a couple of unearthly mannequins stark naked to his surprise. A man inside, the younger Wade, a notorious insomniac bachelor having his Christmas alone with the big dolls. He waved at Cole as if it were an everyday thing to dress a window at midnight on Christmas Eve. Cole waved back without enthusiasm and hurried on to the pay phone outside the five and dime. But it wouldn't take his money. Kept dropping the coin down and out into his hand. He tried dialing and nothing happened and he walked back to Wade's and knocked on the window.

Clayton Wade, without his toupee, looked like a Bartlett pear stuck on top of a fat girl's body. He let Cole in and declared breathlessly, "I knew you was headed for that phone and I could have told you. It hasn't worked since Thanksgiving, Mr. Jones. Miss Saralee Stringer tried to call Paris on it. She was having one of her fits of delusion and thought she heard the voice of Charles de Gaulle."

"Charles de Gaulle?" asked Cole, though the name he meant to say was Saralee Stringer.

"That's right. The president or whatever of France."

"Is that the same Saralee Stringer has a sister named Charity? They used to live out past the pecan grove on the Tallahassee Road?"

"I wouldn't know, sir. She looks to me like she never had a past or if she did she's tried to outrun it."

"She'd be my age."

"She could be your age. Or she could be a hundred. I'm no good at age. I don't look at people by their years, I look at them by their stars."

Cole left that alone and said, "Could I use your telephone to call home? I know it's awful late but—"

Clayton Wade waved away the apology. "Telephone don't care what time it is. You got kids you're thinking of?"

"My girls."

"They're up late or early. It's half past midnight Christmas Day."

"My sister's with them. It's her I'm calling."

"Whatever you like. Phone's in here."

He led him back through the store to the office. Cole for the first time noticed that the man was wearing dark blue silk pajamas with a scarlet cravat. He'd thought it was a suit of some kind but in the harsh light there was no question he was dressed for bed. Wade as he recalled lived upstairs. At least that was what he let himself remember.

He found his hand trembling as he dialed the number. It rang three times and Clayton Wade watched his face carefully. Cole shifted away and Wade said, "You need anything else I'll be out front." Cole nodded as thanks and watched him go and wished

Celine would rise up from her dead sleep and pick up the phone. The thought of it ringing in a fiery house passed through his mind but did not stay. The fifth ring did it, produced a sleepy "Hullo" from the other end and Cole's first words to his surprise were "Where are you?" Then, "Is everyone okay?"

"Cole? Is that you?"

"Hey, Celine. It's me."

"It's awful late, ain't it? You stuck somewhere? You want me to call Mickey?"

"No, baby. No. I'm just checking in. Just saying hello."

"Well, hello. Hello hello hello. Hello there."

"That's it," said Cole. "That's all. We'll see you real soon, alright? And everyone's alright?"

"Well."

"Well what?"

"Everyone here's fine."

"Sleeping I bet."

"Sleeping hard," said Celine. "It's over at the plantation no one's sleeping."

"What's that mean?"

"They called you, a lady did, just after you left. Said Mr. What's-his-name there—"

"Detroit."

"Yeah, Mr. Detroit. He's taken ill apparently and they wanted to let you know. Sounds like more 'en a head cold to me."

"He's dying," said Cole.

"Goodness! Dying! The lady said nothing about that. Said not to bother yourself, it being Christmas and all, but she wanted you to know. I think," Celine said bluntly, "she wanted you to come. That ain't what she said but it's what she said. In my opinion."

"Did she leave her name?" Cole asked, knowing it didn't matter.

"Not Detroit. Though she was family. Oh, it was a nice name, a name you don't put with a person. I thought I'd remember it, Cole, I honestly did but it's gone right out of my mind."

"Valentine," he said. "Quinn Valentine."

"That's it!" she cried. "Oh, I'm so glad you got it, I would have hated to mess you up."

"I better get going now, Celine."

"It *is* a pretty name. I try and put a person with that name and I just can't."

He told her good-bye and hung up the phone. Clayton Wade had the mannequins dressed in pajamas just like his, the same red cravats. The man's lost a screw, thought Cole as he thanked him. He walked the street quickly, grateful to the Catholic faith for making the Mass go on forever so they were just going to the rail as he came in. He watched Karen go up, watched her kneel and receive the host, drink from the cup. The Great Mystery. It was all mysterious to him. The way she bowed her head on her way back to the pew. The genuflection. If she'd run and thrown herself on the altar or handled snakes or spoken in tongues it couldn't have seemed more strange to him than the sight of his wife in quiet communion with a God he didn't know and couldn't see.

Before he went to her he lit his own candle, a thing he'd never done. He lit it with Henry Detroit in mind, though the troubles of a dying man are mostly over, and he couldn't think what to ask for beyond help in *this* life—there was no next as far as he knew. In this life there was a whole raft of people whose troubles lay on them and around them or in their future. Mrs. Detroit, Celine and Mickey, Saralee Stringer, Clayton Wade, the woman he'd have to call Etta, Karen, himself, his children, Quinn Valentine. There seemed no end to it suddenly, nothing a candle could hold at bay or help them walk through. He felt foolish, then false, asking for a better world on Christmas, an easier world. What about all the other days of the year when a savior wasn't being born and a man didn't lie dying? Those days made a falsehood of his candle, burning there with the others like a fox in the chickens. He snuffed it quickly—there wasn't a soul around—and watched the frail smoke linger. "You go on, H.A.," he said, surprising himself, talking to ghosts. "You go on ahead." But he knew how much he'd give to see that man one more time before he disappeared into the gulf of paradise.

RUTHA BROWN

1969

Supper was nothing special. Collards and cold biscuits, some warmed-up gravy, a couple of leftover pork chops. Rutha gave them both to Lewis. After, he took a teaspoon of Nescafé in a mason jar of warm water from the tap. Colored water he called it. He put a lump of sugar in it and sat and talked to her while she did up the dishes.

"There's a man out there come up with something as simple as sugar."

She never knew why he said the things he said.

"Sugar's growed," she told him. "Ain't no one come up with it."

"You ever seen sugar looks like this, growed in a lump?"

"It don't grow in no lump."

"That's what I'm talking about. There's someone out there, Mr. Jack Frost, and he gets this idea to make his sugar different. He make his sugar different, people gonna buy it."

"Why ain't people gonna buy it if it's the same?"

"If it's the same, they got no reason to buy it. They buy it or they buy from Mr. Domino, it don't make no difference to them. Sugar is sugar. You can't do nothing with it but change its shape. So that's what he done."

"You can change its color."

"They already done that."

"You can powder it like for sweets."

"They done that too."

"What make you so interested in sugar?"

"Nothing."

"You go on and sit outside, let me get done in here."

He went and she felt sorry he had no son or daughter to sit out there with him, take an interest in sugar. After a minute he came back and said, "Outside's too cold."

They played cards at the kitchen table. Crazy Eights was her game and Hearts was his. Charlene and Daniel came up on the porch to sing a Christmas carol. "Where's your brother at?" asked Rutha.

"Which one?" asked Charlene.

"Which one? You know which one."

"I got one dead and two over there in Vietnam, and this one here and another one. Which one you want?"

"You sassing me, Charlene? Seem like you are."

"She is," said Daniel.

"Shut up!" said the girl. She looked down at her boots, Dallas's old army boots that didn't fit her and never would. She said, "Roosevelt's at one of his meetings again. Gonna get himself killed without even leaving this dang country."

"Christmas Eve they meeting?"

"Un-hunh. They meeting in the church."

Lewis came out and said, "I wish somebody would stand on this porch and sing something." He went back in and stood at the kitchen window while Rutha helped them get through "Silent Night." Daniel had a high, clean voice, like his mother. He was still a boy. Charlene fought too hard, couldn't hit two right notes in a row.

She gave them a cup of hot milk and molasses and sent them home. Lewis went to bed early and the house felt like somebody else's too-big clothes. Her nieces and nephews had strung those little white lights all over her porch and inside she felt a hundred eyes watching her. Every time Roosevelt came into her mind, she put him out of her mind. She knew his mother was over there doing the same.

She looked at the TV for a while, a program of gospel singers from up near Atlanta. Then an all-white choir from one of the Western states. She'd never seen a choir that big before. They filled a whole church. Her church could have fit into one corner of that church. She thought of getting Lewis up just to see it, but instead she went and made herself a cup of Red Rose.

That television was like having a crowd of spooks in the next room. Gray ghost light washing the walls. Tiny people singing *Hallelujah!* in her window panes. When Dosha and Pearly's children were little they'd come over and watch cartoons before the sun came up, limp piles of pajamas, sleepy-eyed, sucking their thumbs. Lewis was ready for them, making pancakes shaped like lions and monkeys and snakes. The only thing he ever did in the kitchen. Made them wash their hands too.

The feeling of being watched again. She took her tea back to the other room and sat down, then got up and turned off the TV. If there was anyone out there to hear, making the porch boards talk, she wanted to hear him. She hadn't thought about that for a long time. It was those lights making her afraid, and the holiness of the night. This was Our Savior's night, a night full of scares to poor shepherds, which would be her though she hadn't the sheep.

Call them miracles. You could call them that. But scares they seemed to those bedraggled ones who dozed in the comfort of their flocks. They were woken by the light of a comet, as if the whole sky were afire. And their sins jumped into their minds, and their sheep ran and cried out, and their dogs barked and it was a terrible awakening, as if the wolf had come. Imagine. But he had not come. Instead the babe. Only their ignorance kept them from the miracle.

Yet this was no miracle, what bothered her now. Though neither was she ready to call it the wolf. She would like to call it nothing, had prayed it was nothing. Yet here it was, something again.

It had been six years since the big house got built, so it was six years ago in the spring. When the whole plantation came alive with fire, alive being the true and right word for the land's burning which in pine smelled of sweet caramel and caused in its wake a life of pure green lifting from temporary ashes. It was called medicine. It made the hunting good. It swept by her yard, igniting the tall grass across the road, sending the rattlesnakes under. She could see it and smell it and hear it at night cracking and whistling in the woods like a herd of deer, or grunting and chuffing like pigs where the fuel was wet and dense. She could hear pine seeds popping open in the heat, small fragrant explosions that drew the quail from the creek bottoms to feed. And the comic gobble of turkeys finding their way to water or chufa or Lamar Davis the sharecropper's green-wet unburned fields.

Those spring nights after Lewis went to bed she sat on her porch and rocked, watching the moving shapes of men on the road. Two of them were Roosevelt's brothers Clarence and Bernard, another was Dosha's boy Solomon. A fourth man walked in front spilling flame from a long-necked torch till the underbrush ran with fire. Like a pen he was writing the word *destruction* with. She knew him by day, a white man, and had no occasion to fear him though what he was made of was not clear to her then. He was Mr. Luken, the dog handler. He had a wife and a little girl and lived in a house better than Rutha's next to the kennel and close by the plantation house. He was short and thick-chested and drank too much and worked hard. His hair was thick and dark and shone with tonic. His teeth were large and yellow and he had a high-pitched laugh like a woman's. On her way to work Rutha regularly passed his laundry hung up to dry by his wife Miss Rosemary Luken, and she could feel in the look of the cloth and the look of the woman an ordinary depletion that knew no God but meant no harm. Or so it seemed.

That first spring on the land, in this house, after they all got moved from in town, she felt like a queen sitting on her own porch after dark, the long pines sighing and keeping her company after the fire went down low, wiggling along on its belly toward midnight. It would all but disappear. Then in the morning the heat would push it up again, the sun would rouse it and maybe the wind too. It would get up on its legs and walk, or take off at a run, and once or twice she'd seen it run right up to the top of a tree, burning the bark on it black. Lewis said walking and running was what you wanted a fire to do. If it lay down and slept too much it would die, and if it started to fly and jump firebreaks you would have an almighty devastation. He'd seen that happen once and lived to tell it and didn't expect to be that lucky twice. He said not a river could have killed that fire. Right out here on the land. Not a wide cold river.

One night when they were burning somewhere else she thought she'd sit up late just to be alone. The night was thick and open, like an open coat. The darkness felt heavy but she felt like she sat at the entrance to it and the entrance was wide. She dozed some, then woke up and went in to get ready for bed. The lights were off in the house and she kept it that way as she undressed and pulled on her nightgown. But she wasn't quite ready for sleep. She walked down the narrow hallway that divided the house, to the front room with the television in it. There were two windows that gave onto the porch. She stood by one of them and for no reason she could think of looked out and saw rising up out of the ditch along the far side of the road the round white face of a man. It was a deep ditch. He might have been crouched in there. The bulk of his body appeared, his clothes a shade lighter than the darkness. He stepped up onto the road and crossed it and stood looking back at where he came from like a man risen from his own grave. Then he turned his attention to what lay ahead of him, the three houses joined by a common yard. He seemed to study the houses one at a time, the last one being Rutha's.

She pulled back from the window and wished she had a curtain to close against him. She thought she would wake Lewis but she couldn't make herself move. She felt his attention coming toward her, knew he was looking at her empty chair on the porch. Next to it Lewis's chair, but that didn't interest him. She'd left a glass of water out there on the porch railing and wished now she hadn't. It was more than plain curiosity brought him out here in the middle of the night. Who was he? She stood with her back to the wall and her hands flat against it and she could feel him tugging at her. She stepped away from the wall and that was better. She turned to the other window and dared to look out and he was squatting down, scratching something in the dirt with a stick he'd picked up off the road, like he was doing his sums. It was dark all over but less dark where he was, that white face collecting things, stealing things, including the light of the stars. She watched as he scratched some more, then stood up and dropped the stick on the road. Then he just walked off. Walked away in the direction of the plantation house, not out the plantation gate which was where she hoped he belonged.

She woke Lewis and sent him out to take a look at those marks in the dirt, since he could read. He came back and told her there was nothing, no sign.

"You don't believe me," she said.

"Could be there was someone."

"There *was* someone. I seen him get up outta the ditch, onto the road. Then he got real still and it felt like he was sucking in everything he saw."

"What'd he see?"

"The houses here. Certain things. Then he took up a stick and wrote stuff."

Lewis shook his head. "I didn't see no boot mark neither."

She sent him back to bed and finally went herself. By daylight she'd remembered something about the man: He walked like he was barefoot.

She waited up the next night half hoping and half afraid. He didn't come. The night after that again he didn't come. A week went by. They were burning down at Cullis Jones's, down toward the south end of the plantation. The wind came up and she could smell the smoke, the pitchy sweetness diminished by distance but there just the same. Pearly's boys were on that fire most of the night. She went to bed but woke when she heard them clunk up onto their porch, light as two elephants. They must have been tired and they let the screen door bang as they went inside.

For a long time she lay there in the dark, Lewis asleep beside her, breathing in bursts of distant gunfire. She prayed awhile, naming everyone she could think of, but trying to bring the good thoughts forward was like pushing bread through a sieve. She got up and knew where she was headed though she told herself a glass of water was what she was after. She knew he was there before she even looked out. Same place on the road. Same stick in his hand. The moon had grown and she saw by it that he had blackened his face with charcoal. Hands too. His feet were bare and white. He was just finishing up his scratching when she came to the window. She stood well back from it, in the dark, but he saw her, though he couldn't have seen her. He snapped his head up and seemed to know she was there. As if he'd drawn her there. He left the way he did the first time, in the same direction.

She surprised herself by saying nothing to Lewis. And the next morning there were no marks on the road, she looked herself. A few nights later he came but this time he had a dog with him and he walked right into the yard and stood in the shadow of Robert and Dosha's house with his charcoal face pointed at Rutha. She knew who he was then. Imagine him coming right up like that. He'd be on the porch next, him and his dog. It was an old pointer dog, liver and white, a boxy head, thin as a fence. It stood by the man until he touched its head, then it shifted and sat down, looked off into the woods across the road.

That was the last time he came. The dog left prints but the man did not. Rutha glimpsed the dog some months later in the Lukens' yard, sleeping on a pile of bricks that later became a barbecue pit.

She kept her vision to herself and came to believe it was that, a vision, a haint walking at night. And yet she feared it was not. She came to believe Luken meant her no harm, yet the danger of believing so kept her awake at night. She went to the window sometimes, always knowing he wasn't there. Finally she made herself some curtains and the house felt blind to him and she inside it felt blind to him and she knew he wouldn't bother her anymore.

Six years went by and he occupied a part of her mind so small and far away she would have said until that Christmas Eve she never thought of that business at all. The flesh-and-blood man she saw six days out of seven, when he came up to the kitchen of the big house for his coffee. And just as often she glimpsed his wife, and Pearly's Daniel went to school with the daughter. But that was the man not the vision. The man and the vision grew up from the same ground, on the same stalk, but they grew like a Y, and no matter how she came to know the man, knew how he drank his coffee in big hot swallows and ducked his head instead of a thank you, she knew the haint no better than she ever had.

But when he came in on her that night, visiting her mind, she had grown to become a person who could tolerate uncertainty. Who could take uncertainty and turn it to opportunity. Roosevelt had taught her that. She was in no hurry. She gathered herself, finished her tea, touched her Bible (it lived on the arm of the chair where she sat), and got up and went out onto the porch. She didn't look for him, nor did she try to make him disappear. She walked down the porch steps counting them, one, two, three, four, and looked right up into the sky which was the same sky that had so many years ago filled with the comet's light. Tonight there was not one star that shone above the others, but all of them shone together brighter than she'd ever seen, a glittering mass of silver. She remembered the haint's feet gleaming like snow in the dust of the road, and the face that seemed to steal the light of heaven. Well, this time he wasn't going to steal a thing. Not from her, not from anyone on this place. If there was something he wanted he could walk up right now and collect it. She would stand there until he did, out under those burning stars.

COLE JONES
1969

Dark as pitch, tires no more than humming on a hardpan road, and still you could not take the house by surprise. Unless you drugged, muzzled, or killed every dog in the kennel. Up the last hill Cole held his breath and did not wait long. The cry came first from one, then all simultaneously. The sentinel in this case was H.A.'s own, the big retriever by the name of Man.

Gravel was the next watchdog, a short stretch of it in front of the house. H.A.'s old Mercedes and a red Volkswagon in the turnaround. That had to be Frankie. Cole parked over in Osee's spot by the kitchen. He sat awhile, his hands on the wheel, looked out at the dark shapes of the pines that topped the hill to the kennel. Every day but Sunday—and Christmas, New Year's, and Thanksgiving—this is where Osee sat, this is what Osee saw. Went into town in the dark and picked up Geneva Nixon. Maybe Pearly Mae drove with him on a Saturday when she didn't have to get the kids to school. Then he came back and picked up Rutha Brown, or Rutha and Pearly, brought them all up here and they'd get out, taking their own sweet time, laughing, pulling their purses out with them, maybe a shopping bag with an extra sweater, fussing about this pain and that. And he'd sit, Osee would, just for a minute and look out, just like this, look out at something that didn't need him to be a certain way or do a certain thing, just rest. And then he'd get out, walk over to the door, and go in and become whoever they wanted him to be: Friend Osee. Close kin to Friend Cole Jones.

For what ran through a man's veins was only the thinnest form of kinship. The thicker stuff was made—forged, soldered, bolted down—by unrelated strangers thrown together in the same war. He and Osee, they were Southern men together. That thought surprised him. He had never had such a thought before. They were Southern men, fighting a battle inside themselves, here in the shadow of a Northern man's house. Bowing, smiling, and yessirring like vaudeville fools to preserve the ideal of the Southern man, for which they were paid.

Cole closed his eyes, feeling uneasy. A man could be dying inside that house at this moment. Ending his dying on this Christmas Day. Heaving his last breath. But it wasn't this, it was something else that pressed on him, trying to tell him something, teach him something. What came to him was another man's ragged breath, the first time he saw colored blood. He was how old? As high as the counter in his daddy's drugstore. The man came in off the street, the blackest Negro Cole had ever seen, a mixture of blood and spit pouring from his mouth, and his arm, ringed with blood, held tight against his chest. Against his skin the blood looked black, blacker than the man himself. He came in through the front door—Cole had never seen that before—and there was desperation in his face, along with the pain of what turned out to be a series of knife wounds to the chest. The arm was the stopper but it couldn't keep the dark blood back. He staggered in past the scented soaps at the front, and down the shampoo aisle where

Cole had learned to read his first big word: *dandruff*. The man came on. A hissing sound came from his throat, or from the gaps in his chest. Cole peeked around the counter, excited and scared, waiting to see what his daddy would do. His daddy stood behind the counter and Cole could see his legs shaking, he could see his hands nervously patting his thighs. Then he heard his daddy tell the man to leave. He told him, "Get the hell out." He ordered him out the back door, though it meant a longer trail of blood for Cole's brother Ellis to mop up when he got home from football practice. The man hadn't said a word. He staggered out, hissing.

When he was gone, Cole asked his daddy, "Why was that man bleeding?"

"I reckon it's none of my business. And none of yours neither."

"Is he going to die?"

"Someday, like the rest of us."

"Why couldn't we help him?"

"I didn't hear him ask for help. Anyway, you a doctor, Buddy? I'm not. Can't afford a doctor, they come in here looking for free advice. Come right in the front door. Well, I'm not here to give free advice." He went and latched the back door, walked up and locked the front. "Ought to drag him back in here, clean up his own blood."

Cole didn't know what advice was. It was bandages that came to his mind. His mother wrapped a bandage just right. She'd wrapped them for more than one neighbor, and strangers too. His daddy went to get the mop and bucket. He came back and Cole surprised them both and said, "Can I do it? I know how. I'm big enough."

It was a kind of child's penance for the failings of the adults. Not just his father's but the Negro's too. The man had failed to come in the right door, for one thing, and before that he'd failed to avoid the wrong end of a knife. His father had failed to give help where help was needed, failed to treat a wounded man's wounds. A dying man, in fact. Had failed to save a man's life.

Sitting in Osee's spot by the trees, Cole could feel something new, a new discomfort with the memory. It had to do with the difference between his father's failing and the Negro's, and the sense that his own penance would always be for the sins of a man he never liked. It was sense and no more. He caught the vague shape of the thing, but like thoughts of death, the more he tried to grasp it, the more it wiggled away. Like catching night crawlers, something his sister Celine was good at. She saw better in the dark than by day, and she had no sympathy for those creatures. No sympathy to slow her down. Like Cole with dove. He didn't have a feeling for their feeling, and it meant he didn't hesitate, not one instant. Yet he knew people, his brother Ellis, his brother Pete, and others, who deer-hunted and went out of state for bear, and they claimed nothing but sympathy for whatever they brought in. They didn't call it that, in fact didn't talk much about it, but Cole understood what they were saying even if their words weren't saying it exactly. It was connection. It was about getting inside the animal to know the animal, to know its mind. To be able to join with it as if it were the same as you, equal to you at least, and even better and wiser than you (this was Pete's idea) because it allowed you to kill it. If you did the right thing, acted in the right way—and this was also an old Indian idea, Pete said—the animal would do you the great honor of allowing you to kill it. "That's quite a first date," Cole once said, and Pete's answer surprised him. "It is. It's love."

The crunch of gravel—quick footsteps—gave him a start. More and more, lately, he found himself drifting. He turned, put his hand on the door to open it, saw in the yellow light of the veranda a form he knew. Quinn was crossing to him, of course she was, all backlit. He stepped out of the car, dropped his hat on the seat. He closed the door and felt in that one motion he'd cut himself off from the rest of his men. The river had risen behind him and he stood a fool on its banks. On *her* banks, for she owned the ground she walked on—not literally (it would fall to Harry and his wife Kate), but by her self-assurance. "Hello," he said. He held the word out like a bayonet displayed in a museum case. The strength of the sound of it encouraged him. He went forward to meet her and to his surprise she kept on coming, no language to stop her or startle him, and kissed him, her full mouth on his, softly, supplely, then release, though she held his face briefly in her two hands. Only their foreheads touched. They stood just where the shadow of the house began.

"Why?" she whispered. "Why, why, *why* do you make me wait? I thought you'd never come."

"Shhh. Shhh now."

They kept their voices low.

"It's Christmas, Cole."

"It's two hours into Christmas." He breathed the limey scent of her skin. "How is he? H.A.?"

"He's not done yet."

"He'll live?"

"For heaven's sake, he's dying, Cole."

"I know that. I came as quick as I could."

She laughed abruptly. "I'd say you took your own sweet time."

"I had to get Karen home. Was I supposed to bring Karen?"

She ignored that and said, "Who on earth was that woman?"

"What woman?"

"The one on the phone. She was so . . . she upset me. She said she couldn't write anything down, she'd remember it. I didn't think she would. And then . . . then she kept calling you Buddy. Who is she, Cole?"

"A woman at my house?"

"That woman I talked to. There was something odd about her. Could she have been drunk?"

"You must've gotten the babysitter."

"Oh, Lord. I hope she wasn't drunk."

"She wasn't."

"I hope not."

He pulled her in close, felt her shiver, pushed Celine out of his mind. "We better get you inside."

"Why on earth would I want to go inside?"

"You're shaking. You're cold, Quinn."

"I'm not cold. And I'm not ready to go back in. I just got out. And anyway, if I were cold, this would be the moment you'd offer me your coat, not send me inside. I can't do this inside." She looked up at him. In the shadowy dark he could see her mouth tighten. "I've missed you. I guess I'm an idiot. I thought you'd be there at the airport. I thought you'd come to meet us. I was sure you would. Poor Osee. There he was and I just felt awful. I couldn't summon one ounce of brightness. And Seth was a nuisance, acting like a child the entire trip. Leo acts the little man and Seth the child. Oh, Cole," she bounced her head against his shoulder, "I don't even want to talk. Why am I talking?"

He stroked her fine hair. "I've missed you too."

"You have?"

"Sure I have."

"Why didn't you come this week? I counted on that. Every day I was sure this would be the day I would see you. You and Harry would have your powwow. I finally realized I'd have to do it myself, organize a dove shoot to entice you over here. It's set for tomorrow. You and the Cabots and the Moynihans, and who else? Oh, the Chubbs because they're related, and that's all they do is leech off relatives. They're professional leeches. Somehow we all feel sorry for them and out go the invitations—they get invited to *everything,* and return nothing, offer not even a lousy gin and tonic and a nice Camembert. Or a second-rate pâté on stale water biscuits. That would do it. It's the effort. They make no effort. Oh." She stopped herself. "Cole, I just can't not talk. Listen to me. And you're here now, aren't you? I can feel you are. I'm done now. I'll be quiet."

"I like to hear you talk."

"No, you don't."

"I do."

"Months go by, don't they?"

"Six months. Half a year."

"I keep thinking it doesn't matter."

"What doesn't?"

"You know."

"The time?"

"No, the feeling. I keep thinking I won't have it anymore, I'll wake up and it will be gone, I won't have it. But I still do."

"*Don't!*" he wanted to shout. "*Don't! And I won't either.*" But instead he asked, "How's Billy?"

"Billy? He's fine. We don't need to talk about Billy."

"He's here?"

"He was. He was here for the weekend and went back. He flies in again tomorrow—no, it's already today, isn't it? He tried to get an earlier flight, so he could hang stockings with us. But everybody's flying at Christmastime."

"Like Santa."

"Santa," she laughed. "The indomitable Santa bloody Claus. I hate Christmas, Cole."

"You shouldn't."

"Well, I do."

"When's he coming in? I'll go with you."

"You won't go with me. Don't be stupid. Don't *tempt* me."

"Where and when?"

"Tallahassee. He'll be here before the children wake up."

"I'll come."

"You won't come."

And of course he wouldn't. His curfew was the same as Billy's. Karen had promised to skin him alive if he wasn't home before the girls woke up. And she would. Skin him and skewer him.

He and Billy, he thought, two fairy-tale kings whose kingdoms hung on a stroke of the clock. But in the tale, a stronger, smarter king takes time itself and heaves it over the castle wall, seals the children's eyelids shut with a spell that only he can undo. A wilier king. No match for Cole's or Billy's good intentions, for if nothing else marked their reign it was duty—duty dumb as any brick wall. No magic tricks, just a near-impossible wish to be perfect *and* at ease. That was Cole. But of course, like any flawed monarch, here he stood with another man's wife. Another king's wife—the queen—telling her in truth that he'd missed her. And, any minute now, willing to say he loved her. Not to wrest a similar confession from her (she'd as good as given it), but in fact hoping to scare her back to a cool distance, a standing-away he counted on her for.

"All those kids who think they have a daddy because they wake up with one," he said. It sounded bitter. He didn't feel bitter. "Mine included."

"Think of the children who don't even wake up with one." He felt her backbone lengthen, recede. She lifted her head to look at him. "It's guilt, isn't it?"

"What is?"

"What's kept you away. It's guilt." She took a deep breath, looked back at the house. He felt her become formal, felt her retreat. "I'm sorry," she said. "I don't know why I didn't see it sooner. I thought I would feel it first, that's why. Why in the world did I think that? I kept thinking, Well, if I don't feel it, he doesn't feel it, so we're okay. We're okay for another round. That's just what I thought, 'another round.' Two people in the ring together, with every intention of hurting each other, ruining each other."

"That's not our intention, Quinn. You know it's not."

"It's a strong possibility, though, isn't it?"

He didn't think so. Their rounds were too brief, a few nights a year, whenever he came up to New York on business (and once she flew to Baltimore, pretending a school reunion). And never down here. Never in daylight. Never in her bed or his. Always in the antiseptic comfort of a hotel room, and always without reference to Billy or Karen. Though he had knowingly broken that taboo tonight. He didn't believe they were fighters in a ring, or fighters at all. That was exactly what they were not. He didn't believe anyone else imagined it either, a ring with him in it with her. Except Karen. She had imagined it—overimagined it, most likely, and she wasn't placing her bets, not on him. Her hopes maybe. He welcomed her hopes.

As for guilt . . . it was true. Raw, chafing guilt is what he felt, had felt for some time now, though before it had centered on Karen and now it had moved to the twins. It left him full of questions, hesitations, though it slackened nothing in his felt desire. He was made of two men now, the one who went skin to skin with the girl in the back seat of the car, and the one who rapped on the window with the flashlight, who shone that flashlight upon their awkward flesh, revealing them to be human and not too pretty.

He put his hand on the back of Quinn's head, brought it again to his shoulder. She was tall and he liked that. She was almost as tall as Charity Stringer, who was the tallest woman he knew. He hoped his girls would be closer to his height than Karen's, and fuller than Karen, though she had been practically plump when he met her. He thought about Charity's sister, Saralee, and her deluded romance, or whatever it was, with Charles de Gaulle. It was sad the way a sick mind worked, but Cole knew delusions were not only for the unwell. They served a purpose everywhere, even if it was just to give confusion more room to play itself out, wear itself down. And sometimes they spared a person true heartbreak.

"There are times I do feel bad," he said. "I feel guilty. Then it passes."

She snorted. "Men are so much simpler than women, morally."

"Now that's not true. How can that be true when I feel guilty and you don't?" He lifted her off the ground one full inch. "Look who's airborne."

"*Don't* pick me up, Cole. I hate that."

"I know it. It's your punishment for making a cruel and foolish generalization."

"Listen to me. It's not that I'm not capable of feeling guilty. I am. But for you it passes. It comes and goes. It's as unremarkable as waking up and wanting breakfast—"

"It's not one bit like waking up and wanting breakfast."

"But for me it's devastating. I can't go on doing the thing I feel guilty about. That's why I'm slow to feel it. It means the end for me. Do you understand?"

He picked her up again. "Do you see why you're airborne?"

"*No.* Put me down, Cole. I'll kick you."

"Kick me? Women are so much simpler than men, defensively."

She did kick him. He set her down quickly. From the pain of it he guessed she'd bruised his shin. That would be one more lie to Karen—he'd stumbled and hit a rock, or a stump, or fallen over a chair in the house. More ammunition for her disbelief and Quinn had just handed it to her. He felt raw. She'd hit him hard and meant to. It was no good here, so close to the house, H.A., her children. He hadn't intended this here. But then she had come out and kissed him.

"I'd better go in," he said. "It's time for me to see him."

"Oh, I wouldn't bother now, Cole. Don't wake him. If you had come earlier—"

"I came as soon as I could."

He leaned down and touched the edges of the bruise and she said, "It was stupid of me. I'm sorry."

"Last time I got kicked it was H.A.'s old horse Cotton." He stood up. "That was always a one-man horse, that Cotton."

"He still is."

"He's still out there?"

"Henry's making a fuss about putting him down, but he'll never do it. He couldn't. He can't."

"Quinn." Cole reached out, touched a finger to her breastbone, then his whole hand. He spread his fingers, took in the softness of her breasts, the hardness of her bone. "Let's see each other sometime."

She put her hand over his, then drew it back. "But won't I see you tomorrow?"

"Tomorrow?"

"In the dove field. You've already forgotten!"

"But H.A.? He may be—"

"Oh, it's nothing! No, no, it's nothing. He'll be with us. He's—"

"Quinn, you sent for me."

"I know I did. I know. You wouldn't come any other way."

"You mean—"

"Now, don't be angry. I'm the one who should be angry. All these days and you haven't come and I've missed you. All these days when Billy's away and we might have seen each other a little. Suddenly I couldn't bear the thought of . . . of not being close. Of standing in that damn dove field right next to you and not having said a proper hello. I thought you would want it too. If you had been home we might have talked but instead I got that terrible woman who kept calling you Buddy, Buddy this, Buddy that, that terrible, drunk, illiterate woman—"

"My sister," said Cole. "That's Celine, my sister."

Her eyes widened. She started to say something but suddenly the veranda light went out and in the darkness they moved apart. Without a word he turned back to his car and got in, almost sat on his hat. She stood with one hand over her mouth, the other raised in a little wave.

He drove out the back driveway, the way Osee Davis would drive in in the morning and out again in the evening. And he felt the fool, more than the fool, for having believed himself to be at any time any different from Osee, to be the kind of company that rightfully comes in the front drive and uses the front door and courts the king's wife and gets away with it. That was a different man, a different kind of company. That was a man who knew better than to carry on his acts of illicit foolishness in the shadow of the house, because the eyes of the house were everywhere. A man who knew that nothing hidden in darkness or in light could escape for long, or forever, the cool condemnation of those who believed they themselves had nothing to hide.

BYRDINE DEAN

1969

There was one day a year when she felt too fat, too ugly, too old, and that was Christmas. Byrdine wondered if Santa Claus felt the same. At least he could sleep late with a clean conscience, and Mrs. Claus beside him in the bed. Whoever it was said *The touch of a foot in the night is sincere,* that person was a true poet, a professor of the human heart. Of all she missed, it was that scrapey-skinned, under-the-covers brushing of feet that she missed most, felt she couldn't hardly live without. Of course by daylight it was all a personality game again. She'd been with several human beings whose charm, naturally, increased as you moved body-south, but south of there it got even better, into the dumb realms below the ankles. Feet were strong. They burrowed and kicked and clawed and rolled over. They were a mess of calluses or pale as fish in unfished waters. Their bunions made them funny-looking. Some had hammertoes. One drunken fellow who came to have his palm read took off his shoe and offered her his foot. No good. He'd worn the narrative down to nothing and he got too flirtatious when she tried to take his hand. *End of daydream* said Byrdine to herself, out loud. She rolled on her side, sat up, and plopped her flat fat feet on the floor and wished herself a merciful Christmas.

What would she do with this whole day? Linda had a lingering boyfriend, and the girl would go and eat with him and his family, feel bored to death but part of something normal. While Linda's mother, Terry, was off chasing men—or dead in a ditch for all they knew. Byrdine hoped she'd remember to call in and wish her little girl a happy day, but the odds were against it.

Odds were against just about everything on this day. Unless you lived in China. It was a monument to hope and disappointment, this day was. Byrdine's own family—her blood—boiled down to one: her brother Floyd, last seen by swamplight. Once every twenty years she laid eyes on him, and at this moment, on this morning, the world feeling bare and ungenerous as could be, she wished with her whole heart she might spend one more Christmas with him.

She pinched her pale cheeks for a little holiday color and told herself to quit dreaming, get dressed, and get moving. But where to? Suddenly it came to her: "You got a café to run! Someone's got to pour coffee on Christmas Day." And as simple as that, the thing itself saved her, the little turquoise trailer with its yellow counter, wobbly stools, and new blue-painted floor. She put on a clean shift, the one with the stripes running up and down to make her look skinny. She brushed out her hair and braided it and thought about how people could save you too, but they might just as easy come and grind a boot heel on your cold fingers, the ones clinging to the life raft. No animal would do that, not even the meanest bear. To cause suffering was not in an animal's mind. Sure, they'd kill you, but kill you quick to eat you or keep you from killing them. Oh, she'd heard stories of she-grizzlies playing with their human prey, rolling live men up and down hills or tossing them in the air, mangled and screaming bloody murder, juggling park rangers until all that was left of them was their Smokey Bear hat. She thought these tall tales. Or if there was truth to them, the truth had more to do with entertainment, the way her cat, Mr. Burns, batted mice around until the poor little things no longer struggled and danced for him, then he lost interest. Which reminded her, if that fellow, the one in the raincoat with the twin girls, if he ever came back—and he might, yes, he might—she ought to tell him about Mr. Burns and his mice. She wasn't sure whether he, the fellow, was himself mouse or Mr. Burns, but she sensed from him a restlessness, a fatefulness that marked him as a player in this sort of entertainment.

The dogs were waiting for her in the café yard. They sniffed and circled her, a pack of ten or twelve this morning, including one she'd never seen before with a drunken walk. She let herself in and the first thing she did was check on Thirteen. He was still there, hadn't moved a muscle. This would be day six, she thought, and shut the cooler door with enough aggravation to topple a box of something onto the floor. In case it was eggs, she didn't want to know about it. It didn't sound like eggs. She put the coffee on and got some bacon started, made up a pot of oatmeal. Anyone wanted grits she'd make grits, but today she felt like oatmeal. And she might be the only customer, so there.

It was too darn early. A gray sky, stingy and mean-looking, glared back at her through the small kitchen window. It was cold. Not as cold as it could be but damp and achy, the kind of cold that keeps you hunched and drinking coffee all day, which was what she intended to do, customers or no customers. This was the kind of day Santa was having, resting from labors large and small. She'd give her right arm to believe in him and his flying sleigh. She never had, not even as a young child, though she kept her doubts to herself, unlike other children. What she would ask for now was simple: Bring me nothing. Only take *him* away. Undo, if you can—you're a saint after all—the events that landed him here, and dead. Wasn't he precious to someone somewhere? How would they find him? How would they ever find him here?

The dogs started up, an unholy racket, then quit, just like that. Byrdine came out of the kitchen and stood facing the door, waiting. She pushed back her hair. Her palms were damp. The thought crossed her mind that someone had tossed a lump of poisoned meat in the yard and gone on their way again. Halloween, when the kooks came out of their hidey-holes, you never knew what they'd do. Maybe kill an undeserving pack of animals. But Christmas could be like that too. People feeling alone in the world, and crazy.

She turned and went the three steps back into the kitchen and suddenly a man's face rose up at her through the little window over the sink. She put her hand to her chest and let out a yelp and stepped back, but there was nowhere to move. He was a white man. He didn't look like anyone she knew. Under his ball cap his hair was black and shiny and his face was puffy like he hadn't slept good. He stayed looking in at her through the water-stained glass and she counted to ten and told herself maybe he was harmless.

Just then he put his forehead flat on the window and said, "You got a telephone? My truck stopped a mile up the road."

His lack of manners brought her to her senses. "And who would you be, poking in windows, scaring people half to death? I got a telephone, yes I do, but it's reserved for customers, *sir.*"

"Yes ma'am," he said, looking down like a scolded boy. He shook his head. "I'm not the kind of customer you want. Left home without my money."

"You were in a hurry then."

He said nothing. He was the kind of man who could shave three times a day with a sharp razor and still look shadowy around the mouth.

"I tell you what. You come in and do me a favor, I'll feed you."

He hesitated, weighing the debt. Finally he said, "I can do that."

He went around front and for one minute she thought to lock the door on him. But it was Christmas. She should feed him anyway, not put him to work. He came in and she had to ask, "What charm are you using on those dogs that they don't bark?"

"I get along with them, that's all."

He took a long look around and suddenly she felt ashamed of what he saw, the inadequacy of her dream. She felt like she was seeing the truth through his eyes, and everyone else, all those others who'd passed through, they'd been lying to her. The blue floor, it was just pretty paint hiding something that would soon be rotten, or already was. And her yellow counter, the red stools. Ripped and coffee-stained soon enough. Not to mention that cooler, and the leak under the sink, and the gas burner that'd singe your hair if you weren't careful. Who did she think she was, creating a big old monument to herself, a place to make her feel immortal? There was no immortality that she knew of, unless it was a record of wrongdoing. You found those in the newspaper, and in every jail, and in heart after wounded heart. Christmas, people didn't think about things like that. Instead they thought about Mary, who claimed she'd slept with no man, yet got herself a child. They thought about Jesus, the little bastard babe, and they loved Him.

The man's gaze came to rest on her. Byrdine sighed and said, "It ain't much, I know. We got a ways to go yet. I can get you some coffee. And I got oatmeal. Sit down and make yourself at home."

"This ain't home," he said.

"Well, no. It's just an expression."

He wasn't a tall man. He was broad and of medium height and he had no coat, just a dirty white T-shirt stretched tight across his chest and upper arms. He came to the counter rubbing his hands together and she said, "Cold out there this morning."

"Yes it is."

Byrdine poured him a cup of coffee and one for herself. "Looks like you weren't planning on the cold weather." She went and got him bacon and oatmeal and set it down in front of him. He ate like a half-starved dog. At the end of it he glanced up and she said, "Can I get you some more?" He nodded. She brought him a second helping and she could see he'd cut the edge of his hunger because he took the trouble to crumble the bacon into the oatmeal. He added the whole sugar bowl to it, and some salt and pepper and butter. He asked for a glass of milk. She brought it to him and he poured half of it in. The rest he poured in his coffee so it overflowed into the saucer. She didn't like to watch him eat though she couldn't help it. What trouble had brought him here on this morning? A hungry man with a broke-down truck.

She took a sip of her coffee and told him, "You're welcome to use that telephone, but you won't find no garage open on Christmas Day."

He took off his cap and placed it on the counter next to him, reached up and smoothed his oily hair. "I ain't broke down. I'm out of gas."

"A telephone's no use for that."

"I got to call my baby girl. Wish her a happy Christmas."

"Where is she, if you don't mind me asking?"

"At home. Home with her mama."

"Why don't you go see her instead? I'd guess you're not far from home. Can't go far with no money."

He snorted and put his cap back on. "I *said,* I'm out of gas."

She kept her voice even. "We can find you some gas."

He shivered and rubbed his arms and said, "Comes to that I can walk."

"Not in those clothes you can't. You'll freeze to death and turn blue and that'll be bad for your little girl. Men don't think things through. A lot of men don't."

"You know a lot of men?"

"Never mind who I know."

"I bet you know a lot of men."

"There's the door," she pointed. "Any more of that talk and I'll ask you kindly take yourself out the way you came in. Cold or no cold."

He shot her a sour look and she understood then that he was a losing sort of fellow and possibly nothing worse than that. He was a mama's boy who got his blood up easy and went in swinging and lost as many as he won. Though his palm would tell her more—and maybe tell her different. Without thinking she said, "Let me see that hand."

"What hand?"

"That hand there on the end of your arm."

"What for?"

"Tell you your future. Usually I charge for it, but today it's on the house."

"Future ain't nobody's business."

"Not even yours?"

"Least of all mine."

"Well, suit yourself."

She cleared his dishes while he sat whittling his teeth with a toothpick. "Telephone's in here," she called to him, letting the water run hot. "Don't ask me why it is, it just is." She came out and he hadn't blinked or swallowed or even breathed, it looked like. "Go ahead and make that call," she told him. "She'll be looking for you to come home now."

He gazed at her like she had just spoken French or Latin or the language of birds. "Are you crazy?" he said. "Ain't no one looking for their daddy today."

"I thought you said—"

"What I said ain't worth pig shit."

"Hey," cried Byrdine. She moved in front of him, her weight tipped forward, her palms flat on the counter like she was trying to press the whole thing back into the ground. "Don't you use that language in here, *sir,* not when there's a lady present. You ask me, you spend too much time drooping at the neck. You oughtta come up for air and see what the world's about."

He laughed at that, a high-pitched laugh that rose the hair on her arms. Out of the blue he asked, "You're part nigger, ain't you?"

She rocked back, dusted the front of her apron with her fingertips. "White and Cherokee is all I know of. Negro by association."

"It don't bother you?"

"What? To be a mix of things? We're all a mix of things."

"I ain't."

"A pureblood, huh?" She cast him a look that told him she knew better. "You best be getting home to your wife and child."

The man leaned forward. "You ever want to run away?"

"Well, sure."

"I mean forever. And not come back?"

"There's always a reason to come back."

"I think I could go away and never come back."

"You just think that," said Byrdine. "That's what we do is make up a place for ourselves where we want to stay forever. Far away from here."

"In a different county."

"We try and find it but the road don't go there."

"My mama used to drive me all over the state. And into Alabama." He looked up suddenly. "Those were good times."

Byrdine nodded. "Me and my brother too, we went with Mama. We didn't like it though. It was her life, not ours."

"But I know I could do it," said the man. "I could run and not come back. That's why I leave my money behind. Only get as far as I get till the tank runs dry."

"It's Christmas morning," said Byrdine. "They're bound to be looking for you. Got to get you some gas and get you home to your kin."

The man shook his head. "I'll walk."

"Don't be foolish on my account."

He stood up. "That favor, ma'am? You fed me. I said I'd do you a favor."

"You'd do me a favor by letting me find you some gas for your vehicle, or some warm clothes if you're going to walk. I got some of those at home. It may take a little time."

He shook his head. "I'll lose my will if I wait."

"It's will, is it?'

"Yes ma'am. Ain't it for you?"

"Nerves," she said. "For me it's nerves." Then it came to her. "I got an idea. This way you won't have to wait for your warm clothes. Give me a minute and when I call you, you come and help me." She looked at him hard. "One thing it ain't. It ain't pretty."

She went to the cooler and propped open the door. The floor in there was covered with Sunbeam bread. That was all that lay between her and Thirteen and it didn't feel like nearly enough. A mountain range might not have been enough. He was lying across a few big boxes of steaks and she went and stood beside him. "Alright," she said to him, "I'm ready to know you." She reached out and put her hand on the canvas that covered him, took hold of the corner by his feet and started to lift it, started to pull it back, like she was skinning him, like he was some old coon or possum and she was taking away the layer that kept the whole show together, the layer that held the language she could read best. Without skin, a hand couldn't talk to you. But she wasn't skinning him, she reminded herself. She was just lifting up his wraps. She was *un*skinning him, in fact. It was by this steady movement of her hand that he would finally be someone. He would have a name because he would have a face. A face spoke a different language than a hand. It was the first language, the language of the face. And a dead face, did it still speak? Its name, at least, though with difficulty sometimes. She'd heard of those unrecognized in death by their own loved ones. The stillness, it was said, distorted the whole body, but the features of the face in particular. There were many still unclaimed for this reason. But a palm was like a fingerprint. You could read the story of that life after its death, and the story, though it gave you no name, gave you more than a name. It gave you the intention and the struggle that a life had contained. In some she'd seen, it gave you the outcome. Which was always death. Though only a few palms bothered to mention it.

She arrived at Thirteen's waist, the top of Leon White's trousers to be exact, and was considering the difficulty of removing them, which was difficult enough on a live man, if she remembered right. He wasn't going to help her, that was for sure, but neither was he going to tickle and smooch while she was trying to get the business done. Leon, for all his dimness, had more than kept up his part of the bargain in dressing the body—it seemed like one eternity ago. He'd even done up the zipper, buttoned the button. Now she set out to undo his work. She touched the cold skin and broke down a little, started to shake, told herself, "He's *dead,* Deedee." It did help her.

She felt living eyes upon her and looked up and sure enough, there was the fellow. "Stand there and keep the door open," she told him. "Look the other way if you have to." He started to come in and she said, "All you got on is that T-shirt? Go get my jacket and put it on."

"I don't need no jacket."

"You're going to catch your death in here, mister."

"Looks like somebody already did."

"Never mind that. I got a good set of clothes here going to waste, and I intend to get 'em for you."

"A dead man's clothes?"

"They came off a live man, but what's the difference? Clothes is clothes."

She started inching the trousers off Thirteen's hips. She didn't care to think about what lay below, the dead sex. Oh, she didn't care to envision that at all. "Could you help me here for half a second?" she said. "Every time I try and roll this boy one way, he wants to roll back the other."

"He's fighting you."

"Oh, he's done fighting."

"Ma'am?" He stepped beside her. "Who is he?"

"Just a dead man is all I know."

He was quick and skillful with the body. He started right in, didn't recoil as she'd expected him to, and within a minute they had Thirteen's trousers down at his ankles, the whole rest of the business blowing in the breeze. And he didn't flinch at that either, as many men would have, seeing the prize parts lying useless—all mortal that place that was supposed to mean *forever.*

With the trousers off, Byrdine worked the canvas up to the shirt collar, leaving only the head still covered. "I owe you a debt," she told the fellow. He was unbuttoning with a skill she'd never experienced in her own men. Well, the true test would be the hooks on a brassiere, and Thirteen wasn't going to provide that opportunity.

"You don't know how he died, or when?"

"Nosir. I just own the cooler he's living in."

"Living?" He barked a high-pitched laugh.

"Living's just a word, mister. It would be an answered prayer," she sighed, "if someone came to claim him. It would be the Christmas present I've been hoping for. If this day was like that day, when the big old star stood over the stable and said, 'Hey! This is the place. This is the one you've all been looking for. Here he is, your little king.' 'Cause don't every mama think her boy's a king?"

"Yours did?"

"Yes she did. Oh, she beat Floyd, beat him 'cause she couldn't beat her boyfriends. And then she had her boyfriends beat him just to prove her loyalty lay with them, not us, so maybe they'd stick with her, warm her bed. We'd stick with her 'cause we had to. She knew that. And Floyd, Floyd'd stick with her 'cause he was foolish for her, dumb in a way. Dumb about people. His heart didn't work right after a while. When his heart hurt, that's when he felt he was where he ought to be. But he was her little king alright. When he was tiny she would of done anything for him. What are you looking at? You're looking at me strange."

"Floyd was his name?"

"Yessir. Anything wrong with that?"

"I hope there ain't."

"You hope there ain't. Now what does that mean?"

"It means I got no business being here."

"But we got to get his shirt off yet."

"Leave it on," said the man. He took hold of the canvas and started to pull it down over the body. "Cover the whole damn thing and call someone. Get it out of here."

"But it belongs somewhere! He belongs to someone!"

"For Pete's sake, woman." He stopped and looked at her. "You say you can read the future. Well, what about the past? Take his hand."

"Take his hand?"

"Ain't his life right there on his hand?"

"It's a dead man's hand! I don't need to read no dead man's hand."

"And here I thought it was on the house."

She was frightened. She wanted to burn the whole darn trailer down, and everything in it. But flames couldn't touch it, not the part she wanted destroyed. She took the body's hand—he was no longer Thirteen to her. He was about to have a life of his own, and for one free moment he was just "the body." When she pried open the fist he'd died with, he was as familiar to her as he'd always been. That hand. She didn't have to read it to know it. The long scar that was his lifeline. He'd cut it on a broken Co-Cola bottle back when he was five or six years old, back when he was still his mama's little king. Their mama's little king. "Hey," she said. "Hey, Floyd. It's me."

"You don't want to uncover his head," said the man.

"I think I do. It's the rest of him don't deserve to be naked."

"He's gone now. There ain't nothing you can—"

"Stay here with me."

"Ma'am, I—"

"Stay," she ordered, and though he put out a hand to stop her she lifted the canvas up and over the rest of her brother. There was little left to recognize. She guessed he'd taken a baseball bat in the face. Several times. Then maybe been run over. "Why'd they do it?" she cried, straightening up.

The man shook his head.

"I know it was more than one of them. I know that." She turned her face into his shoulder and her hands clawed at the sleeves of his T-shirt until he took her wrists and pried her off him and pushed her backward. She landed against the cooler wall.

"Now get a hold of yourself!"

"Me?" she whispered. She pushed off the wall and came right up close to him. "You're telling *me* to get a hold of *my*self?"

"Just take it easy."

"My brother's dead. His head's smashed in. I'll take it easy when I'm good and ready to. Now you go, and don't you ever come back. Stay home. You got a home and family, stay there. Do me a favor. Pull your head up and see what you got. 'Cause I got no one. Right there. That mess of blood and bone right there. That's my only kin."

She waited until she heard the door close behind him. She waited for the dogs to bark but not one of them did. She turned to her brother. She got down on her knees beside him. "Floyd," she said. "I got to ask you, Floyd. What in the world am I going to do now?"

RUTHA BROWN

1969

"Lewis," called Rutha. "Come take a look at this."

Lewis came grumbling out of the bedroom where he was putting on his after-church clothes. Rutha stood in the kitchen. She still had on her fancy hat, the black one with the decoration on top—it looked like a propeller. Lewis and Osee and her nephew Roosevelt, and even Dosha's Robert who hadn't smiled in fifty-two years, they all called it her "heliocopter" hat, said one day it would lift her off the ground and take her up over the trees. Was that all? Up over the trees? If she was going somewhere why not make it home? Back down to Florida where the sun came up over the ocean and the little flies bit behind your ears and she'd once seen a drunk man—dead or drunk (she'd hurried on)—with his lips so covered with crawling flies it looked like he was chewing. Or trying to speak. Maybe he was.

"Look out here," she said, and pointed.

"Lady in an automobile," said Lewis. "What else am I looking at?"

"That's it."

"Well?"

"Look who the lady is."

He shook his head and started to laugh. "That ain't Odetta."

"It's Odetta alright."

"Since when she learn to drive?" He stepped out on the porch and called, "Good morning, Miz Jackson. A merry Christmas to you." He nodded at the car. "I guess you done outflew Santy Claus."

"Mr. Brown," she greeted him. She was a tall, thin woman, bent over some, older than Lewis by an unknown number of years, though it was rumored she was close on a hundred. She still had her teeth, blamed that on the benefits of chewing tobacco. She walked without the help of a cane and heard everything that was said within half a mile of her and saw at such a great distance there was little that went unnoticed by her in the entire southern half of the state. She was not God-fearing, yet she did not believe herself to be at the center of any universe. If she worshipped anything it was that weasel-faced dog of hers. Lewis looked for it now. It usually came running out from behind Odetta's long loose skirts, ready to sink its teeth into the first friendly fool it met.

"Where's the weasel?" he asked.

"He don't like the motorcar."

"You didn't leave him home now, Odetta, did you? Wouldn't do to leave that dog home."

"He never been left home, Lewis. Never will."

"That's good. He might just bite you when you get back."

"He don't bite me. Where's Rutha at?"

"I thought you could see into Alabama, Odetta. Must be slowing down some. There's Rutha behind the window. She's been waving at you."

Odetta had come halfway across the yard. "Couldn't find her under that hat."

"That's her heliocopter hat. She get excited in church, she start to fly right up and out the window."

She laughed and said, "Lewis, Lewis, Lewis. All that church-going's wasted on you. When you gonna sit down and figure out what you *believe?*"

He said nothing, walked down the porch steps to give her his arm. She took it and said, "He get under the seat and won't come out. He just stay under there, shivering and shaking. I don't know what he believe, but whatever it is it make him feel scared right down into his bones."

"The day I weigh four pounds I'm gonna be that scared too," said Lewis.

"Day you figure out what you believe, you may do some shaking."

Rutha came out and said, "Merry Christmas, Miss Odetta. I see you learned to drive."

"I did, and a merry Christmas to you, child."

"Where's Honey at? He ain't sick, is he?"

"Scared," said Lewis. "Scared a Odetta's driving."

Odetta swatted his arm. "I drive better than you do, Lewis Brown."

"Let's hope so," said Rutha. "Now where we off to, Miss Odetta? I know we going somewhere. They don't come to you no more, you go to them?"

"This one can't come to me. It's a body needs laying out."

Rutha's hand flew to her mouth.

Lewis said, "Who is it?"

Rutha shook her head. "And no one said one word at church."

"It's a white man," said Odetta. "He got a different God, a different church. And he ain't news. He been dead a week."

"A week!" cried Rutha.

"Kept in a cooler. We'll do our work in there. But go on now, get what you need."

"Miz Jackson, I got a Christmas dinner to cook. The man's been gone a week, what's one day more? Can't he wait?"

"He can, but she can't."

"Get my overcoat," said Lewis. "You'll need that if you going to spend Christmas Day in a cooler."

"Who's he belong to?" asked Rutha, going into the house.

"Miz Dean. Her brother."

Odetta was little more than a fair driver, overall, and on corners she was poor to fair. The car was big and wide and must've been hard to steer. It didn't brake too well either. Rutha didn't blame the dog one bit. It lay under her seat and moaned. She would've got under there too if she could've fit. At one point it lost control and a terrible stench filled the car. Odetta said, "No matter how bad the stink of life, it beats the stink of death, don't it?" Rutha said nothing, just looked straight ahead. On the corners she closed her eyes and prayed to Jesus, though she hated to make Him work so hard on His own birthday.

Finally she said, "I didn't sleep good last night."

"Dreams?" asked Odetta.

"No ma'am. The haint came back. I couldn't sleep for a long while after that."

"You sent him away this time?"

"Went out to meet him is what I did."

"You did?"

"Un-hunh."

"Bet he don't like that."

"No, he don't."

"That's all you can do."

"I know it."

They passed right by Miss Dean's house. Rutha said, "You gone on by."

"How you know this place?"

"You sent me out here one time. Me and Roosevelt. We walked."

"I remember that." She kept on driving. "She own a café now. It's this one here on the right."

They pulled into the yard. There was no car there. Just a pack of mean-looking dogs. "This it?" asked Rutha.

"She said just a short bit after the house."

"Did she say blue?"

"No."

"This place sure is blue."

"What's that sign say?"

"What sign?"

"Sign right above Santa Claus. Right above his sled."

Rutha saw the letters and put her mind to them until they made the word *Etta's*. "Etta's," she said.

Odetta nodded. "That's what she said, Etta's."

"How'd you know I could read that sign?"

"Little bird told me. Name of Roosevelt Davis."

What business did Roosevelt bring to Odetta? Rutha wondered. "Is that the same little bird taught you to drive?"

But Odetta wasn't listening. She had her eye on the dogs. They had moved in from the edges of the yard and stood around the car, a few of them with their front paws up on the car. Honey quit his moaning and started to growl. He came out from under the seat, still covered with his own indignity, and went for the throat of the nearest big hound but the window stopped him. "You better wipe him down," said Rutha. She shooed him over to Odetta. "I don't care if it's better than the stink of death, I still don't want it all over me."

She got out and clapped her hands and all the mean-looking dogs slunk away from her, then bounded back, wagging their foolish tails. One of them, with a stumbly walk, looked so familiar to her she almost cried out, almost called it Chad. It was impossible. Old Chad would now be fifty years old. She went and got her bag from the back seat of the car. Lord, it weighed enough. What all did she have in there? A ball of wax, some string, two pennies, a yard of linen, a pair of good scissors, a nail file, cotton, a bottle of rosewater, a pocketknife, some sandpaper, a little hammer and a box of small nails, lipstick, talcum powder, pomade for the hair, rouge for the white folks, bobby pins, a piece of charcoal, a bar of Lux soap, Jergens lotion, a jar of lanolin, large curlers, small curlers, an electric iron (for clothes and hair), a washcloth, clean towel, roll of tin foil, chewing gum. She asked Odetta, "What would I be needing chewing gum for? I put it in here, now I don't know why."

"Takes the tension off. That's why I carry tobacco." She tucked her little dog under her arm, got out of the car.

"Where you taking *him?*"

"In."

"In?"

"I told you, he don't like the car."

"He got to like it better than being a big dog's dinner."

Odetta ignored that. "Get my bag, please."

They started across the yard, Honey shivering and whining in Odetta's arms. Rutha came behind, saying another prayer to

Jesus. And He did take them halfway over before the pack came in on them. Cool as could be, Odetta turned and told those big dogs "Shoo!" But they were curious, kept on circling round. Honey started growling and yapping. He was scared and wild as a little monkey. He wiggled free and jumped right down into the middle of all that mess. He showed his teeth and barked so hard he bounced. Odetta said for him to get right over here now. Rutha dropped her bags and went for him but he skittered away toward a couple of blue-skinned hounds. He growled at them, put his shoulders back, got his ruff up. He stood like a tiny horse on those delicate little legs. She could just imagine the sound of his bones breaking, the neck and those fine legs snapping like pole beans. Why, that whole dog could fit in a bowl. He could climb right into your pocket and sink to the bottom of it. What made him see the way he saw, blind to differences and dangers?

Someone shouted from the café and just like that the dogs cleared out. Except for one. Rutha saw Honey flatten down and fly at the legs of the straggler. It was the stumbly-walk dog. Honey got him and the old thing yelped, thought he'd got bit by a snake. He limped off out of the yard, started walking the road. He sure looked like old Chad, same black tip of the tail, same bald spot on his rear end.

Miss Dean called out, "That bat-eared fool dog of yours, Odetta. He can't always be counting on his good looks to save him."

"He don't need to," said Odetta. "He got you."

"Come in, come in. Bring him in here before he stirs them up again. Who's that you got with you?"

"It's Rutha," said Rutha.

"Rutha? Rutha Brown?"

"Yes ma'am."

"You all come in." She held the door open for them, gave Odetta a hug. "I remember that night like it was five minutes ago."

"What night?" asked Odetta.

"The night I met Rutha."

"Yes ma'am," said Rutha. "I do too."

"I never hear a word from Roosevelt no more. I guess he's all grown up now."

"He is."

"He think he is," said Odetta.

"You tell him hello for me. Will you do that, Rutha?"

"I will."

"He was so tiny."

Miss Dean looked bigger and whiter than Rutha remembered her. And older, though she was some years younger than Rutha. Of course she'd never seen her in broad daylight. She remembered one night when she came and picked up Roosevelt, took him to the cypress swamp. He came home talking about devil's eyes. "Devil's eyes?" asked Rutha. "What's wrong with you?" He started to cry, asked her if he had an uncle who was white. She said no, he didn't have no white uncle, no white aunt, nobody. He was colored. All them was colored. What'd he want a white uncle for? He told her he didn't want no white uncle. Just wondered if he had one. "You don't," she said. "Good," he said. That was all he said. And no more about the devil's eyes.

Miss Dean had a mess of black hair kept back in a braid. Rutha didn't remember all that hair. And she wasn't pure white. You could see that. She had Indian blood in her, same as Rutha.

"Ain't this a pretty place," said Odetta, looking around. "You done all this in one week?"

"Six days," said Miss Dean. "I just finished up the floor yesterday. Paint's still tacky over in the corner. I didn't expect to be open on Christmas Day. What all can I get you? I got Coke and ginger ale, cream soda, root beer. I'm making up a fresh pot of coffee now, and I got tea."

"I'll take coffee," said Rutha.

"You still like plenty of cream and sugar?"

"Yes ma'am. You remember that?"

"You run a café, that's all you remember, how they like their coffee."

"You didn't run no café till a week ago," said Odetta. "Six days. You always had a mind like that, Deedee. That's just the way you made."

"Put that dog down, Odetta. You see he's wiggling to get down?"

"Yeah, I do. But I don't want him to do his business inside. He like a place, he do his business there."

"I can't stand to see that dog wiggle. Put him down. Some business ain't going to sink this day. What are you drinking, Odetta? A nice hot cup of tea?"

"I'll take a Nehi."

"One Nehi and two sweet creamy coffees. Come look at this kitchen while you're on your feet. That's the cooler over there. That's where he's laying. Oh, my poor Floyd," she cried out. "I can't hardly believe it. I can't even cry tears for him."

"You will."

"I know they're in there. I just can't get 'em out."

"Miz Dean?" said Rutha.

"Call me Deedee, okay?"

"Deedee. Okay. You got some paper towel here? That dog already left his mess."

"I told you he liked the place," said Odetta. "You go and sit down, Deedee. Rutha and me'll get the coffee."

"Rutha'll clean up the mess," said Rutha, "then she'll get the coffee. Why don't both of you go on and sit down. Pretend like you're my customers. Go on."

They sat on their stools and Rutha heard Odetta say, "He got enemies? Someone he owe some money to? Or do you know did he put that thing where it don't belong?"

Deedee said, "I wish I knew."

"Don't wish that."

"I do wish it, Odetta. The way they took him out, you'd wish it too. You'll see. It'll make you want to—"

"No, it won't. It ain't the kind of thing you fight, it's the kind of thing you say, 'Well, that's over now. Let's keep on going.'"

"He ain't your kin."

"No, he ain't. My kin's long dead and gone, just about every one of them. Went the same way he did."

Deedee sighed. "I thought I'd call the sheriff in the morning."

"Sheriff know about it already. He come eat in your café, don't he?"

"No one's said one word in here. I won't allow it."

Odetta laughed. "Naw, they just wait till they get out in the yard. Deedee," her voice got soft, "it ain't easy to hide a dead man, and a dead man in a cooler, it ain't possible. Now that sheriff, if he'd a wanted to ask you something about it, don't you think he would have by now? He know all about it, things you never want to know. That Floyd's a jailbird, been in and out of there like it's a motel. He's no better'n a nigger to them. You look for justice it's going to be nigger justice."

"Aw, Odetta."

"That's what it's going to be."

Rutha brought the coffee in. "Miss Odetta," she said, "we got everything but Nehi."

"What do you recommend, seeing you ain't got Nehi?"

"Well, I like a root beer. We sell a lot of Co-Cola, too. Co-Cola's our most popular drink. After that come ginger ale. How am I doing?"

Deedee looked up and said, "You're doing so good I'm going to give you this place. The counter, the brand-new painted floor, these stools, that sign out there, and that damn cooler. You can have 'em all, Rutha. Take the whole place. Take the dogs too. Take the customers. This place is a morgue, it's the home of the dead."

Rutha said, "There's a dog in the yard looks an awful lot like Miz Detroit's dog Chad. The first Miz Detroit."

"It walk funny?"

"Yeah."

"I never seen that dog before."

"It's gone now. Took off down the road."

Odetta said, "I'm going to be a ghost soon if I don't get nothing to drink. What would Floyd a drunk, Deedee?"

"On a dare, anything you can think of. Any kind of liquor or anything else. Antifreeze. Antifreeze mixed with Dr Pepper, that was one of his stunts. Gasoline. I saw him drink that. Anything that might kill him quicker than ordinary life, that's what Floyd would a drunk. Have a Coke, Odetta."

"It bother my insides."

"Have a ginger ale then."

"I'll have a nice hot cup of tea."

Rutha went and put the water on to boil. She stood in that little kitchen and thought of Lewis all alone on Christmas. She should've looked in next door and asked Pearly and Osee to send the kids over, keep him company for a while. Eunice wasn't coming in till the evening. She was a grown-up woman by now, the oldest, with two of her own children, two twin boys. Eunice, Dallas, Clarence, Bernard, Roosevelt, Charlene, Daniel. One of them gone to his grave already, two over there in whatchamacallit, and one . . . what was he doing, exactly, Roosevelt? Walking out into the world and claiming it was his? She hoped he was right. She believed he was. It was his safety she prayed for, not the accuracy of his mind. She wondered if Deedee here had prayed for her brother's safety, prayed every day, knowing there was not one thing to do but pray. Pray and wait for him to live or die as the Lord saw fit. She guessed she had.

The water came up and she made a cup of weak tea—just a couple of dunks—and put a slice of lemon on the saucer and took it out. Miss Odetta was patting Deedee's hand, not saying a word, just patting her hand.

"You got a cold cup of coffee here," said Deedee. "Sit down and I'll get you some hot."

"I'll drink it cold," said Rutha. She sat down. "I like it cold."

"Where'd that dog go?"

"He's under the stove."

"That's where I'd like to be. I know we got to go in there and get him ready. But I do wish we could just be like Honey, sleep under the stove. Wake up and it'd be a dream. Wake up out of it into a regular Christmas."

"Have some of this," said Odetta. She slid a tin of tobacco to Deedee. Deedee pinched a wad into her cheek and slid it back.

They were quiet awhile. Rutha had been in such situations when the family, the loved ones, kept on talking, kept on telling their stories to bring the dead back to life. And in situations like this one, though they were rare, when there was nothing to say, not one word that would comfort or cure the sickness of grief and surprise. She had not heard how this man had died. She had not asked. It was not her custom to ask. She was there to do what experience had taught her, to perform the task of preparing the living for death, by preparing the dead. It was always a satisfaction. In the washing and dressing of bodies from which life had so clearly flown, those who continued to live in their body, who had to, saw something. It happened almost every time. They saw that death was an emptiness but not an end. They saw that life was also an emptiness and did not end in death. Bodies, cool to the touch and no longer elastic, had but an hour, a day, a week before been different bodies, busy with the inner chores of life. The notion of *absence* descended upon those who handled the dead, the sense that there was more than one country to be at home in, that there was more than one world. Yet there was only one world. There were worlds inside this world, and one of them was death. It was like this cup of coffee, sweet with sugar and light with cream. You couldn't separate it into coffee, cream, and sugar. You couldn't even separate it from the cup. If you did it would change its shape. Maybe it wouldn't be coffee anymore but a mess on the counter, a stain on a dress. This shape-changing was the only difference between the ones who grieved and the one they grieved for. To be so close to death themselves, to lay their hands on death and wash him and dress him and know he was their loved one and was not, this is what people needed and so rarely sought out. White folks in particular. They'd rather call Rutha to do it, close the door.

Cold coffee always strengthened her mind. She was ready

now. And that fellow was good and ready. "I'm going in there," she said. She stood up. "Take a look at what we got." It surprised her, that short walk to the cooler and all she was thinking about was Lewis. Not Lewis alone at home with the TV on, waiting for her to cook him his dinner, but Lewis as he would be one of these days, lying there like this man was now, the Lewis she'd be walking to someday to wash and dress him—to prepare him. And it surprised her: She was not the least prepared.

LONGBROW

1929

Lewis Brown had two men with him, one of them with a fresh wound on his cheek. They started looking that night and searched until sunup. Lewis's sister Cordelia brought out a field breakfast of corn cakes and venison sausage, a tall pot of coffee. The men went through it without talking, then they sat with their backs up against the blackened trees, smoking and resting.

Cordelia said, "That cut need tending, Abel."

Abel raised his head. "Un-hunh."

"You want to come back with me? I can give it a good washing and cut a bandage for it. It look like it ain't bled yet. A thing like that, it do better if it bleed."

"I'll come by once we found him."

"Who says you gonna find him?"

"If he's in here, we will."

"Who says he ain't asleep in his own bed?"

"He ain't."

"Them ones set this business slept the whole night long in their own bed."

"Ma'am?"

"Burn down your daddy's fields is what they trying to do."

"Miss Cordelia, we the ones set this business."

"How come it come back on you like it did? Come in behind you till y'all squeezed in like hogs in a pen?"

"Wind took it," said Lewis.

"Wind and a bunch a devils out there riding the road."

He got up. "If we ain't in before dinnertime, bring it here."

"If you ain't in before dinnertime, best you can do is pray for him." She gathered up the breakfast things. Before they left she said, "If he's out here he's down in the creek. If he got half the sense an animal got, that's where he'll be."

They came in at noon with Mr. Detroit and she put a fresh sheet on her own bed and put him in it. Lewis carried him like an armload of wood. The man's arms and hands were bad, and the eyes stood open like two empty drawers. The soles of his boots were burned thin. Lewis tended to him while she got dinner ready. She sent Abel in to tell him to come and eat.

"He say go on without him," Abel said.

"You and Jackson sit down." She went in herself and told Lewis, "You go on in there and eat. I'll watch him."

He had the man's shirt off him. He'd had to cut it off him. It was a mess of char and blood but he'd folded it like it was fresh laundry and laid it on the chair. He was wrapping the arms with a comfrey poultice she'd made up that morning. A cloth lay across the man's eyes. She said, "Ain't he got no one in that big house to tend him?"

Lewis said nothing. He had a sponge and he sponged the man's chest.

"He got a fever?"

"Un-hunh."

"Where'd you find him?"

"Down in the creek."

"After dinner I'll send Jackson on to the house. Maybe they'll come out here and get him in a motorcar."

Lewis shook his head.

"We can't keep him here!" she whispered. "Is that what you're thinking? Listen to me. He ain't ours to keep. He'll draw trouble to us, just like he already done."

"He didn't draw no trouble. Trouble fell on him same as us. It were the wind."

"This my house, Lewis. This my bed he laying in. He ain't laying in your bed." She thought a minute. "I won't even send Jackson. I'll go myself."

She fixed up Abel's face and set him and Jackson to work on the pump which hadn't been drawing good. She said she'd be back to feed them supper.

"Miss Cordelia," said Abel, "if it's like you say it is, it ain't a good time to be out on that road."

"Never mind that road. Ain't a road in this country fit for a Negro woman to walk on. Don't you know I know that?"

Back in the woods was the Negro road, a highway the width of a woman's shoulders. She ran along it toward town, raising up a red dust that settled on her calves and the skirt of her dress. She was tall as a man, Miss Cordelia Brown, taller than her brother Lewis and as wide as he was skinny. She had no man of her own and would not be looking for one any time soon, not until she couldn't split and carry her own wood or fix her own roof or kill her own rattlers in the yard. She was grateful to those boys for setting their minds to the pump, but she'd learn to fix her own pump before she'd set up house with a man, just to have him handy. She'd rule her own life as long as she could, and as long as she breathed air she would not work in a white man's house. She'd work in turpentine along with the men before she'd lay a white woman's table. She'd always worked alongside the men and outworked most of them in tobacco or cotton, and she could run a mule team good as any man, and go home at noontime and fix dinner and get a wash out and go back and work until dark.

And yet she ran along the Negro road, afraid. She ran like a field mouse under the shadow of the hawk. No matter how fast she went, that shadow rode her and rode her. She hated her fear and she hated her running and she stopped often and set her shoulder against a tree and waited for her heart to slow. Then she moved on toward the white man's house.

Geneva Nixon looked out the kitchen window and saw a big dark woman coming along the drive, old Chad following silent behind. That poor dog hadn't uttered a breath since Miss Caroline passed. He followed close with his head and tail down. The woman paid him no mind, just kept on coming like Mr. Detroit's motorcar. Geneva had a big belly on her—her second child—and her feet were swolled up like two melons. She called out to Aunt Annie who was full-blind now but could hear just as good as anyone, and Aunt Annie called out to Miss Rachel the cook, and Miss Rachel told the new girl, Rutha, to go on out there see what that woman was after, and Rutha went. She stepped out and stepped back in and said, "Why, it's no one but my Lewis's sister." Then she burst into tears.

"Go on and see what she wants," Miss Rachel said.

Rutha went out again. She was crying and trembling. It was bad news the woman brought, even blind Aunt Annie could see that. Geneva at the window could see that and she put a hand over her belly to shield the child. The woman came on and Rutha went to meet her. They were close to the same size, and next to them old Chad looked like a rag blown loose off the laundry line. He went to Rutha and picked up his head, which meant he was ready for feeding time. The stranger woman stopped and said, "That dog oughtta be taken out of his misery."

Rutha said, "Tell me it ain't Lewis."

The woman nodded at the dog. "See the way he looking at you?"

"Just tell me it ain't."

"It ain't. Look at him looking at you."

"He just hungry," said Rutha.

"Naw. He wanting you to send him on."

"I can't kill no dog!"

The stranger woman shrugged her shoulders. "He still gonna ask it."

They came up to the kitchen door but the woman wouldn't come inside. She was covered with dust and she'd walked all the way from Magnolia. Geneva brought her a glass of water. She'd never seen the woman before but the woman told her, "This your second child."

"Yes ma'am."

"Something you afraid of?"

"No ma'am. I ain't afraid of nothing with this one. Just my feet swoll up."

The woman nodded and handed her the empty glass. "That's good water."

Miss Rachel fixed a plate of food for her but the woman wouldn't touch it. She was a strange woman. She had a man's hands and a scar at the base of her throat that looked like an arrowhead. She told about the burning, about Mr. Detroit laid out on her own bed and Lewis tending him. She said she needed a fresh set of his clothes and a motorcar and someone to drive it.

"You looking to dress a man or a body?" asked Aunt Annie.

"I told you, my brother's with him."

"I ain't asked who's with him."

"He'll live. 'Less someone come out there and burn down my house with him in it."

"Don't say such a thing!" said Rutha.

"What all made this fire go wild?" asked Geneva.

Aunt Annie said, "Ain't you heard the wind, girl?"

"There weren't no wind at my house."

"You got a man in your bed, ain't never any weather."

"Man in my bed! He don't fit in my bed. Look at the size of me!"

But the stranger woman said, "It weren't the wind. It were men set that fire."

"That's right," said Miss Rachel. "It were men. It were Mr. Detroit and your brother and that other help they got. That's what they go out to do and that's what they done. Burning. The wind gets up it look like the devil hisself come to pay a visit."

"It were the devil hisself," said the stranger. "It were a bunch a devils."

"These devils," said Miss Rachel, "what business they got burning a white man's land? You mean they given up on the Negroes?"

"Negroes ain't got land," said the stranger woman. "The only land they got is what they borrow. They borrow it and work it till someone come along and burn them out, then they still gotta pay their rent on it, crop or no crop."

"Abel Davis lose his crop?" asked Rutha.

"About half. His boy almost lost his left eye too."

Miss Rachel said, "They set the whole plantation on fire to get at one sharecropper's fields? That don't make sense."

"He ain't a friend to them," said the woman. She was lifting her feet up like she was walking on hot coals.

"Who ain't?" said Miss Rachel.

"He ain't." She nodded at the house.

"Mr. Detroit ain't a friend to who?"

"Them devils. They see he got his Negroes living right here in his own house."

"They ain't fond a Yankees," said Aunt Annie, "but they ain't never tried to burn one down."

Geneva said, "I don't like this talk. I'm going in and sit down."

Aunt Annie said, "You go with her, Rutha, before she scare that child right out of her. Make her soak them feet." Rutha went and Aunt Annie called after her, "Gather up some of Mr. Detroit's clothes."

The stranger woman said, "That dog there ain't fit to be around no child, born or unborn."

Aunt Annie said, "That's all he got left, that dog a hers. He'd put me down 'fore he'd put down that dog." She laughed and shook her head. "Look at me, just an old slave woman who can't see no more how far she come and how far she got left to go. Every morning on my way down I count the stairs, and every evening I count 'em on my way up. Same every morning and same every evening. But one day they gonna fool me. They gonna be one more or one less and that's when I know my time is come, 'cause that's the only thing I got that don't move around on me. Everything else move all around and upside down and one day we working for nothing 'cause we ain't no one, and the next day we someone, working the same work we always done, but now they only give us enough to buy half a meal and half a bed and half a roof and half a life, when in slave days we got all that. We got all that like we was children. Like we was the dog here. We was worth money is what it was. We was like that motorcar out there. You pay your money for a thing like that and you feed it and wash it and put it inside at night, or you might as well throw your money in the road. I know about money." She laughed again. "I been watching it all this time and I seen what it don't do and what it do do, and I seen him all tangled up in it like a fish in a net. His daddy never was like that. No, it come from his mama. He can't get away from it. He don't even know he want to. But he don't like it. He don't respect it. He just learning that now. I guess that's what he's doing laying there on your bed, laying there thinking about something he don't think about here in this big old empty house. I seen him born," said Aunt Annie. "He weren't born here but I seen him in a dream that night he was born. That was the beginning of my blindness."

The dog got up out of the shade of the house and came toward the women, sniffing the air. "He smell the master on me," said the stranger.

"He just an old slave like me," said Aunt Annie. She said to the woman, "I ain't heard your name."

"It's Cordelia."

"Well, Cordelia, however long it take you to get here, it gonna take you to get back home. The only motorcar we got went out with him yesterday. He didn't say nothing about when he'd be back, just said he was helping Lewis with the fire. Was they on the north end or the south end?"

"North end. North of Cullis Jones."

"The barn and horses, they all gone?"

"I ain't been there to look. I come here soon as they found him and brung him in. He can't stay in my house."

"He can't go nowhere neither," said Miss Rachel. "Not till his sister come."

"When's his sister come?"

"We never know till she get here."

"Ain't there no doctor can come get him?"

"Could be. Long as the rain holds off and that road don't wash out."

"If you scared a them devils," said Aunt Annie, "and them devils is after him like you say, best you can do is leave him out there and you stay here with us. Miss Mary she be by in a day or two. That's his sister. She come down to be with him, and she gonna bring us a motorcar. Now, smell that?" She held her face in the air, flared her nostrils. "It's fixing to rain. It'll rain good and wash away that devilry."

"Don't know about no devilry," said Miss Rachel. "It'll sure enough wash away the road."

"Devil need a road," said Aunt Annie. "These days he do. Now when I was a girl, seemed like the devil was young and strong, not lazy like he be today. He didn't need no road. He didn't need no wagon. He didn't need no horse nor mule. He walked on his own two feet like we do, walked all over, spreading his mischief. He was alone. Then the freedom time come along and he was never alone after that. He was scared to walk alone, so he found other devils and walked with them, and then they all got up on horses so they could walk faster, and wagons so they could go longer and farther and spread their mischief to all kinds a people, people who didn't expect the devil to be coming down the road looking for them when they done nothing but raise up their heads and say, 'This my life now.' Well, these days we got a different kind a devil. He go by motorcar if he can, or he sit still and wait for you to come to him. He own everything, so he know sooner or later you gonna come to him. This a different kind a devil alright. That other devil, I could meet him and keep my head up and say a word or two as I passed by. This one. This one sit in his motorcar with the window rolled up and he don't let me see his face, he don't let me see who all's in there and how many he think it gonna take to bring down one old blind woman like me."

"Ain't you afraid?" asked Cordelia.

"Afraid? Afraid a what? What can this devil do to me? Nothing he ain't already done."

"You living here in a white man's house, that don't make you afraid?"

"I lived around white folks all my life. They some good ones, they some bad ones, same as colored."

Cordelia shook her head. "I don't understand 'em."

"You ain't been around enough of 'em."

"I keep away from 'em."

"That's what make you afraid."

Miss Rachel said, "You better get on back home if you're going. Or come inside if you're staying. Come on in out of the rain, Aunt Annie, 'less you going on to Magnolia too."

"Magnolia don't want me," said Aunt Annie.

Just then Rutha came steaming up to the door, her face all popped out with perspiration. "She gonna have her baby right there on the floor!" She pushed a bundle of clothes at Cordelia.

"No she ain't," said Miss Rachel. "She gonna have her baby in a bed. This house got plenty of beds." She went on inside.

"It's coming!" said Rutha. "It's coming quick!"

"Boil up a pot of water," Aunt Annie told her. "Boil up two or three. I don't like it," she shook her head. "The ones in a hurry coming in, they the same ones in a hurry going out." She turned to Cordelia to tell her go and help Miss Rachel get Geneva comfortable, but even with her old blind eyes she could see that woman was gone.

HENRY DETROIT

1929

Blindfolded as he was, he could not judge time, and the need for it came on him like a great thirst. Over and over again he asked Lewis what time it was and the answer came always in increments of gray, until there was no gray left in the sky but darkness, and time became equal to his own blindness and therefore ceased.

Lewis brought him food he could not eat and bathed him with cool water and vinegar. He did not sleep but floated above himself, anchored by the smell of meat and ashes—his own smell. The room was close. He tried, with what he recognized as his tongue, to beg for air.

At last he dreamed of the French girl, the nanny, her dark hair shining like olives, her thick calves, ankles nonexistent. She had a smudge of fur across her top lip and the hair in her armpits bushed out darkly against her white uniform. He woke and Lewis held something to his lips, thin and oaty. He took it in.

After that, when sleep wouldn't come, nor dreams, he lay awake and remembered. His son, sitting in his nanny's lap, reaching for his mother in the car ahead. The French girl inconsolable, hugging the child while he himself felt nothing, was aware only of his duty to follow the hearse at an accurate distance, not crowding it. This required all his attention, for which he was numbly thankful.

He suspected they'd had to dynamite the ground—he did not ask. It was the first bitter week of January, a winter as cold as any he could remember. He did not feel the sun though he saw it coating the snow and the bare black tar of the road. The hearse slowed and stopped and he did the same, knowing he was expected to step out of the car into the cold blank world that awaited him. He felt unprotected and unprepared, a man whose bones are exposed, whose teeth chatter so violently they break the glassy hush of the grave. His sister Mary appeared at his window and he cracked it open but did not move nor consider moving from behind the wheel. She passed in a cigarette, one of her Pall Malls, and said, "Dearest. Whenever you're ready." She walked back to the car behind and got in beside her husband Chauncey.

He shared the cigarette with the French girl and did not mind the intimacy, did not see any way around it, did not care. Finally he took the baby from her and held him close, let himself enjoy the softness of the boy's cheek and the milky smell of his head. The girl said, "He must have his hat on before we go. It will be a long time in the cold, no?"

"I hope not."

"I have never felt it so cold. It is better, I think, we live in the plantation. The baby is happier there. He can play outside in nature."

He said nothing. The girl dressed Tim in hat and mittens and zipped him up and they were ready. The boy seemed excited, almost elated, babbling away in his nurse's arms, and he wondered, suddenly, why he hadn't heeded his sister and left the girl and the baby at home. Mary joined them, Chauncey walking behind, tall and lean and inclined slightly forward like a native porter bearing on his back the memsahib's burdens. They made their way to the graveside where the sight of the coffin suddenly made Tim cry. Mary took him but he kicked at her and screamed until his whole tiny body convulsed and she quickly gave him up to his father, who passed him to his nurse.

Two days earlier he'd stepped off the train in Washington D.C. to smoke on the platform, one of the girl's terrible harsh Gaulois. The night solemn and cold around him, the unfamiliar heat in his lungs. He'd glanced at the back of the train, the baggage car that housed his wife. It struck him fully then, the full force of it for the first time.

She had been a pretty smoker. He'd enjoyed watching her handle a cigarette. A cigarette and a glass of gin fit nicely in her hand. The other hand talked to people, had talked to him the first time he saw her, at dusk across a swimming pool. What had it said, that hand? Only that she was bored. That she was young and hopeful and already bored. *Come talk to me,* it said. *Come deliver me from Chauncey Chubb's wan soliloquy or I will go mad.*

And so he had. Sent Chauncey packing off to Mary who was lost in a corner with some old beau. Caroline thanked him. She was twelve years younger than he and not the slightest bit interested in marriage. To *anyone,* she emphasized. Within three months they were engaged, and three months later married. And yet she had foretold the truth: Marriage interested her not at all. She seemed as dulled and bored by it as any party. Was there something, he wondered, to which she might react with love and energy? A child, surely. But when the child arrived she was listless, depressed. She called the little one her jailer. When she cried at night "I have no maternal instincts!" he held her and quieted her and assured her she did, of course she did, they would come in time, they would come.

But he guessed they would not. And the nanny had instincts enough for all of them, maternal and otherwise. She was a bosomy girl of seventeen, passing as twenty-one. Her hair was dark and smelled of olives, and it inspired in him a great laziness, a desire not to think about the months to come. Timmy would need her now more than ever. He would ask Mary what to do.

Sleep came, dreamless, and while he slept Lewis went away and a woman came. Her breath was hot and she bathed him roughly and pulled the pleasant darkness from his eyes. Light came in, shapeless light. He struggled, thrashed his head until she laid a clean cloth on him. She dressed him in clean clothes that smelled of bleach and tobacco.

"Where you been?" she said.

He could not imagine an answer. But across the room a man said, "Me and Lewis went down and found the horses. Fire took the barn. Musta took that old mare belong to Miss Caroline. That old Alabama."

"Mules too?"

"We ain't seen no mules."

"They gone back in the woods is where they gone."

"Miss Odetta, there ain't no woods."

He'd lost all direction to the fire and around him everywhere was partial devastation, yet enough living fuel to call a firestorm back to him. He walked forward. Silence, like thick brown layers of cloth. He thought the flame had deafened him until from the low wet haven of a creek a deer whistled, then crashed upward out of the ooze that stank of rot and hid clusters of cottonmouths, he knew, yet it had saved the life of the animal and would save his if he stayed with it. The deer fled, white tail bobbing against the black ruin.

And the fire did come back on itself that night with a hunger. Like some fat wildness with appetite insatiable for its own flesh. Tearing off its own shoulder, howling and cracking in pain then turning to devour its own belly. He had not thought of the noise of the fire as the pain of the fire, but the staggered screaming of trees came to him—though he lived little in his imagination most days. He was ever afterward willing to admit the sentience of everything he touched. This changed him, charged his life with an edge of madness.

He met other dumbstruck men in those woods, though some were dreams and delirium. He followed the creek and heard in its slow stutter the babble of a wild clear stream, the trout-grounds of a younger man who looked like—was it?—himself. When orchards swept Long Island and the ground gave off the scent of fruitwood, roots scrabbling downward to infect the soil with acidic sweetness. Stumbling through raspberries, his bamboo rod held high as if to lure the sky closer, wet to the waist and a creel full of brookies. The boy stops and kneels, forgets fishing, fills his mouth with a taste so red and tart he feels stung by bees. Then the sweetness afterward. That day's lesson seared in his mind: *Look everywhere. Turn around. Look. See.*

One man wore a pink gash on his cheek. From his hair black blood poured in cupfuls. He squatted and washed in the creek and looked up at Henry with doe's eyes, then fled in terror, his bare black feet shining.

Another rowed the little creek stiffly, back and forth from bank to bank though it was but an armspan across. Another held a slab of ham to his face with his fists.

The night deepened and spread out through the trees. The sounds at the edge came to him like sharp stones pelting his face. His arms and hands felt like he had beaten himself with a rope. He sniffed his wrist and the meaty warmth of it frightened him, a flaying he could not remember. He lay down in the creek with a longing for snow. Pines worth good money smoking above him and the smell of caramel breaking his waves of nausea. The fire burning itself out now, darkness imprisoned like black sheets behind bars of flame. He lay on his back and felt the possibility of snakes and the certainty of clay clothing him in a cool red silt. He let his face go under and sucked in water between his teeth. Raised up again, let his tired head float and felt winter come for him at last.

ROOSEVELT DAVIS

1969

The way the sun caught in the clouds made it look like the barn was on fire and Roosevelt hurried up the road past the kennel, knowing he'd feed after, on his way home. They barked in a lazy way, disinterested—they knew him too well. He could see flames leaping out of the new hay, baled and stacked four times his height (he'd stacked it himself). But it was the sun, a beautiful illusion that made his heart pound. He stood in the many shafts of light that suddenly fell downward and asked the source of that light to steady his hand, to create a clean death. He was no Christian—not in the way others were. Books led away from an easy belief to a more difficult faith, which was growing in him as he stood. The shotgun in his hand seemed strange to him. The same gun Dallas had used to change the life of everyone who knew him. It seemed unnecessary, the gun, for soon enough and without it the old horse would go. He would walk to the high end of the pasture, bend his knees to the earth, and let his head go down for the last time, the milky eyes open but blind. The gun was but a bucket of cool water, Roosevelt knew, from which another old man might drink, drink and wander to his own death feeling done with death, sated, feeling merciful and complete.

He turned to the pasture and saw the horses bunched by the trees at the far end. Mules too. He set the gun against the barn and filled the manger with hay and spilled two pails of oats in the trough. Two shells in his pocket. Two in the gun. Three more than he'd need. He called the horses in. They came steady and slow, swaying from side to side like cows. Old man Cotton came as far as the hayrack and stopped there, lifting his long blind head to death. Roosevelt walked out to him with the halter in one hand, feed bag in the other. But an old horse was not a dog and Cotton spun away from capture, the easy promise of a full belly. He leaned against the air as if pushing it aside to make room for his own last fast walk through it, and Roosevelt stood looking after him.

Alright. He would wait. The horse had gone to where he intended to lead him anyway. Mr. Detroit had insisted it be there, at the high point. The gun was back at the barn and he went to get it. He saw the way the ground had darkened, how the shadows had swum together. He should have come earlier—he could have, but it was Christmas. The horses were drinking, noisily pulling water through their long lips. So different from dogs. And the patience of the mules feeding at the trough, looking up from their grain to gaze at him. Huge box heads and Oriental eyes, blowing through their nostrils, turning to feed again. He liked it. He liked the clean grassy smell of the animals. Their manure. The great size and strength of their bodies.

The gun was not there where he'd left it, pointed to the sky.

She was not ten yards away, sitting under the live oak. "Hey," she called. She was wearing a pink dress and the gun lay across her lap. "Look what I got. Hey, I know you. You're Roosevelt, right? You work for my daddy."

"That's right," said Roosevelt, wondering had he flicked the safety on? He hadn't. He felt the barn wall close at his back.

"When I do this," said Brenda, stroking the barrel, "if I close my eyes it feels so soft and silky. It's pretty. It's pretty to touch. Mama says all guns is ugly and bad but this one's not. This one's pretty. You're Roosevelt."

"Un-hunh," he nodded. "Brenda, you put that down now. Put it down."

"But I like to touch it. Daddy don't let me touch his guns."

He moved toward her as slow as he knew how. "What kind of guns he got, your daddy?"

"You mean what are their names?"

"Yeah. What are their names?"

"I don't know all their names. I know he's got one like this 'cause I seen him do this before." She lifted the gun and started to fit it to her shoulder and Roosevelt said, "Wait now, Brenda."

"No, *you* got to wait, Roosevelt," she laughed. She held the stock in her armpit, the barrel pointed at his knees. "We'll play a game. You don't come no closer now till I say so. Ready?"

He nodded.

"Good. Now come closer."

He took a step to the side.

"That's *side*ways!" she cried. "This's a game Daddy plays with Mama. Won't you play it with me, Roosevelt?"

"I'll play it with you. But first you got to help me."

"Help you?" She looked at him suspiciously, then she laughed. "You don't need no help."

"I do. I need your help."

"No you don't. It's a trick!" she cried. "Look out, I got the gun on you! It's a pretty gun. The gun don't like to be tricked."

She held the barrel steady at his knees. Her hands had not yet found the trigger but he guessed she knew of it, knew where it would be, knew how to use it and knew nothing of what it could do, what it could end and begin. He eased his way forward. She looked at him in disbelief. "That's not the game!" she cried. "That's not the game, Roosevelt!" Startled now by her own duty to do something, she didn't know what. He saw her arm move, her hand slide backward on the barrel, the trigger there within reach if she wanted it, and he did what his body told him, which was to open his mouth and talk. "You like to read?" he said. "I like to read. What books you reading now, Brenda?"

"You're not supposed to move! And don't talk!"

"I like to read 'cause I can go somewhere, I can go all over the world without moving. I can go back in time, or into the future, and I can go into other people's minds and find out what they're thinking, find out what they're like."

"I don't care!" she cried. But the barrel drooped and she said, "The girl captured by Indians is the book I like."

"I like that book too."

"You know it?"

He nodded. He was almost within reach of her.

"Mama read it to me and then I grew up and read it myself. She likes the Indians. And they like her. And then she has to go back."

"To her people?" said Roosevelt.

"To her family," Brenda nodded. "But she runs away from them and back to the Indians. Then she marries an Indian. Then the Indians kill her family. It's sad, but then she has babies."

He reached and took the shotgun from her and she seemed hardly to notice. "How many babies she have?"

"Sixteen!"

"A lot of babies."

"Un-hunh."

He broke the gun and took the shells out and put them in his pocket. He said to Brenda, "How we going to find these Indians?"

"Find them?" She laughed. "That's not the way it works, Roosevelt. They got to find you!"

"They always got to find you?"

"'Course they do!"

"Well, I guess I already got some Indians."

"You do? No, you don't. You're tricking me again!"

"These Indians came to me when I was just about your age."

"They captured you?"

"Took me out to the swamp."

Brenda's eyes widened. "They tried to kill you?"

"Tried to tell me something, that's what she did."

"It was a *lady?*"

"In all kind of ways, it was."

"Where you going, Roosevelt?"

He took the gun and put it in the tack room and saw it was almost dark, knew he'd have to be using it in the dark. "Let's take you home," he said.

"But I don't want to go home."

"You stay out here you'll get captured by Indians."

"I will?"

"Un-hunh."

"Well, I'll go with you."

They walked up the road together and she was quiet until the end. "What're you doing with that gun, Roosevelt?"

"I've got to put old Cotton down."

"The horse?"

He nodded.

"You mean kill him?"

He nodded again.

She shook her head and said, "I don't know why can't they just let him die."

"'Cause he's too old."

She looked at him like he had spoken a great mystery, which in fact he had. The sense of it eluded him as well. He watched her into the yard (and never would set foot in there again by his own choice). She turned at the door and called to him, "What did she try and tell you, that lady?"

"She tried to tell me you got to go away before you can come back. You got to leave your own people sometimes, to find your own people."

"That's all?"

"That's all."

"Well, thank you for playing with me," said Brenda. "It ain't much fun, Christmas."

Just before darkness came in earnest, the horse lowered his head to the gun and allowed Roosevelt to take his life. The great body seemed at first unmoved by the explosion, then the first tremor came, and the second, and a last violent shaking before the forelegs buckled and the shoulders went down, pitching the head sideways onto the earth. A groan came from the throat, from mouth and nostrils the frothy blood, and Roosevelt thought of Dallas, for the first time thought of him as a man killed not by his own hand but by a world that raised him up and used him up and stood before him with the gun. He had lowered his head to the gun, Dallas had. He had gone down quiet and taken no one with him. Like a good horse, a noble horse. You couldn't call nobility in an animal cowardice in a man.

He walked back across the field of shadows, the shot still ringing in his ears, and he knew he would never again allow himself to be used this way, to create another's death. Anyone could kill. A child could kill. It was what you did with your own death, when death stood in front of you, or sat in front of you in a dirty dress under a live oak. It was what you did then and said then, whether you bargained or quit, walked toward it or ran. You were most alive then, standing in front of your death. It watched you. All your life it watched you. And finally you were alive as you would ever be, watching it back.

LEWIS BROWN

1969

Lewis had the whole long holy day to think on what he believed, and he sat down at the kitchen table intending to turn his mind in that direction. But it was an old man's mind, full of gravel, full of foolish starry shapes and dusty roads untraveled and the weak cry of birds at dusk and the *caw-caw* of crows in the morning. And blackbirds seemed to fall from above as he sat, and a heat touched his legs, and a hunger came over him. He pushed himself up and found an old brick of yellow cheese and an old slab of cornbread the size of a book. He sat down again and ate, and drank a jar of colored water, sugar and Nescafé. He believed in blackbirds, yes he did. Now, was that enough? That might be enough. But oughtn't he think on it until he could say why?

Flocks of them in every corner of the sky. And all through the middle too. Birds so thick you felt pressed down by them, and then just as suddenly they came, they went. They had a sharp, uneven twittering, and when they settled in the trees and rose up out of them they twittered ceaselessly and seemed to lift the branches right up with them. Oh, to raise your gun up into that vast commotion. Empty both barrels: drop a dozen. And in your hand they were nothing much, but no one just like another either, each of them its own weight, its own story dressed up in feathers. And that was what he believed.

Satisfied, he stepped out onto the porch, sat down in his chair, and closed his eyes, resting. *Blackbirds,* he'd tell Odetta. *Blackbirds!* she'd say. Why, Lewis Brown, that must be what fill that head a yours. Rutha! We got a man here say he believe in blackbirds, and Rutha'd say, Well, that's right, Miz Jackson. That's my Lewis. That's my man. That's all the reason I marry him, Miss Odetta. On account a them blackbirds.

They living inside his head! say Odetta.

Worse things live in a man's head, his Rutha say.

Like what?

Like ghosts. Like human ghosts.

And he rests his eyes and thinks back on the time when ghosts was all there was, and the poor head of Mr. Henry Detroit was dancing with ghosts, crying with ghosts, the poor heart of Mr. Henry Detroit. He went and got himself another wife and child then, and then another child, and Lewis, though he'd longed for that, had never had it. It was a sorrow to him, to him and Rutha too. And this also he believed: You did not tell the Man upstairs what you wanted, you saw what you got and wanted that. Now Rutha, she'd gone away from that. She'd gone a different road. She done her walking and her talking and her wanting. But it didn't bring her no child, did it? Did it? She'd learned her letters now, and she could speak just as good and hard and loud as she could always sing. She sang to Jesus. She loved her Jesus. But now she told Him what He could do for her (Lewis had heard her prayers). And there was Roosevelt. He was her child. Soon he'd be a grown man and all the rest of it, and he'd come and be company to her, play her a game of Crazy Eights or watch the TV. Did he know that? He ought to know that. Lewis would tell him. That he was her child.

He heard a *clump clump clump* on the steps and opened his eyes to Charlene with her big old overalls on. She always did go for overalls. She had a shiny new chain around her neck, tucked into the bib, and he said, "Lemme see what you got there," and held his hand out like she was a wild animal come to be killed or tamed.

"Daniel give me the chain." She fished it up and flipped it outside her overalls. Dog tags, and something Lewis had never seen before, a circle with what looked like a bird's foot inside it.

"What's that all about?" he asked.

"It's a peace sign. Ain't you never seen a peace sign?"

"What all's it mean?"

"It means peace."

"It means we gonna get some peace, or we gonna give some peace?"

The girl considered. "Give. We gonna give some."

"That's how we get some," said Lewis. He felt like an old, old man, almost done with answers, and full of questions. "Least that's what I hear."

The girl put the chain behind her overalls again and told him, "They called. They want you to come up. They all going out somewhere and ask could you come up and sit with him. They ask for Aunt Rutha, I told 'em she gone out and it was only you." Lewis said nothing and the girl said, "I didn't tell 'em you would, I told 'em you might."

"You go on and tell them I'll be there. Fast as I can get there I'll be there." He stood up slow. "And that smart mouth a yours ain't no good. It don't do no one no good. You got a smart head, you oughtta put that in front, put that mouth behind. You want to give Dallas some peace, you put that mouth behind. He done some things he wished he hadn't of, but he was a good clean boy inside. He had respect. Someone come and say, This what I need, he give it to them. He don't say, Oh maybe he give it to them. He give it to them. You standin' in his shoes, those big old boots a his, you oughtta know what that mean, walk in his boots. He's tryin' to tell you what it mean. Just you ain't ready to listen."

"I'm all ready to listen," she said. She hooked her thumbs on her pockets and clomped on down the steps. At the bottom she told him, "Just maybe I don't hear what you hear." And she clomped on home.

He shook his head. He should have told her a merry Christmas at least. He went on inside and put his church clothes back on, looked a little while for his good overcoat, then remembered he'd given it to Rutha. He wondered was she wearing it now, and was she thinking of him as she did whatever she did (he truly didn't know) to bring a body closer to its grave, to bring the body and the grave together—so often people tried to keep them apart. And this one stuck in a cooler. . . . A chill went through him—not of cold, but a sense of the violence of the end—and then a car horn honked. He looked out the window and there was Miss Frankie come to get him. She was parked right where Odetta had parked. Seemed like it was a day for the ladies.

She stood at the bottom of the steps (that was manners) while he came out and closed the door behind him, stepped across the porch feeling like a dressed corpse himself in those fancy clothes.

"Wow," she said. "You look great."

He laughed.

"You do. You really do."

"My church clothes," he admitted.

"Oh, Lewis, they're wasted on church!"

"Everyone got their own way to go to church, Miss Frankie." And he thought of the blackbirds.

They got in the car. He knew better than to try and open her door for her, like a gentleman—she'd just holler. It was a small car, the smallest car he'd ever sat in, and his legs were bunched up in front of the dashboard. He could almost rest his chin on them.

"Go ahead and slide your seat back," she told him. She showed him how and he flew back like he'd had all the air knocked out of him and they both laughed. She got the car turned around and he took one look back at the house and surprised himself thinking about his sister Cordelia. She'd passed away ten, fifteen, twenty years ago, he couldn't remember, but she stood in his door now and motioned him to go on. She had a basket of walnuts in one hand and the other hand shooed him down the road.

Miss Frankie drove fast and too far over in the ditch, turning her head to talk to him, two fingers on the steering wheel. "I'm sorry about this, Lewis," she said. "I mean, to get you out on Christmas. I was against it."

"It don't matter," he said.

"No, it does. It does matter. You wouldn't get us out on Christmas. Or any other day," she added.

"Well. That might be so."

"It is so."

"It don't matter," he repeated. "You got the corner coming here, Miss Frankie."

She moved the wheel an inch and they went slopping around. She didn't slow down and Lewis wondered if he didn't believe in that too, the body flying through space to arrive among other bodies, ignoring the curves in the road like they were just so many unborn wishes. Of course there were curves you couldn't see. You were curving all the time, Roosevelt had explained to him. You go from here to there, you go to Tallahassee, you look like you travel a straight line, you feel like you travel a straight line, but you don't, you know you don't, 'cause you're still bound to the earth and ain't the earth round? To move was to bend. Now, that's what he believed. *Odetta,* he'd say, *forget them blackbirds. To move is to bend.* He'd stand by it.

Miss Frankie was saying, "Papa wouldn't go. He'd think it was a ridiculous waste of time. He was like an old bear, Lewis. Well, *was?* Was, I guess. He's not like an old bear now. He's not like anything. But he was like a bear, a hibernating bear. You couldn't get him out of the house to go anywhere, even before he got sick. He'd hibernate all year round if he had his way, never set foot out the door. For sure not to go to some dumb cocktail party to sit and listen to all the old alcoholic biddies flatter him. This is Dad's idea. This is so Harry. To drag us all out to make an appearance." She dropped one wheel into the ditch and out again. "He couldn't be flattered, could he, Lewis? Papa."

"No. I reckon he couldn't."

She roared on over the bridge at Bully Creek. Lewis looked down. Mighty little water.

"He was easy to admire, though, wasn't he?"

"He was. He was easy to look up to."

She went quiet and Lewis settled against the seat, craving rest and feeling released. It wasn't long they climbed the hill past the kennel, the dogs strangely still as statues, waiting for food and an end to their idle day. But it was wrong, their stillness. They didn't throw themselves against the fence or chase their tails or utter a cry, and though Miss Frankie didn't pay no notice, Lewis stiffened, wondering.

At the top of the hill he marveled at the way the house rose up out of the tall grasses and pines, out of all this good hunting land, and seemed at home in it. Seemed not to master it but to disappear into it, in this way calling attention to the land itself, which was the jewel, the way no house could ever be. He had never, not once, arrived here by the front driveway, and it stirred him to see it.

Of course she sprayed gravel all over the porch and the good green grass under the live oak tree. The tree was doing poorly, casting a poor shade, many of its branches dying or dead already. But it was this that grew the grass, thought Lewis. A healthy live oak often rules a patch of bare ground. Miss Frankie got out—only then did he know they were not still moving. He got out too and she came around the car and told him, "We won't be long, Lewis. Those guys already went over. It won't be more than an hour. Maybe two." She rubbed her forehead. "Oh, God. I hope not more than that. I've got to get Seth. Then we're off. But Mars won't want to leave Papa for long." She started toward the house and Lewis followed her. "This thing's at the Moynihans', this shindig. They've got an art deco indoor pool, otherwise I wouldn't go at all. Seth?" She opened the door and he slid his hat off and followed her inside, cool and dark as a tomb, the brick hallway. The boy came from the kitchen, eating a piece of cake. Lewis smelled the caramel—Geneva's best cake. The boy ate from his own hand, without a plate. Miss Frankie said, "Look at the mess you're making. There's icing all over the floor."

The boy shrugged. "Man'll get it."

"How did the dog get in here?"

"Papa wanted him. I went and got him."

"Mars'll have a fit."

"He's okay. He's not on the bed."

"Still, you should clean that up. In case Man doesn't get to it."

"He'll get to it. And if he doesn't, that's why we have servants."

"You're a pig, Seth. You know that?"

The boy only laughed, and Lewis guessed there wasn't much he didn't know about how to light a fire under Miss Frankie. He'd always been a boy who liked the heat of destruction, who stood at the edge of things then suddenly ran to the center, touched a torch to the ground, then ran away again and hid in the woods. It was easy not to like him and most people didn't. But Lewis found him too predictable to cause much bother. Inside himself he was a sad boy, not bedeviled as Rutha thought but sorrowful and lost to the world like so many his age. They wanted the world to make room for them, to move over and leave a place for them and teach them how to fill it. Well, it didn't go that way, the world. Whatever you got you got. And some would say there was ways to get more than where you started but Lewis didn't believe it, he never had. It was all inside, and there wasn't no one gonna move over, and there wasn't a whole lot of teaching gonna happen that wasn't already waiting inside you to be uncovered and learned. Rutha thought different. Lot of people did. But Lewis was older than all that and he thought the way he thought and that was good enough for him.

He hadn't seen the boy in some time. A year or two. He hadn't grown taller, but more narrow. His face was thinner. His lips were two thin lines. He squinted and worked his brow when he spoke, like he was trying to make out something in the dark. He was delicate as a girl and knew it, and all the lit fires and orneriness could not change it. His hair was thin and straight and cut close to his head—not one of those longhairs. It made his forehead look wide and empty.

"You didn't even say hello to Lewis," Miss Frankie told him.

"I was getting to that," said the boy. He put the last of the cake in his mouth, held up his sticky fingers, and said through a mouthful of cake and icing, "Sorry. Can't shake hands."

"You just enjoy it," said Lewis.

"I'm trying to." The boy swallowed. "I'm trying to enjoy everything, Lewis. I've decided to become a hedonist. What do you think of that?"

"Well. You do what you got to do."

"Hedonism. Definitely. You ought to try it, Lewis."

"Cut it out, Seth," said Miss Frankie. "Lewis, let me take your hat."

"She objects to everything," said the boy. "Icing. Hedonism. Hats. Even nuclear war. She's a flower child, Lewis. Did you know that? Frankie the flower child. Peace, love, and Frank Zappa."

"If you're not ready," warned Miss Frankie, "I'm leaving without you."

"See what I mean?" said the boy. "She'd leave without me. Without *me,* the life of the party." He shook his head. "These are trying times but they make men out of us, don't they, Lewis?"

"Nosir," said Lewis. "Nothing make a man out of us 'less we're ready to be a man."

The boy smiled. "Janis Joplin. You stole that line from Janis Joplin."

"Grow up, Seth," said Miss Frankie.

"I want to be just like you."

"As soon as I get Lewis settled with Papa, we're going."

"Hey, everything's copacetic."

She led the way down the hall to the room at the end. Lewis had once carried a hospital bed into this room. It was the only time he'd seen her cry, Mrs. Detroit. The sight of that bed, the way it lorded over the whole room. The next day he and Osee and a couple of Osee's boys and Dosha's boy Solomon, they carried it out again. Miss Frankie went in and he went in behind her. She sat down in the chair beside the bed and the dog came from the corner of the room and put his big brown head on her lap. Lewis stood at the foot of the bed and the man in the bed opened his eyes and saw the girl and closed his eyes again.

"Papa?" she said.

The man rolled his head toward her, like a heavy rock.

"Papa? Lewis is here. Lewis Brown. He's going to sit with you for a little bit, then I'll come back and sit with you, okay? You okay?" The man gave no sign. "You remember Lewis."

The man said, "Lewis doesn't remember me."

"Of course he does. He's right here."

"No."

"Yes, he is."

Lewis came beside the girl and she got up and he sat down in the chair. The dog went back to the corner. The man said, "It isn't Lewis."

"Yessir," said Lewis. "It's old Lewis."

And the man seemed to know him for a moment, then forget. He closed his eyes again and Miss Frankie said, "I'm going now, Papa. See you later."

"Alligator," whispered the man and smiled weakly, just a shadow crossing his mouth.

Miss Frankie touched Lewis's shoulder and nodded, and he nodded back. He heard the boy say something to her out in the hall, something he couldn't make out and had no wish to. The car started up and rolled away, making a crackling sound across the gravel. Lewis settled in the chair, looked around him, then quickly felt he shouldn't, that it was not right. The particulars of a man were here, but not only that, it was Mrs. Detroit's room as well, and the room of their marriage. He glanced briefly at an open drawer and saw without meaning to a thin strap, something womanly spilling out, and he was ashamed.

For a long time he sat, sat and rested, looking at nothing but his own hands in his own lap. He turned them this way and that, the pink of the palms, the dark of the backs, the nails ridged and cracked and too long. For a long time he could not look at the man. He remembered a time when he had sat just so beside him, bathing his wounds from a basin of vinegar water. All afternoon and into the dark night. And it seemed but a minute ago. It was. It was but a minute. These lives were short. They expected nothing of a man. It was a man did all the expecting. He looked at the man's hand, the long yellow fingers bent and clawlike, scratching the sheet, scratching and scratching, like a slow dog digging up a bone. The eyes were closed, the head almost hairless now and the face drawn smooth and tight across the forehead and cheekbones, the chin stubbled with today's whiskers. He was the wrong color altogether. Lewis put out his own hand, next to the man's, and scratched too.

The man opened his eyes. "Lewis. Lewis Brown." He reached for Lewis's hand and squeezed it. At the sound of the man's voice the dog got up and came to the bed and put his front paws up on the bed and before Lewis could stop him he leaped in a sudden burst and stood across the man's legs, solid as a table.

Lewis laughed. They both did. Lewis said, "You get off a there now. Man! You get down now. Man! You hear me?"

"Hears what he wants to hear," said the man.

"You all filthy from the kennel and you standing up there on that nice clean bed. You get down now, hear? Down! What's the matter with you, Man?" The dog sat down and Lewis shook his head. "That's one kind a down. Let's try another kind a down."

The man spoke sharply to the dog. "You listen to Lewis." The dog hung his head and lay down.

"He know he got us beat," laughed Lewis.

"Just a great big lunk of a dog."

"He taking up half the bed though."

"I don't mind. There's plenty of bed. An empty bed is . . . is nothing but empty, Lewis. At night she's here, and more and more during the day. She comes and lies down like we're new again. I want you to see she's taken care of. Fed and watered and loved. Will you do that for me, Lewis? I know. I don't even need to ask. But there are fools out there. Her own children. You know there are fools, Lewis."

"Yessir. I know it. Fools and fools."

"Blind fools."

"Yessir."

"And Lewis . . ."

"Yessir. I'm here."

"Tell Cole. Tell that Cole Jones."

"I'll tell him."

"Tell him to marry that wife of his."

"I'll tell him."

"Thank you. Thank you, Lewis." And the man reached for his hand again and clutched it and did not let it go. "You saved my life," said the man.

Lewis bent his head. "Well now."

"I was close to death. I wouldn't have lasted the afternoon."

"You was bad. You was real bad."

"How you found me I'll never know."

"My sister. She the one knew."

"Your sister."

"She say if a man got half the sense an animal got, he be down in the creek. And that's where you was, what was left a you."

"What was her name, Lewis? A regal name."

"Cordelia. Some call her Big Cordelia."

"Cordelia. Of the bare feet."

Lewis laughed. "Yessir. She never did wear no shoes. She never had no shoes."

"Shoes aren't everything."

"Nosir. Fact, they ain't much."

The man still held his hand. He brought it up to the top of the sheet, right below his chin, and Lewis didn't know but he might kiss it or some other such thing, and he prepared himself though for what he did not know. The man said, "All that night I lay there, I lay there half-cooked and half-blind, knew I would die. And by the end of the night it came to me. It came to me, Lewis. The place came to me. The place I'd always had a strong feeling for, my own place, an affinity. It was the creek. Bully Creek. I hadn't known it until I passed the night in it and then I knew it to my bones. Bully Creek. That's my place. The way Cullis Jones's was hers, and your bed is yours. That's why we built here. The creek. Can't come in or go out without crossing the creek. Little trickle of a creek until it rains and swells up like a muddy vein, then down it goes again. The filling and the passing and the emptying. Right now it's empty. That's my guess, Lewis. You crossed over it today. It's empty."

Lewis nodded.

"Good," said the man and patted Lewis's hand and let it go. "Smell that?"

"All I smell is that dog."

"At the window. You'll smell it there." Lewis went to the window and the man said, "What's the light doing? I see only gray."

"That's about all there is to see is gray. Be dark in a little bit."

"Do you smell it?" asked the man.

"What kind a thing am I smelling?"

The man laughed. "You have to decide that with your nose." It was good to hear him laugh.

"My nose smell all kind a stuff." The window was cracked open and he leaned and put his face to the air and took big gulps of it, like it was cool water. "It smell the grass. Out there by the pool. That come and go, that smell. And it smell something else real sweet. Different kind a sweet. Mmm-mmm, that's sweet."

"Tea olive," said the man.

"Tea olive. And I get a little smell of the earth. Earth smell. And there's a fox or something passed by not too long ago. I get a scent a that. Like a skunk, but not strong like a skunk smell. Rain. We gonna have some rain. Smell like tonight or tomorrow. And the trees. They smell like sugar. And something else now, it's coming. Peaches. Here it come again. Un-hunh. Peaches? Wrong time a year for peaches."

"My rose," said the man. "It's my rose. The Marechal Niel. Oh, *smell* it, Lewis!"

Lewis took one last drink of the air—it tasted like plain air but it surely smelled like peaches. He came and sat down in the chair again and the man said, "Now you better be on your way."

"Nosir. I don't need to go nowhere. That's why I'm here."

"Lewis, Lewis, Lewis! Not after dark. Along these roads? All kinds of fools and ghouls. Go!" The eyes shone. The thin arm rose and waved him away. "I can't keep you safe," he whispered. "I'm no good. You haven't even got a coat on."

"Nosir. I won't be needing no coat."

The dog whimpered and twitched in his sleep, all four feet running.

"Take mine," said the man. "I insist, Lewis. You must take it. What would I do with a coat? It's a hell of a night and they've burned us in our rags and hung us and stolen our skins right off us . . . never mind a coat . . ."

Lewis put a hand on the bed beside the man. "Shh, shh. You just rest now. We gonna be alright. We gonna make it."

But the man struggled to sit up, shook with the effort and fell back again. "Oh, Lewis, look at me. I'm here to stay. And all these years I've had no word, navigating blind, a covered bridge, the stream below undrinkable and all her wheres and whys hung out, the flash of the spade on a day so cold it froze thought itself. Unthinkable. Happiness doesn't fall, does it? It rises. It becomes or doesn't and splits a man right down the middle. Fishing his own waters for what cannot be caught. Cash it in! Cash it in!"

Again he struggled to rise, his excitement growing, and Lewis felt like a man pushed out on the track, the dark weight of the train bearing down on him and his legs not yet working, his mind not yet understanding the meaning of the looming shape. The sound is what awakens him, the alarmed whistle blowing, and so it was with Mr. Detroit who sank briefly into a dying man's madness, strange utterances arising from his throat and a confusion in every part of him, a dark confusion of time. He wandered, it seemed, in a burning place, and years ago, and Lewis knew it well, both the when and the where. And he could do nothing. Then he understood, and there was one thing he could do and he did it. He took off his shoes. He stood up and the dog stood up and shook and sat down again and Lewis shooed him from the bed. He went around to the side that was Mrs. Detroit's and he pulled back the blanket and the sheet and lay down. He rolled toward the man and took him in his arms. Only his Rutha had ever been there, in his arms. The man babbling words that weren't words, just a language made of noise and sound and worry and deathly fear. And he told him it would be alright though he himself had no doubt it would not be only that. He lay the length of the man's flesh, the man's body barely yet a body under the soft, worn pajamas. He said what he thought a mother would say, what his own mother might have said had she had the time and inclination to soothe. She did her soothing elsewise—those sweet walnut pies. And the man's breathing slowed, and his tongue became still, and in Lewis's arms all the hardness went out of him and he softened and cried with no sound at all, but the shiny wetness.

Slowly Lewis let go and got out of the bed. He straightened it as best he could. The dog jumped to the bed. The man wanted to come up a little and Lewis fixed the pillows under his head. He sat down again and the minute he did he heard the shot. It came from the direction of the barn. A single shot. It sounded like a sick man's cough.

"That's the end of it," the man whispered, his eyes unclouded and shining.

Lewis nodded.

"God bless him, that's the end."

They sat in the darkness and said nothing. Lewis got up to put a light on but the man said, "Not yet. A little more darkness. My eyes . . ."

"That's right."

An immeasurable amount of time went by. The man slept. Lewis started to sleep but woke himself up tilting forward out of the chair. He put his shoes back on to keep himself awake. At last he heard a door open and close, though he had heard no car, and it wasn't the front door but farther away, in the kitchen. The long hall. Unsure steps. Then a known voice calling, "Hello? Hello-o?"

Lewis cleared his throat and said, "Back here in the dark."

"Who is it?" said the man.

"It's Roosevelt."

"Roosevelt. Give him some light."

The boy came in and he had a drawn look to him and there was blood and hay on his coat. It was a good hunting coat from last year's Christmas. He looked at the bed and said, "Well, there's Man. There's my missing dog." The dog raised both eyebrows, lifted his head. "I'm sorry to bother you, Mr. Detroit, but when I went to feed tonight I seen a pen open and a couple of dogs gone. One of them was Dixie, and Man been in with Dixie for the last few days. Dixie come back soon as she know it's feeding time, but when Man don't show up I figure I better make sure he's up here."

"Roosevelt?" asked Mr. Detroit.

"Yessir?"

"Is that you?"

"Yessir, it is."

"Well, you're something."

"How's that, sir?"

Mr. Detroit shook his head slowly and said, "I'm not sure I can explain it. Maybe another time when I'm not so . . ."

"Another time," said Roosevelt. "You look like you could use a rest."

"I could rest, couldn't I? Let the water rise up."

"Look like a rest would do you good."

"Let's rest," said Mr. Detroit. Then he added, "Read to me while I close my eyes."

"Read?" asked Roosevelt.

"Anything." The voice grew weaker. "Anything at all. Rowena's side of the bed. Look there. Whatever she's got. Read it."

Lewis gave Roosevelt the chair and he himself stood by the window looking out at the fallen night and in at the reflection of the lit room behind him. The man in the bed. The boy who would become a man. The man who would soon be nothing, who, Lewis felt, finally wished to be nothing. The boy who would become a man to discover that a man becomes nothing. Cannot bring his knowledge with him, cannot bring his books or his children or his grandchildren or his great sweeping plantation, or his mind in any form, or his body in any form, his acres of pines and swamps and winter wheat and planted benne and chufa, all of it he must leave behind. He must leave behind the sons. He must leave behind the woman in his bed. He must give up every hope for his family and his land and know that the land at least will be torn apart without him and go on and become a ruinous nothing like him and perhaps rise up again in a different form as he may. Lewis lifted a hand to his throat and felt the pulse there, his own pulse, and knew it would not beat much longer. The boy began to read. He had a good strong voice and he read without hesitation. Even the words he could not know, had never heard before, had never seen before, he read them as if they were already in him, waiting to come out.

And the boy read:

In the uncertain hour before the morning
Near the ending of interminable night
At the recurrent end of the unending
After the dark dove with the flickering tongue
Had passed below the horizon of his homing . . .

And Lewis slept standing at the window and woke to more poetry, for surely it was that.

We shall not cease from exploration, read the boy,
And the end of all our exploring
Will be to arrive where we started
And know the place for the first time.
Through the unknown, remembered gate
When the last of earth left to discover
Is that which was the beginning;
At the source of the longest river
The voice of the hidden waterfall
And the children in the apple-tree
Not known, because not looked for
But heard, half-heard, in the stillness
Between two waves of the sea.
Quick now, here, now, always—
A condition of complete simplicity
(Costing not less than everything)
And all shall be well and

All manner of thing shall be well
When the tongues of flame are in-folded
Into the crowned knot of fire
And the fire and the rose are one. Lewis?

Startled. To hear his name in a poem.

"Lewis?"

He went and stood by the boy and put his hands on the boy's head for he understood what he was trying to say outside the words of the book. He gazed at the bed, at the small size of a man who has emptied his last breath into the world. "Yes," he said. "He's gone on."

ASHES

1969

The man emerges from the garden, camellias in full bloom and the colored maid with her pruning shears there to take them for the table. She does not see him. There is no one to see. She sings softly to herself, *Jesus, oh sweet Jesus, abide with me.* Out of habit the man steps off the path and she passes him and could pass right through him without knowing it until she has gone by and the wind blows the scent of him to her. He stands only an arm's length away. She raises her face, quits her singing, clutches the shears in both hands, and turns and runs to the house. He wonders what has frightened her more, his presence or his absence.

Rowena cannot sleep at night and sits in the chair by the window, his pajama jacket pressed to her face, breathing in the scent of him. The bedroom is dark and she can see beyond the tops of the pines a thin moon rising. She feels him waning. This is the third night.

On the first night his scent was faint, subdued by illness, the smells of medicine and soap. On the second night she held the pajama jacket to her face and found his own strong sharp sour-bread smell in the cloth. But tonight it is going, almost gone. She wishes the hours would not pass and take him from her. She wrings the jacket as if to squeeze the last juices from it, as if they will fall into her lap, drop by drop, the last juices, the last traces of him. She knows every woman, every woman who has loved and buried a man, has done this, or wished to, and never spoken of it, held his clothing to her for the brief, vanishing comfort of his smell.

She goes to her bureau and though there is not enough light to see it she puts her hands on the brass canister that once held her grandfather Sherman's cigars. She runs her palms across the metal. It is thin, dented in several places, the shallow dents of roughing it and outdoor life. A deeper dent that speaks of a bullet, and for a moment she hears the scream and gunfire, a buoyant bugler far away across the ruined field where lives lie useful as bulwarks. She clutches the canister to her, sits on the bed, his side of the bed, and says to him, implores him, Come back.

She moves once more to the chair and watches the late moon vanishing, the first light walking toward her out of low frowning clouds. She's tired and cold. She covers her knees with his pajama jacket and lifts the canister's lid. Inside, the unfamiliar chalky smell of what was his body, and the bones sharp as chipped arrows. Today they will throw his ashes in the creek. Yesterday she and Frances scattered him around his roses. The youngest one, Lucy, with them, amazed at the rubble death is: "But his bones are so little!"

"Dearie, that's just what's left of his bones."

"I guess he doesn't need his bones."

"No."

"But I need my bones."

"Yes you do."

"And Frankie needs her bones."

"Yes she does."

"And you need your bones."

"For a little while longer."

"Mine," said the child, "I'll need for a long long time."

Pearly Mae steps inside and leans against the door, fanning her face with the pruning shears. Rutha's ironing the good tablecloth for the buffet after they throw him in the creek. She sets down the iron and says, "What in the sweet Lord's name come over you?"

"Nothing," says Pearly.

"What kind a nothing?" says Rutha.

"He's out there," Pearly says.

"Well of course he's out there. Ain't no one put him in the ground. He's wandering. He'll be wandering a long time. Can't throw a man to the wind and expect him to settle down."

"I didn't see him," says Pearly.

"Un-hunh."

"He come on the wind."

"That's right."

"Well what do I do?"

"Whatever you was intending to do," says Rutha.

"I was aiming to cut some camellias for the table."

"Go on and cut 'em. He won't bother you none. He just wandering, that's all. He just looking for his body."

"I hope he find it," says Pearly.

"He never will," says Rutha.

His body, though it does not remember itself, remembers a time long ago when knowledge was the smell of blood and water, the scent of the lion's kill and the rock-cupped rain.

When the milk in a woman's breast warned away strangers, its blue sweetness traceable, like the sigh of a knife. And men moved across the land like rivers, the clover air drawing them on, the wild roses, sedges, bulrushes, magnificent flocks of blackbirds scorching the sky, darkness of wings multiplied by wings by wings by wings. And bodies were husks, raw, dank smells encased in rapture and death.

Cole Jones lies across the body of his wife and thinks of Bully Creek bridge. And the creek below, its smell of earth and ripe dampness. Karen shifts beneath him, throws one arm around him, and moves him off her so she can go check on the girls.

"The girls are just fine," says Cole.

"I want to make sure."

"It's the middle of the night, Karen. They're sleeping."

"Still," she says. She sits up. "I think I want to make sure."

He pushes her down on her back and she looks up at him in disbelief. She turns her head to the side and he takes her chin and turns it toward him and says, "Look at me."

"I can't, Cole."

"Karen."

"I can't."

He lets go of her then and she curls on her side, her knees to her chest, forcing him away. "I'll check on them," he says, and when he comes back she is pretending to sleep but he kneels by her side of the bed and tells her he is sorry. He puts his hand in her hair and tells her he would like to get to know her again and like for her to get to know him. She says nothing. She stretches out in the bed and reaches for his other hand and presses it to her forehead. "We both try," she says.

"We do."

"There isn't anyone else I want to try with, Cole."

"I know."

"Come up here and hold me. You look like you're saying your prayers."

I am, he thinks, and he gets up and climbs into bed beside his wife, and she lies on her side and lets him run his hand along the length of her. At the curve of her hip he waits. He waits for her to want more. He waits for her to want what he wants and finally she shows him she does.

Charlene Davis doesn't want to go to no funeral, even if they ain't gonna lay him in the ground. Even if there ain't no cemetery, no hole, no big old coffin. Just a little box with that whole man in it. That's what she gonna be, no worms squirming all over her insides and outsides. Yuck. She gonna be burned up and set free, like him.

Anyway, she got a boyfriend now, and she and Jerome gonna have some fun, drive around in the car, go bowling, see a show. They got plans. And they gonna someday make a baby. Someday. Maybe. And they gonna get married. If they like each other. You don't have to like each other to make no baby. They'll make that baby and see.

She knows one thing. Never again is she gonna listen to someone alive do the talking for someone dead. Dead can talk, let 'em talk. Right now she's trying to listen to the hole inside her that says fill me, trying to hear if it's Dallas or her own child wanting to be made. Or maybe it's both. Maybe that's what it is, that's how they talk to you. They get inside everything you make. One day you see them, you see them looking out your baby's eyes. You look at the baby. He's your baby. You look away and look back and who is he? He's one of them that's gone and wants to stay with you and has to stay with you till a soul don't need a body. How long is that? she wonders. And who all's inside me?

She gets her blue jeans on and a white blouse and a pair of bright red high-heeled sandals, pretending it's a summer day. The jeans are tight and they look good on her. She takes the sandals off and carries them in a paper bag. She calls Jerome and tells him to pick her up on the road, don't come by the house, and she goes out on the porch and down the steps and out onto the plantation road like she's just getting some air. Stretching her legs. Around the corner she starts to run. She's barefoot, with her shoes in the bag, and the cool clay feels good and the way her heart's pounding feels good. Scared? She ain't scared. She's excited. She smells the trees. She hasn't smelled the smell of the trees for a long time, since she was a kid. Since she was a kid and her and Roosevelt used to play pony and they'd gallop in the yard and up onto Aunt Rutha's porch and she'd come out and stroke them and give them a carrot. A carrot and a cookie. Then they'd run away and gallop in the yard again and sometimes they'd go out and stand by a tree. Stand by it and hang their heads down and pretend to be horses sleeping. But that's gone. But the trees are still here, smelling up the woods with caramel. She stops at the gate and walks through it and looks back and sees no one running after her, hollering at her, and she walks out onto the road and puts her red shoes on and walks down the road toward town.

ACKNOWLEDGMENTS

I would like to thank Ann Baker, who accompanied and encouraged me through the conception and shaping of this work. She read every one of its numerous drafts, and the influence of her comments and suggestions appears on every page. When my energy flagged, she saw the solution and drove me down to Georgia to reacquaint myself with the taste of field peas, and roast quail in brown gravy, and the smell of tea olives and gunpowder, and the sound of dove roosting in the live oaks. She knew the senses mattered deeply to this book. I thank her for her insight, and most of all for her unwavering belief in the story's power to heal and illuminate.

To my brother Stephen Erhart I owe a great debt of gratitude. His early editing of the manuscript rerouted me when I most needed direction, and his insistence on each character's fulfillment of his or her destiny was invaluable at a time when I felt I held a handful of beginnings, and no endings. I appreciate every moment of the many hours of work he gave to this book. Without his literary hand to guide it, it surely would have been a thinner, less satisfying fiction.

Other contributors include Mary Jane Ryan, who helped me wrestle with form, and my uncle Charlie Chapin, who served as creative liaison between the world of fiction and the tangible world it seeks to recreate. In other words, he welcomed me and my fabricating ways into the place he calls home. Any inconsistency between the two worlds, as well as any overstepped boundary, is my responsibility, not his or anyone else's.

I credit the poet Eileen Myles with the line *The touch of a foot in the night is sincere.* My niece Claire Erhart generously provided me with her favorite word, *up*. My father, Charles Erhart, offered opera expertise, and Stephany Brown and Rose Houk proofread the manuscript. Bobby and Wanda Thrasher weighed in on road paving materials, and Karla Baker advised me on canine diseases of the sixties. I read many accounts of the Civil War and cut my teeth on one in particular, *The Civil War: An Illustrated History,* by Geoffrey C. Ward. General William Tecumseh Sherman's letters, which appear in these pages, are a product of my imagination, as is his granddaughter Rowena.

Finally, I would like to thank Emilie Buchwald, my editor, for having the faith and resilience to take on this book. In her hands, it truly became the work of fiction I set out to write more than a decade ago, and I can think of no greater tribute to any creative effort than to be the swan song of an admired and accomplished editor.

ABOUT THE AUTHOR

Margaret Erhart is a writer and teacher who lives in Flagstaff, Arizona. Her commentaries have aired on National Public Radio, and her essays have been published in the *New York Times.* Her novels include *Augusta Cotton* (Zoland Books) and *Old Love* (Steerforth Press).

THE MILKWEED NATIONAL FICTION PRIZE

Milkweed Editions awards the Milkweed National Fiction Prize to works of high literary quality that embody humane values and contribute to cultural understanding. For more information about the Milkweed National Fiction Prize or to order past winners, visit our Web site (www.milkweed.org) or contact Milkweed Editions at (800) 520-6455.

Visigoth by Gary Amdahl (2006)
Crossing Bully Creek by Margaret Erhart (2005)
Ordinary Wolves by Seth Kantner (2004)
Roofwalker by Susan Power (2002)
Hell's Bottom, Colorado by Laura Pritchett (2001)
Falling Dark by Tim Tharp (1999)
Tivolem by Victor Rangel-Ribeiro (1998)
The Tree of Red Stars by Tessa Bridal (1997)
The Empress of One by Faith Sullivan (1996)
Confidence of the Heart by David Schweidel (1995)
Montana 1948 by Larry Watson (1993)
Larabi's Ox by Tony Ardizzone (1992)
Aquaboogie by Susan Straight (1990)
Blue Taxis by Eileen Drew (1989)
Ganado Red by Susan Lowell (1988)

MILKWEED EDITIONS

Founded in 1979, Milkweed Editions is one of the largest independent, nonprofit literary publishers in the United States. Milkweed publishes with the intention of making a humane impact on society, in the belief that great writing can transform the human heart and spirit. Within this mission, Milkweed publishes in four areas: fiction, nonfiction, poetry, and children's literature for middle-grade readers.

JOIN US

Milkweed depends on the generosity of foundations and individuals like you, in addition to the sales of its books. In an increasingly consolidated and bottom-line-driven publishing world, your support allows us to select and publish books on the basis of their literary quality and the depth of their message. Please visit our Web site (www.milkweed.org) or contact us at (800) 520-6455 to learn more about our donor program.

Interior design by Linda Koutsky
Typeset in Perpetua 12/15
Printed on acid-free 50 lb natural paper
by Edwards Brothers.